A Sacrifice for LOVE

ALSO BY SHELLEY KASSIAN

Contemporary Romance

Places in the Heart:

A Sea for Summer, Book 1

The Thurston Hotel:

A Lasting Harmony, Book 5

The Women of Stampede:

The Half Mile of Baby Blue, Book 2

Historical Romance

A Heart across the Ocean

A Gentleman for Christmas

Shelley Kassian writing as Abby Lane

Dark Fantasy

A Reign of Blood and Magic:

The Scarlett Mark, Book 1

The Ebony Queen, Book 2

The Immortal Blood, Book 3

A NOVEL

SHELLEY KASSIAN

—A Sacrifice for Love—

Published 2017 by Shelley Kassian (shelleykassian.com)

ISBN: 978-0-9948385-9-9 (Print edition)

Design and cover art by Su Kopil, Earthly Charms
Copyediting by Ted Williams

DEDICATION

To those who Sacrifice for Love.
But especially to those that serve in the ministry,
Hoping to make a difference in our world.

PREFACE

A Sacrifice for Love was written years ago when I was a member of a Protestant congregation. The story relates the fictional telling of a priest falling in love during a period of religious conflict, a time when Father Martin Luther challenged principles of the Roman Catholic Church, such as indulgences. In the ensuing years, he's instrumental in writing a German translation of the Bible, and ultimately the birth of the Lutheran religion. This was the perfect period to set my story.

I had taken an avid interest in the clergy, in particular priests not being able to marry, especially given that prior to the year AD 1139, priests were able to marry and many had wives and families.

I'm sure there are many reasons why the celibate rule became clerical law. Although in the 2017 year, it's surprising to me that the rule still exists, forcing priests to choose between their vocation and the love of a partner. Some priests have left the church for this reason.

I felt that spirituality had to form a part of the written work of this book. I've tried to temper the religious oratory as while I once wrote inspirational romance, that's not my focus now. Not wanting this story to become a sermon, I've revised the text to keep the focus on the romance.

I don't mean to offend anyone with a faith background. I hope if you choose to read this book, you'll see Mathias as I do: a hero compelled to the ministry, who offers his compassion and service for the betterment of the community.

Also please note, sexuality is expressed in explicit sensual terms in the latter chapters. I considered removing these love scenes, but in the final stages of production decided to keep the original intent of the narrative.

Mathias and Sophia's story is worthy of being told, and in fairness to my characters, their love story has been collecting dust since 1994!

I hope you enjoy, *A Sacrifice for Love*.

Shelley Kassian

ACKNOWLEDGMENTS

I thank my colleagues, Brenda Sinclair and Katie O'Connor, for beta reading this book prior to its publication. Their advice contributed to the story plotting, further developing the story. Their suggestions added depth and deeper meaning to *A Sacrifice for Love*, making the novel a better book.

Thanks to Su Kopil for the cover art and designing a logo for my name. I love the final design!

Thanks to Ted Williams for his editing expertise, which brought continuity to some elements of the manuscript. I especially appreciate the attention to detail and his knowledge of language.

Finally, I thank my family who always support my publishing efforts! They share my Facebook posts, indulge my story ideas, and spare me the time to do what I enjoy best. Write!

And now these three remain,
—Faith, Hope and Love—
But the greatest of these is Love.
1st Corinthians 13:13

CHAPTER 1

NEAR LEIPZIG, SAXONY

Damn you, grim reaper! Sophia mused, missing her father and hating that she'd never see him again. Her life had lost meaning since the passing of Lord Dedrick Baldemar. She reclined in an azurite armchair in her father's Yellow Chamber—more of a library than an office—waiting for the solicitor to speak. The interior seemed dour, devoid of laughter and gentle teasing, too silent without her father's booming voice. It didn't matter that a spring breeze whispered through an open window, or even that the sun sparkled brightly beyond the windowpanes. Not even the birds chattering in the leafy trees outside lifted her spirits.

Life had stopped, sullen as death inside this room—but she didn't suffer alone. Numb, she endured the ugly pauses and suffocating presence of her stepfamily.

She glanced at her hands in her lap, perused her stepsister, Alisz, sitting on the opposite chair, but couldn't bring herself to even look at her stepmother, Lady Wendeline, an iron poker wedged between them, heavily veiled in black.

A full week had passed since the night Father had died, and she likened the horrible eve to a dream she couldn't awake from. The days passed at a snail's pace, and the nights; a hellish reliving of tragedy. She recalled Father's sea-blue eyes as he clutched at his chest, struggling to breathe.

You'll be all right, Father...

But she'd been wrong. Good had not come to pass. Instead, a family's solemn vigil had taken place, followed by a man's burial. Life pressed on, the world whirled in motion, even though silence, grief, and disturbing utterings permeated the manor house. Seven days had sifted through the hourglass and still, she felt numb. Sadness gripped her, constricted her heart; she couldn't stop crying.

Father, I'm not ready to be without you, or to face what is to come, alone...

And now before her father was cold in his grave, his attorney arrived to read the Will. He sat at her father's walnut desk. It wasn't right. It was too soon.

Sophia wasn't ready for estate disclosures, but her stepmother had insisted: *"We must soldier on, present a brave face to the world. After all, Dedrick would want his dependents to press forward without delay, rather than suffering sad afflictions of the heart."*

A SACRIFICE FOR LOVE

The woman had made it sound clinical, but perhaps she was right. Father had never been one to postpone business.

Alisz was quieter than usual. It was perplexing to see her attempt at gravity. Her stepsister enjoyed getting the better of Sophia as often as was possible. Minor jokes and biting jabs, but perhaps grief had fashioned some respect. After all, Alisz had lost a father, too.

"We've gathered together to read the Last Will and Testament of the Right Honorable Lord Dedrick Baldemar," Sterling said with a sigh. "If you're ready, ladies, I will share the disclosure."

"You may continue," Lady Wendeline stated, showing no emotion. "We're ready."

Sterling glanced at them, raising his eyebrows, tapping thick fingers on the parchment. "This is the last Will and Testament of Lord Dedrick Baldemar. I, Sterling Richter, his legal authority and executor, do hereby declare that the statements so listed are true, and are his intent and his alone."

Sophia swallowed when he paused. "Carry on," Lady Wendeline said.

"The estate of Baldemar Manor is bequeathed to Lady Wendeline, but at her death, the property and all physical assets shall be deeded to his sole surviving daughter…" He paused, scrutinizing the document. "This is strange. I don't recall this stipulation?"

"And why would you remember the legal assignments?" Lady Wendeline asserted, "given that you're new to the file."

"Yes, but my father apprised me of the estate before he retired, but perhaps he was mistaken as the Will clearly states that Alisz is the sole surviving daughter."

"What of me?" Sophia asked, perplexed at the news. "There are two surviving daughters, not one."

He looked directly at her. "You're to be given a yearly stipend of one hundred and fifty thaler. Should you marry, this sum will become your dowry and you'll receive no further allowances from the estate."

"Something must be wrong. I'm the first-born child. Surely I should inherit the estate in the event of my stepmother's death. Not Alisz."

"You can't possibly," he said with a frown, appearing concerned. "As you're not the natural born daughter of Lord Dedrick."

"What are you talking about?" Sophia rose from her armchair. "Of course I am."

"According to this Last Will and Testament, you are not. I'm sorry, Lady Sophia, you must brace yourself for it appears that you're not of legitimate birth; for all intents and purposes, you're a bastard."

"Preposterous!" she yelled, stepping forward, placing her hands on the desk. "I most certainly am not."

"Shocking," Alisz said with a smirk. "Who would have thought?"

"I don't believe it," Sophia cried out, stepping backward, tears filling her eyes. "Lies! A cruel joke is afoot here."

"Thank you, Sterling," Lady Wendeline breathed, her serious-minded facial expression never changing. "Is there any more to be disclosed?"

"Some minor allocations to the servants."

"We don't need to hear of these allowances. The relaying has been quite shocking. I think I need to lie down."

Sophia turned to her stepmother, only slightly able to see her stony glare through the black netting. "Did you do this? How did you manage it?"

"Sophia, I'm shocked at your behavior, but don't embarrass yourself with accusations when the truth has been exposed."

"I can't believe this. What will I do?"

"Stripling," Lady Wendeline remarked, disguising her irritation, "just because your mother didn't comport herself as a proper lady should, doesn't mean we'll force you into the street. You still have a yearly stipend and a home at Baldemar Manor, despite your illegitimate heritage. Dedrick was very fond of you, as you know."

A tear slipped from her eye. She wiped it away. "But it can't be true."

"I'm new to the file," Sterling mused, scrutinizing the paperwork, "but the Will appears to be authentic," he relayed dryly, closing the file. "However, I'll need to investigate to ensure there's been no tampering."

"The Will was kept at your firm, so how could such an undertaking be possible?"

"Indeed," Alisz said, uttering a nervous chirrup. "I'm sorry, Sophia."

"So it's true?"

"I've only just realized that we're not sisters," Alisz winced, her lip quivering. "This is the saddest part."

"Oh please, as if you've ever cared about our relationship," Sophia retorted, standing her ground before a rotten seed. "You treat me abysmally."

"Now, girls," Lady Wendeline chastised. "None of that. I'm sure Dedrick had his reasons for keeping this secret, but he wouldn't want discord in this house."

"He loved my mother," Sophia murmured, tears continuing to fall. "I know that's true."

"It appears so," the dowager acknowledged, gazing at her wrinkled fingers, "since he was quite prepared to care for you, even with the stain."

"I can't bear this any longer."

Sophia strode across the space to the outer hallway, rushing from the room. She needed to escape this calamity. Her only thought was to retrieve her horse, Maraclese; the mare her father had given her on her sixteenth birthday.

Her father, he wasn't her father…

The fact that she wore a sumptuous lead-tin yellow mourning gown and was not dressed appropriately to ride didn't slow her down.

"A lie," she sobbed, crossing the reception hall and soon passing through large oaken doors to the south-facing portico. "My life is a lie!"

CHAPTER 2

*F*ather Mathias, a parish priest, listened to the mourning din of chapel bells pealing for a deceased friend and teacher. Normally, he appreciated the sound of the carillons, but on the first breath of a new day, he was grateful when the metallic clang finally ended. The night had been long, difficult, and the reticence calmed his anxious mind.

Shrouded in a black robe, the uniform of his calling, fatigue, grief, and the Bishop's deathbed confessions kept him seated on the last pew inside the sanctuary. Admissions of guilt brought him to this quandary. He needed time to think. Needed to find some wisdom, strength, and the peace that the sanctuary offered. The loss of a fellow clergyman raised more questions than answers, answers he couldn't resolve from biblical knowledge or even the cold silver cross that lay entwined between his fingers.

Why couldn't he forget the confession? Let its heavy worry go? The secret that Bishop Eberhardt had kept, never confiding the truth until it was too late? Where had the sin taken his dear friend, perhaps to Hell? But even though an earthly suffering had ended, a human passing brought a development of darkness.

There was more to lament than the passing of a man. The Bishop had succumbed to his next spiritual life with great discord and regret. He was a well-versed teacher and his lessons had conveyed key principles to the secular world. His faith had seemed unshakable, and his fiery sermons had been a testament to glory. Mathias would miss his vim and vigor, but it was difficult to accept the confession of physical weakness.

The cleric had proclaimed to serve God for the benefit of his parish community, but for a time he had enjoyed the sexual love of a woman, and had committed the ultimate sin. Fornication.

Weary, Mathias sighed, releasing pent-up fatigue with a single whoosh of breath, and then leaning against the wooden backrest, he closed his eyes. The exhaustion threatened to pull him to his own inner darkness; a cross he could not dismiss after experiencing endless hours of anguish. He was certain that long after the memories faded; Bishop Eberhardt's final words would haunt him forever.

"I love her still!"

Throughout the Bishop's final hours of life, he had proclaimed to love a woman. The tears had seeped from his sunken old eyes as he spoke of his regrets. He had spurned a woman's love for the commitment to his church and parish community. Yet, if he could experience his youth again, he would sacrifice all by marrying his love and raising a family within that devotion.

Mathias shook his head. It was too late for love to find a way. This admission aggrieved him the most. *What would he do if he should ever face such a quandary?*

Swallowing, Mathias attempted to understand. His friend's regret had been so profound that passing peacefully had been difficult. However, Bishop Eberhardt remained steadfast to his vision of womanly love to the very end, crying out—

"—Liebling."

Despite being moved by his final words, he could not act on the advice given. Like the Bishop, he had made a commitment. He too had lain before the altar of Christ to receive his anointing. His vow must not be lessened because a clergyman on his deathbed cried out a woman's name, begging of her forgiveness. Faith could not alter its way because a man urged you not to meet the same fate.

Although every drill of theology enforced his beliefs, he could not deny the sad ending. A mortal man alone on his deathbed with a priest attending him, his ancestry lost, waiting for death to come.

"Rejoice in love should you find it—"

Mathias opened his eyes, scrutinizing the ivory lines of the cross, hoping he'd never face such a predicament. But what soul wouldn't desire love?

So deep in thought, he barely noticed the door opening, allowing a nuance of light and wind to filter through the narthex, alerting him to a presence. He turned to the sound. A woman wearing a black cloak eased the double doors shut, entered the sanctum and then quietly walked past him with her head held low.

He watched the young woman. From where he sat on the pew, he could almost detect the anguish buried within her awkward step. Carried painfully within soft lady shoulders that slumped forward in dismay.

She stopped briefly at the altar to light a taper; now two candles glimmered in the grayness. This done, she sat on the first pew. Her quiet sobs only confirmed Mathias's suspicions.

As he watched her where she sat, curiosity overcame him. Compelled, he stood and walked down the aisle, leaving his Bible and cross behind. She didn't raise her head nor shift her sullen form at his footfall. As he neared, he observed her hands clasped together tightly, her knuckles white.

White with what, sadness, fear, shame? He leaned toward her, placing his hand on her shoulder. "My lady, what brings you to the chapel so early in the day?"

She turned her head at his question, revealing a porcelain face framed with a maze of auburn ringlets and curls. Helplessly, he gazed into an emerald visage, bathed with the tears of fresh morning dew. He denied that he felt the flutter of his heartbeat as she stood, tears streaming down her lovely face to collapse into his arms.

"Father…"

"Lady Sophia?" he asked, holding her against his shoulder while she sobbed. "What's wrong? Do you need my counsel?" He tried to detach her hold, but she clung to him, her fingertips gripping his shoulders.

"Oh, Father, bless me with your wisdom. I'm in need of your counsel. All is lost in the world; ruined, destroyed, broken..."

"Come now, it can't be as bad as that."

"I assure you, it's horrible," she declared, releasing her grasp. Turning to the altar, she swept away the tears. "There's no mercy in this world, only age-old sin that rises from the depths of the grave to destroy my precious heart."

"But sin is forgiven," he said through his fatigue. "Your faults shall be absolved by the grace of God through your confession. Perchance you wish to speak about your burden?"

She cast him a wary glance before returning to the bench, her hands clasped in her lap, her gaze scrutinizing a silent and peaceful Madonna. "You misunderstand, 'tis not *my sins*," she emphasized, "requiring forgiveness or penance. A blatant lie needs to be set right, as well as my former fiancé's outrageous behavior. He has ripped my heart out of my chest to lie at the foot of another woman. My sister, Alisz, a poor example of sisterly love, steals the man who is rightfully mine. My mother made it possible through her wrongdoing."

Mathias sighed heavily, and then sat beside her on the pew. "Dear lady, there are no easy answers to the afflictions that burden even the strongest souls. But I can promise you that when you trust in something greater than yourself, you'll be delivered from your pain."

"I wish I could share in your convictions." She shook her head, obviously not convinced. "But as of today, my destiny and trust have been destroyed. I shan't be known as Lady Sophia of Baldemar Manor. Forever more, I'm simply Sophia, a bastard child. And the man I believed to be my father, is not my father! I shall never know whose life-giving seed damned my birth. That secret is buried with my mother."

"And how did this matter come to pass?"

"What? I'd think the answer obvious," she blurted, turning away from him with shame. "It was acknowledged a week past at the reading of my father's will."

"I'm sorry," he said with a frown. "That must have been terrible news to receive."

"It was shocking." She started to wail anew. "I don't know whether it's the truth, a bad joke, or a well-crafted lie. I feel numb inside."

"Even so, you won't be faulted for your parentage," he said, attempting to console. "Aye, the community will think differently about you for a time, but you are the same kind woman."

"I'm not the same. Already, the societal classes dismiss me as if I carried the plague. My friends won't speak to me. They scrutinize me with accusatory eyes and taunt with ugly catcalls. Why? I've done nothing wrong."

"I won't turn you away and neither will our Heavenly Father."

"That doesn't help me much. I assure you, the good news shared inside the church doesn't often extend to the community outside your doors. People are brutes."

Mathias tried a different approach. "I suspect that a father once loved a child even though the daughter was not his own. Lord Dedrick favored you well if I remember correctly. Am I right of it?"

"I believe my father loved me." She hiccuped, fresh tears rolling down her face. She wiped them away hastily. "He always demonstrated kindness, compassion, and his love. But he would beget this wistful expression from time to time. I would say to him: 'Father, why are you so sad?' He wouldn't tell me. 'It matters naught,' he would soothe, a tear slipping from his eye. I pretended not to see the fullness, but I glimpsed the sadness all the same."

Reaching for her hand, Mathias entwined her fingers within his hand. He knew his support shouldn't be offered this way. The Church, his religious authority, decreed such affection as blasphemous.

We must keep our boundaries!

Right now, he didn't care about opinions. He'd heard them frequently enough by his peers, even by his own family who had applauded his rise to the priesthood. He knew she was a woman; he wasn't blind to the temptation. But surely a loving God wouldn't fault him for having a heart. To hold her hand might seem wrong, but providing faith and hope through healing touch seemed right.

Furthermore, Mathias didn't want to be alone during his own time of sorrow. He was in need of someone else's kindness and their conversation helped him to forget his own struggles.

"You spoke of a sister. How does she figure in your troubles?"

"The unworthy scofflaw marries my betrothed for her paternity is stronger and truer than mine. She rejoices in my sorrow, so rich is her new-found bounty."

"Your fiancé, Franz if I remember correctly, does he have a say in this change of affairs? Surely, he would honor the betrothal contract?"

"No, Father. He will not; he cannot. The agreement stipulated that if either party were proven unworthy, the marriage contract was to be dissolved. His family prides itself with great esteem and bloodlines are chosen with particular care, much the same as a well-bred horse if you must know. You understand, Father; he would never be permitted to marry a bastard."

"Yes, of course. But why would your sister marry in your stead? I understand all else, but this turn of affairs speaks of a horrible injustice."

"My stepmother saw to the deed." She laughed through her tears. "To the satisfaction of all parties. This man offered words of love. He courted me relentlessly, but now that my parentage is uncertain, he walks away. How can he allow this erroneous affair? 'Tis painful enough that he chooses another, but that thine other is Alisz?"

Mathias held her hand firmly, offering his strength of will as her voice began to break. *Too many evils in the world*, he reflected sadly, just as she'd indicated. What could he say that would change anything?

"In time, you'll find someone else to love."

"I shall not think of another," Lady Sophia declared. "I could never consider loving another man. I don't know what to do. My life is over. I shall never be able to hold my head up high again. How will I reside in a manor I once called home in the wake of wedding preparations? How can I take myself there again?"

"Faith," he whispered solemnly, filled with despair for her pain. "You must dig deep to find it."

In need of comfort himself, he hugged Lady Sophia, pulling her against his chest. She came willingly into his arms. He had thought her sorrow spent, but fresh tears spilled forth in a torrent of anguish.

"Let it out," he said with a sigh, feeling her warm female form pressed against his chest. He persuaded himself to believe that in the wake of his sadness, her warmth brought a healing balm to his own mourning. He held her for what seemed like an eternity. Until he ached from the giving of his strength and the receiving of her own. She fell fast asleep. He could not deny her the peace; so intense was her suffering.

"What now?" he pleaded to the sacred space, listening to the soft inhalations of her breathing.

Another lamb trusted in him. Lifting Lady Sophia into his arms, he wondered why a length of robe should garner such faith and trust—a man stirred beneath its folds—a human being who grappled with desires no different than other men.

Sometimes, Mathias admitted that his vocation didn't seem fair. Sure, he'd welcome the life that the Bishop had spoken of. A wife. Children. Something solid that he could leave behind, but he'd surrendered his wants to bear the sacred doctrine.

Mathias retreated from the sanctuary and left the church, carrying Lady Sophia across the outer courtyard, taking her to his simple house. He couldn't bring her to the Bishop's home; ill humors infected the space.

I should wake her up. Force her to go home. But he couldn't bring himself to disturb her peace. Instead, he took her to his bedchamber with her arm draped trustingly on his shoulder.

He thought about how other men with blood pumping through their veins would respond to such a situation. Would they woo her in the privacy of their quarters, dispelling her pain and suffering as fortune's advantage?

His father would tell him to court the sin, and '*forget the priesthood'*. Lars Rohland had voiced an opinion on the subject, prior to Mathias's ordination. He hadn't wanted his son to sacrifice his soul; he still hoped a son might change his mind. He'd encourage a tryst, support taking Lady Sophia into his arms, kissing her sweet lips, and it had never been difficult to look upon her beauty.

His mother on the other hand was proud of the pious achievement, and in particular the rise of the Rohland name. He wasn't sure if she remembered that her second son was no more than a mortal man with a human soul. He had his urges, but squashed them down.

Somewhere in the great beyond, Bishop Eberhardt scrutinized him with an avid interest, perhaps cheering him to a new calling. The thought offered no comfort.

Mathias walked through the archway that led to his bedchamber and eased Lady Sophia onto his bed. Sighing after, he considered the woman sleeping, her chest gently rising and falling. He covered her with his woolen blankets, and then approaching the side-table, he lit a waxen taper. Then went back to the sanctuary to find solitude in prayer.

If not for a sudden tragedy within his family, his life would have been very different.

—*Marcos*, it should have been you.

CHAPTER 3

*T*he light of a full moon streamed through thick panes of glass, illuminating Lady Sophia where she slept cuddled into Mathias's pillow. Unknowingly, she breathed in a mix of masculine musk combined with the clean smell of lye soap, soon awakening to the wane of the evening sun and the dwindling cascade of a beeswax taper.

At first Sophia didn't know where she was lying, but a moment's glance at the simple room reminded her of where she might be. The walls were barren, the only adornments a wooden crucifix and a miniature replica of the Madonna. A side-table lay beside the bed, and a small wardrobe stood beyond the footboard. The room was simple, tidy, clean, and it surely belonged to Father Mathias.

She didn't feel particularly nonplussed by the fact that she was reclining on his bed. After all, the man was her spiritual teacher, and a friend. She cradled the woolen blankets closer to her chest, clinging to the warmth he had graciously offered. She could trust him. Somehow, there was comfort in his gesture and she was grateful.

Sophia reflected on their earlier conversation, wondering why she had revealed so much? And yet she wasn't sorry for running at the mouth. Sharing the burden of her shattered life had created a positive effect on her mental attitude. She felt better, as if the dialogue had eased some of her burdens. Lost in thought, she didn't hear Mathias's approach until he stood before her.

"You're awake. You slept through the day, evensong is done and the night has come. But no matter, you needed your rest. Are you hungry? I've kept a pot of stew warming on the hearth. After refreshing, perhaps you'll join me for a bite?"

"I'm sorry, Father, I see that I've inconvenienced you." She slid her fingers through the curls that funneled at her forehead, sighing heavily. "It would be wrong to burden you further."

"It's no great difficulty. I've seen to your comfort, as any good friend would do. Would I send you away hungry?"

"You've been kind and understanding. It won't be easy to pay proper homage to your generosity."

"It's important to care for our lambs," he said with a smile, "but if you're of the mind to recompense; the offering plate needs to be filled every Sunday to safeguard the work we do in the Lord's name. But allow me to escort you to the kitchen, before your meal becomes cold."

Sophia stood on weary legs, stretching. Releasing her cape from her shoulders, she attempted to straighten a rumpled crimson dress, failing miserably. Then she followed the Father to the kitchen with the cape draped over her arm.

She fought with the unruly strands of hair that played about her face while studying Father Mathias intimately. Although he was tall in stature, his footstep was neither clumsy, nor loud. And though he seemed thin, she was certain that beneath his cloak hid a solid mass of man. She had warmed to his advice, finding his words as strong as the broad shoulders she had leaned against. She chastised herself for thinking such inappropriate thoughts. He was a man of the cloth and yet the musings continued.

He's handsome. *I wonder why I've never noticed this before?*

His amber gaze portrayed an expanse of knowledge and Sophia knew he was gifted in educational pursuits. She'd heard his sermons often enough. He wasn't like other men she had known. The men who reflected chiseled statues of granite, whose bodies were strong in stature, wide in girth, handsome even, yet they held no heart to equal the measure.

Franz was such a man, she reflected sadly. She'd found out too late.

Father Mathias portrayed a subtler image of masculinity. His honest expression could have been molded from basic clay. The features were not crudely defined. His eyes were well set and edged with just enough lines to gain him a sense of maturity. He had a well-defined patrician nose that was neither too large nor too small, but adequate for a full face. She frowned as she thought about his mouth, his lips, which were fully capable of kissing a woman.

His voice, she sighed, was an endowment from… heaven. She'd always admired him. Always felt like his homilies reached a place that needed to be tended to, as if he were speaking directly to her.

Sophia stopped her foot pace, for Father Mathias had turned unexpectedly at the archway to the kitchen. Had she not stopped quickly, she would be against his chest.

"Lady Sophia, I must beg your pardon for the lack of conveniences. I'm a simple man; I have no need for the abundances that society types require. I don't wish to offend you, but if you need to relieve yourself, there is an outhouse to the west of the kitchen doors."

She grimaced, glancing downward at the wooden slats of flooring, then upward again to his earnest expression. "Father, if it is offensive to offer thy healing touch, express peaceful words, and provide nourishment as well, then I'm truly offended. Indeed, I'm grateful for your kindness. I will use your facility and then I will welcome the meal that you have prepared for me."

Sophia accepted his hand, appreciating his slight smile, as he led her to the back entry. He helped her out the door and showed her the way to the facilities. Before long they were seated at the table, enjoying a savory stew before the flickering flames of the fireplace.

"Lady Sophia, have you thought about which course of action would be suitable for you now? As your priest, I feel it is my duty to advise you."

She spooned little bits of lamb and potato into her mouth, chewing thoughtfully. "Father, I have thought of little else but my situation. However, I haven't had much time to consider the future. I suppose I'm doomed to live out my life as a spinster. Who would have me now?"

"Have you considered joining a community of sisters? The sisters at the monastery do good work. Perhaps such a vocation would welcome you and gain you a purpose."

Sophia stifled a smile. "Such a lot in life is not for me," she intoned, nibbling at her lip. "But I don't mean to offend your kind regard."

"It's only a suggestion. A religious life is not meant for every soul."

"My stepmother would approve of such a commitment. Alisz would pack my suitcase and escort me to the abbey herself. In fact, she has suggested the notion, but such a life is not for me. I feel no calling or compelling need to serve, only a desire to follow a good direction through life."

"There need not be a calling, my Lady," he said with a serious expression, "just a will to serve. A determination to do good for others and therefore good for one's self."

"Such an existence wouldn't fit well with my lifetime goals. I want the love of a husband, the promise of a family. I'd like to be a mother, but with my lineage stained, finding a husband is futile. Regardless that I have much to offer the right man."

"Which is what, my Lady? What can you offer?"

"My goodness," Sophia quipped, dropping her pewter spoon. "I know you didn't mean to offend, but you sound crass."

He leaned backward in his chair, staring at her intently. "I didn't mean to insult. Come now. Answer the question. What can you offer the right man?"

"A minor income, I suppose," Sophia said with a grimace. Then grasping her implement, she spooned the last forkful of food into her mouth. "I should be grateful for the pittance my father gave me, though I suppose he's not my paternal parent any longer. It's not much, but I thank him for his consideration all the same. I only wish that Alisz had not stolen Franz."

"Lady Sophia, surely you won't seek vengeance. Though your stepsister has done you wrong, you must not judge her actions."

"My stepsister?" Sophia said with a sad inflection. "No, Father, I won't seek retribution. Vengeance and dirty trickery is commonplace to that spoiled brat. I won't sink so low. I would seek justice, the truth if real facts can be found. But I have burdened you long enough. It's time to take myself home."

"Allow me to see you there safely. The hour is late."

"My thanks, but no. The sun, though on the horizon, has not set fully. I'll be safe. Thank you for your guidance and your hospitality."

"This house is a sanctuary to those who need solace. Should you fall into despair during the troubling days ahead, don't be afraid to seek me out."

"You're very kind," she said with gratitude, accepting his arm. He escorted her from his house to the corral.

"Will I see you on Sunday?" Mathias asked, opening the gate.

"Will you offer any hope from the pulpit?"

"There's always a message to be received, if you're keen enough to hear the meaning."

"I'll be there," Sophia mused, mounting Maraclese. "After all, attendance is mandatory."

"Rules don't stop some from staying away."

"Rules aren't my motivation, you've captivated me," Sophia said with a smile, glimpsing a mystery in his eyes she couldn't quite grasp. "Perhaps you're only fishing for another soul to save, but whatever the reason, I'm hungry for more conversation."

He smiled too then, as she nudged her horse in the side. "Until Sunday."

"Good night, Father."

She felt his heated stare on her back as she galloped away, in no hurry to return to the manor house. If the truth were to be known, she didn't want to go there. The place didn't belong to her anymore, she felt inferior and unwelcome in a once beloved place, but where else could she go?

SOPHIA CONSIDERED her stepfamily as she approached the gates of Baldemar Manor. She'd never thought of them in a negative manner before her father's death, merely accepting that they were somehow family, related through marriage and sharing the same space. But now—Christ's nails, there was separation. No more than a strained existence of strangers living amongst each other, a forced presence of obnoxious opinion too freely shared. Knowing this, it was not a complete surprise to find Lady Wendeline waiting for her in the Chintz Chamber.

Sophia had been prepared to make her escape up the staircase, but when she heard someone familiar calling her name; she lowered her head resignedly and walked into the room.

Lady Wendeline, sitting confidently across the room, was small in stature. A seductress at heart, she was beginning to show her age, but she still possessed a finely cut figure. Likely, she already had designs on some poor unfortunate creature of the male persuasion.

Sophia knew that look, it promised vengefulness. For even now, her gray eyes suffused with the temerity of a serpent and holding a tongue with venom, ready to strike. She swallowed, waiting for the vitriol.

"It's appropriate, I suppose, that in the wake of your father's will, and everything we've been forced to endure this past week, that you arrive home at a lamentable hour. It's no surprise that you would compromise a moral upbringing, confirming a poor-breeding pedigree. Thank the dear Lord that your supposed father was not here to witness such a brazen demonstration. He would then know that his value of your person was misplaced."

Sophia approached Lady Wendeline slowly, giving her time to think of an appropriate response. She held her head high and her shoulders equally square. This horrid woman wouldn't make her uncomfortable in her own home.

"Hmm." She smiled partially, almost enjoying the coming battle. "It's appropriate, I suppose, that you speak of my, as you say, adoptive father. He was a kind and fair man, blessed with a keen intuitive sense. He saw through your vengeful and wicked ways years ago."

"Dedrick would turn in his grave if he should hear you speak to your stepmother in such a manner. It's obvious that you've learned little respect from your elders, or Alisz who is very much a lady. This is another sign of your appalling genealogy."

"Leave the dear departed man out of this." Sophia laughed angrily in her face. "If he doesn't sleep peacefully, it's because he unknowingly fell victim to the lure of your temptation."

"It's a good thing, too, or he'd have no children of his own."

"You wound me."

"You must face the truth, sooner or later. Instead of carrying on, running about crying, feeling sorry for yourself."

"The truth? You dallied your sexuality as if you held Eve's apple in your hand. You used your figure to bridle and constrict my father's heart. He bit, fed, and you rejoiced, soon delivering a killing blow."

"He was a good man. I cherish his memory. However," she said, grasping black beads that lay on a garment of staunch black silk, wrapped around her neck, "he was not your father."

Lady Wendeline dropped the beads and stood abruptly. Sophia stepped backward, a gasp coming from her lips. "You hateful woman, I could strike you for saying it out loud."

"Insolent child," she declared, the anger flaring red from her neckline to her cheeks. "How dare you speak to me like this. I've done nothing to deserve your anger. I don't have to sit here and listen to your impertinent bearing."

"Quite right, Mother dearest, you do not. For I have had quite enough of your ugly jests. I promise you, I'll prove you wrong. Sleep well."

"If only you could," she bit back, approaching where Sophia stood. "Then, we'd all sleep better at night."

Sophia turned on her kid slippers and walked in an unhurried fashion to the staircase, hurrying to her bedchamber. Crossing the threshold, she walked into the room, immediately feeling the chill. Funny, she thought, for it was dark. Adeline, her chambermaid, always kept a fire burning in the hearth and a candle lit on the mantle. It was then that she noticed the scent of jasmine. She scowled, even before the voice penetrated the gray fathoms of air.

Damn. She was not alone.

"Tsk, tsk, tsk, mine sister," Alisz clicked her tongue disapprovingly where she lay on Sophia's bed. "How wanton of you to arrive home at such a late hour. Though I hardly blame you for seeking escape from your quandary, shouldn't you conduct yourself more respectably?"

Sophia approached the fireplace shaking her head. Bending down, she reached for a poker and stabbed at the coals. They were still hot. She reached for a taper and placed its wick against a smoldering log. When the wick erupted into flame, she placed the candle back on the mantle.

It angered Sophia that her stepsister could rest so easily atop her bed as if this belonged to her, too. Despite everything that had changed with the reading of the Will, she wanted to toss her from the room, but that would be no easy task. For Alisz did as Alisz pleased, much to the discomfort of everyone.

"It hardly matters to me what you believe," Sophia replied, facing her. "Only if you decide to gossip, please ensure the conversation is interesting."

"Oh my dear," she laughed deceptively; angering Sophia, "Of late, there's a wealth of information to confide to our friends and acquaintances. Well, with your revealing heritage and my wedding preparations. I thought you might be interested in knowing some of the details. 'Tis why I waited for you to come home."

"I'm not interested in your upcoming nuptials," Sophia said, clutching a chair nearby for support. "Even you for once could have some compassion and let it be. Marry Franz and have your bitter-sweet revenge, but leave me alone or you shall rue the day you ever interfered in my life."

Sophia watched her sister carefully checking her manicured talons. She wished she could wipe that impudent smile from her face. *What was she hiding?*

"Franz, he is a handsome specimen of a man, is he not? From your experiences, Sophia, do you think he will master the marriage bed?"

"How dare you ask such a question; I won't respond to such a retort."

Undeterred, Alisz raised herself to a sitting position and swung her feet off the side of the bed. "Come now, surely a woman as experienced and as well versed as you, is not embarrassed by such a question." She grinned, licking her lips. "Franz is a man who I can imagine is quite adept with his handling. A man such as he wouldn't be satisfied with a woman of a shy nature."

"He's an honorable man. A pity he's forced to wed a scheming woman such as you. He will not want you."

"I assure you that he does." Alisz stood, paused in thought, and then re-arranged her pretty-in-pink silk skirt with a skillful flourish.

"What lies do you shed now?"

"I didn't think it was possible, Sophia, but perhaps your upbringing has taught you some valuable lessons. You're still a blessed virgin. I'm shocked, but not surprised. Your entire life you've been a dreadful bore and too much the simpleton. It's just as well, for I wouldn't want my future husband soiled by your contact."

"You go too far."

"Not far enough," she mused, sauntering closer. "Sometimes, one must act in accordance with what will better thineself. Of course, some individuals get in the way, but they are people and people are expendable. Even a sister is dispensable. Of course, I mean you no harm, but I must act in my best interests."

Anguished tears pooled in Sophia's eyes. She reached for the nearest object within her reach as Alisz walked to the door; a porcelain dove. She threw the trinket with the force of the pain that constricted her chest. Her aim fell short, and the bird struck the doorjamb, shattering into a myriad of jagged bits.

"Sweet Jesu, Sophia!" Alisz's laughter irritated her eardrums. "Even at this you miss the mark. You're simply not a worthy opponent."

"Get out!" Sophia screamed, motioning menacingly to where the leper stood. "Leave my room!"

"Good night, bastard girl," she snickered as she left.

"Why are you always so cruel?" Sophia yelled, then closed and locked the door behind her departing sister, soon crouching over broken shards of porcelain. She retrieved the fragments, cutting her finger in the process. As droplets of blood stained the flooring, angry tears fell.

Leaving the rest of the remnants on the floor, she carried herself to bed fully dressed in her red crimson evening gown. She thought herself free of her tears and yet they continued to slide down the contours of her face, saturating her pillow.

"I've lost everything I once held dear," she croaked, hitting the pillow with her fist. "Everything."

It was a long time before she fell asleep.

CHAPTER 4

When Sophia reached the crest of the hill, she pulled on the reins, urging her mare to a more leisurely trot. She had allowed Maraclese to lead the tumultuous chase galloping recklessly across the scattered prairie. Hoping that the whisper of the wind rushing through her hair and biting at her face would lessen the pain. But a wild ride had not achieved the desired effect; it was time for the master to exert control.

The hour was early. The sun's rays had barely risen over the tree-lined hills. Sophia loved this time of day when the world was garden-fresh. She closed her eyes, reveling in the crisp breeze. It carried the scent of heather, mixed with a pungent musk, filling her with a certain calm. But then Maraclese nickered, which urged Sophia to open her eyes.

A man approached on horseback from the other side of the wood. As the distance between them lessened, she knew it was Franz. She felt like showing him her back, knew she should urge her horse in the opposite direction, but no, instead she waited silently and watched her former fiancé ride closer.

She studied him where he sat tall in the saddle, clenching and unclenching his gloved hands. He was a handsome man and he dutifully carried himself, befitting his station in life. She missed his affection. Sweet kisses and warm caresses had offered an all-consuming passion. He appeared the same, except he was not the same honorable man.

She considered the lack of concern for his appearance this morning. His lackluster brown hair held an untidy wave and a sizable growth of beard covered his face. Sighing, Sophia swore the whiskers only added to his features.

But beneath the rugged appearance, she sensed a lack of confidence. Though he looked his fill in her direction, he glanced away often, unable to maintain proper eye contact. His hazel eyes seemed shaded with the melancholy of suffering, perhaps guilt, too.

Sophia freed her gloved hand from the reins as if to reach out to him, as if to comfort him in their mutual pain. But she was not free to touch his dull locks any longer; indeed, he was hers no more. She didn't greet him as he neared, instead detached herself from his observation, weighted her hands on the pommel and waited for him to speak.

"I thought I might find you here, Sophia. I want to speak to you, if you would agree to hear me out."

"Have you come to offer hope?" she said with a sigh, as if that tiny inhalation of air might release the weight constricting her chest. "When last we met, you were steadfast that our love was lost."

"I need you to understand."

"I understand completely. A man full grown has made his choice, or should I say, his father and mother have made it for him. Doubtless, Alisz will look stunning in white taffeta, though gray woolen is more her lot. Will you be happy with your new bride?"

She studied him closely; he peered at the ground. "I will try. I must."

"You bastard!" Sophia cried out. "Why have you sought me out; to twist the knife deeper inside my chest? What could possibly be gained from our conversation? You've taken my love, stolen my heart, shattering everything!"

"I have only obeyed my parents' regard. It's my duty given that I'm the heir to the estate. But even with Alisz as my wife, I could have you still. Don't you understand, I want you still—"

"Have me still? What more can you expect me to give? Regardless of my circumstances, I have my pride."

"Sophia, please. We can work this out."

"There's nothing to work out. You have chosen Alisz."

"I didn't wait on your presence to argue, or to talk about your stepsister. Were there any other way, she wouldn't be my intended. It's an impossible situation and one not to my liking, surely you can see that."

"What I see, Franz, is a man who promised to love me." She regarded him without malice, without desire, but with open contempt. "You knelt on your knees, embraced my hands within your own and pledged to me an undying love. You whispered, speaking with great passion, asking me to make you happier than ever by becoming your wife."

"Yes, I remember it well." He glanced at her shyly, his voice whisper thin.

"I remember…" Sophia chirruped, her voice nostalgic, breaking. "I was filled with a tremendous joy."

"The moon paled in comparison to your emerald eyes that glowed brighter than the most luminous star in the heavens. You bewitched me," he said, reminiscing, his eyes filling with liquid at the recollection. "There's no one more beautiful than you, so stunning a creation you are. It was true then, it's true now with the beginnings of a new day."

"Please stop." She looked away, unable to bear the purposeful look of ardor. A weaker woman would have fallen prey to the lust he displayed, her faith clinging to the scraps of a possible future. Sophia could not bear to fall victim to such folly.

"Sophia, I will not give up on us, no matter what you say."

Through her peripheral vision, she watched him jump down from his roan stallion. Heard him approaching across the soft earth, and finally felt his hands on her own, his hand grasping hers where she held the reins, his other massaging her thigh. As she turned to look at him, tears blurred her vision. She quickly wiped them away.

"I can honor my duty, and still hold what matters."

Sophia closed her eyes, trying to ignore the avid sensations. God help her, but she didn't want his fingers to end their rhythmic pursuit. She searched for the strength to beseech him to stop.

"Why do you torture us, Franz? Why?"

"Because my darling, I love you. Surely you can see that my love is pure and unchanged. Were there any other way, I would lead you down the aisle this very minute. But I'm decreed to wed another and although that woman has come between us, this marriage cannot replace that which lies deep within our hearts. I don't love Alisz!"

Sophia grasped Franz's hand when his fingers wandered, attempting to touch her belly. The soft flesh was as warm as she remembered. She almost brought his fingers to her lips. Almost.

"Franz," she murmured as her mare pawed the earth, "can't you see that this wedlock business has already wreaked its devastation? If your words of love are honorable, then reject your parents' decree and take my hand in marriage as we had planned. I won't share you, especially with mine own sister!"

"Although my love for you is strong, I cannot defy my parents' directive. It would mean snubbing my heritage and everything that is important to me. Disobeying their authority could mean disownment."

"I will not give my children the same fate that has cast doubt on my life. I will not raise bastards." Wrinkling her face, she released his hand, pushing it away like some bad disease. "I thought I was important to you. You proclaimed your love yet again."

"I do love you, Sophia." He appealed in frustration. "But this marriage need not come between us. This match is no more than a blind obligation, a preferred pairing between a man and a woman, nothing more, nothing less. We can have each other still. If only you were not so obstinate! Be open to a union of sorts."

"You refuse to listen—I'm a lady, Franz Altbusser, such a life is not for me."

He grabbed her hand again. The vice-like pressure caused pain. "Is it really such a terrible notion?" he quipped; his facial expression became pinched and anger fired his hazel eyes. "We would be free to love each other. Free to explore our mutual passions without restraint. And I, my darling, could provide dearly for the woman I love. *I want you*; can you not see the need burning in my eyes? Look at me!"

She faced him then, shifting on Maraclese, but something in his scrutiny filled her with shame. "I will not entertain such a notion. You've made a choice. I won't allow you to entertain us both."

In his greed, he grasped her arm tightly, causing further hurt. "You witless bitch," he ground out cruelly. "So high and mighty with your faulty airs, when you're no better than a serving wench. You won't receive a better offer."

At her wince, he released his hold and stepped away. His fingers left a bruising impression on her tender skin, but his cruel words cut to the bone.

Blinking back tears, Sophia nudged Maraclese in the flank, urging her mare to a safer space. "I have lost a great deal as of late, I will not lose my pride as well."

"Pride will not keep your bed warm at night, Sophia."

"Regardless, my answer is no. It must be no, you heartless fool."

"I would have given you everything," he ground out angrily. "A country manor house far away where rumors could never reach. Servants, clothing, jewelry, anything your heart desired. How can you spurn my affections this way?"

Sophia gasped, greatly offended. "I have not spurned you. You know the truth of the situation."

His voice turned to ice. "I know what has caused this turn of affairs. You're a bastard—a damnable bastard. It pains me to remind you; your sordid past has brought us to this place. You're no longer worthy to marry a noble man. You should accept my offer, for it may be the last one you receive."

The words, combined with his ugly tone, hurt more than Sophia could possibly imagine. This man who had spoken passionately about their love moments before, had quickly turned a knife in her heart. Had he really loved her, or was her suspicion of lust more accurate? Was she a plaything to be admired, owned? She wouldn't be kept, by him or by any other man. She would be loved and respectfully married.

She nudged her horse into a gentle stride, which took her away from where he stood. "It's very sad, Franz, for I did love you," she mumbled, choking on a sob. "But the role of mistress will never be mine. I may be condemned to a state of bastardom, but my children, should I be so blessed, won't share the same fate."

"You're weak." He threw back. "I don't know what I saw in you."

She wiped a tear away. "God is as merciful as he is kind. If there is a man anywhere in this rotten world that is worthy of my love, I know he shall find me."

"Always remember," he called after her, "that this was your misplaced determination. You'll regret it one day when you're a disillusioned virgin, alone and unfulfilled in your bed. No gentleman will want your sullied hand."

She urged Maraclese to a trot, tears sliding down her cheeks. She didn't comment, nor look back, but his final comments couldn't be forgotten.

No gentleman will want you, no one will want you, seemed to whisper repeatedly in her thoughts.

She allowed her mare to lead her where she may. In her despair, the grasses mingled together to form a solid mass of green. Moments later, Maraclese was lapping up water from the White Elster River.

Sophia dismounted into the fast-flowing water, hardly sensing the cold fluid that licked at her kid leather boots. The water flowed past her ankles, soaking the hem of her dress, but she didn't step onto the safety of the embankment. Instead, she allowed her tears to carelessly flow and fall to the riverbed. Somewhere in her mind, thoughts tumbled together into a torrent of confusion. In her pain, she really wondered if perhaps Franz's perception of her was correct. Would any man see past her sordid history, considering her a worthy enough match to wed?

Franz himself was not willing to forego his parents' wishes to take her hand in marriage. Why then, would another man take such a risk? *His opinion must be correct in this nasty state of affairs*, Sophia sighed sadly. He was a man of the world and as such, he knew what fellow comrades would think of a woman such as her. A fallen woman condemned for the rest of her life.

No marriage offers would be forthcoming. Men would seek her skills as a mistress only. No longer the lady she thought herself to be, the name *'bastard'* seemed to echo to the reaches of her soul. The wordplay wouldn't stop. Indeed, the shame seemed stamped on her forehead for everyone to see. The shame was too great to bear.

Sophia removed her cloak and swung it over Maraclese's back. "Fair lady, I shall miss you," she whimpered, stroking the horse's shoulder. "You have been a loyal and trusted friend. For that, I thank you. But you shall find another owner. Take care, my girl," she said, patting her rump, urging her away, "find your way home."

The river was vast and the current strong. Sophia guessed it wouldn't take long for the woolen fibers of her dress to weigh her down. She didn't cry at this point, she would go silently into the night.

She watched the water tumbling with the current, quickly moving downstream. The fear of death collected at the corners of her heart, quickening her breathing. Yet panic was no deterrent. Trembling, she stepped further into the torrent, the water now at her knees. The sounds grew stronger, compelling her to move to a peaceful purpose. She need not be afraid. Death was a quiet thing, still and motionless and not filled with pain.

Even so, her steps slowed, the water reached just above her knees and she paused. The icy cold brought on convulsive shivers. Sophia gasped, taking a huge gulp of air. She looked back at the bank—to life, and then to the deeper, faster moving current—to certain death.

One step further could mean the end of her life, her dress would weigh her down and the water would wash her into its jaws. But back at the embankment life waited; would hope live there too?

Sophia stepped backward, wobbling on her feet, hesitating.

It was not like her to give up so easily. Alisz had enjoyed several victories as of late. Would she gain one more with this death?

Stop. Hurting herself was a mistake. Sophia pivoted toward hope, wanting to return to the safety of the riverbank, but the movement was too swift. She wobbled on a rock, losing her balance and plunging to her knees.

Suddenly cocooned by cold water, Sophie choked out a gasp, fought for breath, and was soon shaking from the bitter chill that threatened to deprive oxygen from her lungs. She struggled, trying to keep her head above the churning flow, but the fast-moving current grasped at her chest, dragging her ever deeper into the rush of moving water. She tried to stand, but her limbs refused to respond, suddenly paralyzed from the crushing cold.

"*Help…*" Sophia cried out, choking on the river water.

She couldn't save herself. The water swept over her, threatening to pull her under. She tried to whistle for Maraclese; perhaps she could grasp the stirrups and pull herself from the water, but she shook with cold and her breath eked out in a smothered whisper. She was afraid to move.

But it was not her day to die.

She cried with relief when someone grasped her arm and pulled her none too gently back to the safety of the shore. Soon standing on feet that threatened to give way and gasping for breath, she shivered from the cold, clinging to the person who held her. Pushing strands of hair away from her eyes, she suspected her former love had sought her out. Yet it was not Franz that greeted her embarrassment.

CHAPTER 5

*M*athias shook with concern, trembling from the scene he had just witnessed. It was not like him to anger so quickly, but Sophia's naiveté and careless risk of precious life fueled his emotions.

"Why?" he bellowed, gripping her shoulders. "Why have you attempted this nasty business?"

Quiet, shaking, and dripping water, Sophia scanned the ground guiltily. Her face scrunched up and it appeared as if she might cry. "Pa, pa, pain," she spluttered, her lips blue. "Too much."

None too gently, Mathias tipped her chin upward with his fingers, forcing her to look at him. "Is your life so worthless that you wouldn't ask for help? You could have sought me out. I would never turn you away! Where is your faith?"

"I'm—sorry—" she cried out, shaking violently. "I wasn't myself," she sputtered, gasping for breath. "I yearned for release from my frustrations, but I came to my senses before it was too late, only I tripped on the folds of my dress, and fell. Had you not come..."

He released her and bent downward to squeeze the water from the folds of his robe. "Lady Sophia—" His voice softened, rising back up. "Had I chosen an alternate path, had I altered my course in any way, you would have met with a terrible fate. You could have," he paused, shaking his head, "drowned. Do you realize the risk you've taken?"

She nibbled at her lip, stepping awkwardly to her horse, her dress clinging revealingly to her chest, buttocks and thighs. Dry, he imagined the emerald hues would flatter her delicate eyes, but wet, *well*, he wouldn't think about her female form.

She reached for her cloak, which was draped on her horse's back. "I'm aware. I came close to death's door."

"Let me help you," he muttered, approaching where she stood. "You'll catch your death of cold if you don't remove your gown." He took the garment from her hands and held it high to shield his view.

"Can I trust you to keep your eyes averted?"

"I'm a priest, I've sworn my vows."

"You're still a man."

"Take off the gown."

"Oh, very well. But do be a gentleman."

Mathias closed his eyes briefly as she untied the laces of her bodice, but he opened them too soon, only to witness the creamy flesh of her bare shoulder. He silently berated himself for being a curious man and didn't chance another look until the cloak was safely secured around her shoulders. She held the wet woolen garment awkwardly in her hands.

"It's the most dire of sins to seek an unnatural ending to your life. Had you succeeded, you would never have known God's grace. Your place in his kingdom would have been lost, with your soul cast into purgatory. Doomed to spend eternity in the shadows."

"Is there really such a place as purgatory? How can you be certain that it exists when you've never seen it? What of heaven, or of hell?"

He turned her to face him. "I have not witnessed these places, yet I have faith in their existence. Men and women are free to doubt, free to ask questions; I rely on the gift that God gave humanity; a Son who miraculously arose from death. By Christ's rising, those who believe in him shall have everlasting life."

She peered intently into his eyes, and then turned away to drape the wet garment over her horse's back. "I believe in this testament, Father, but how does the premature loss of my life cast me into purgatory? I'm not a stained person, neither am I evil or impure."

"I never meant to imply that you were bad, every human carries their sins."

"I made a mistake. Surely I would be forgiven."

She turned to face him. Mathias hardly realized he was caressing her with his eyes. Her cloak cracked open, giving him a glimpse of supple skin. A beautiful innocence drew him a step forward as he imagined mortal men would be drawn. An alluring woman, vulnerable in her pain, a lamb he must lead to safety. Could he show Lady Sophia that her soul was worth saving, that her life held promise? Would saving her wage war against his own destiny, thus destroying him? He realized whatever the cost to himself, he couldn't let this sweet woman perish into damnation.

"It's not for mere mortals to decide the ending of their lives."

"You misunderstand. I didn't mean to take my life. I slipped. I fell."

Her murky eyes creased in concentration, her brows shot dubiously inward. Her unspoken thoughts only confirmed what he suspected. "I think you're lying."

"All right, I confess it." She lifted her arms wide in frustration. He took a deep breath as more skin met his sight. "I lost hope, but I assure you, I've come to my senses."

"You must not lose faith. Hope shall be found, you only need to look to receive its light," Mathias entreated, scrutinizing the sky. "This world offers many gifts, the air we breathe, the blueness of the sky, the birds that fly unhindered through its space. Sometimes, we find our answers in the simplest of places."

"Hmm," she snorted, shaking her head. "Answers are never simple in my experience."

She must have noticed that he was staring at her bosom, for she grasped the folds of her cloak and squeezed the fabric together, closing the gap between. Frustrated, he grasped her elbow and led Sophia to a large oak tree that grew along the bank. An expanse of leg came into view from beneath her cloak. He hoped his indrawn breath and momentary lapse of movement went unnoticed.

Reaching for her hand, he splayed her cold fingers across the bark of the tree. Ever so gently, he massaged her knuckles; mindful of her big-eyed expression and how quiet she suddenly became.

"This tree has grown in this place for at least a hundred years, withstanding the tests of Mother Nature and man's plunder. It has provided a home for many an animal and shade for the traveler. If we were to chop it down with no thought to the loss, a home would be destroyed and we would enjoy its shade no more."

"It's not the same thing. A tree does not think?"

"What of this, then," he replied, taking her hand in his grip, pulling her close, and placing her palm where his heart beat strong.

"I don't understand?" She sighed, nibbling at her lip. "Is this some sort of lesson?"

"Of sorts." He might have imagined it, but he thought her breathing took on a different rhythm. She became quiet, gave him fleeting glances, had difficulty looking at him. "I want you to understand human purpose."

"By touching your chest?"

"By feeling the pulse of my life, the steady rhythm of my heart. This is my life rhythm beneath your hand, a steady beating force. Should I suddenly decide it should end, I have betrayed my promise."

"I've always learned lessons from your lectures, but surely your heart's purpose is simply to power your body, not your mind?"

"Of course, but through my sacrifice, I can offer hope to those that struggle. It doesn't matter what the struggle is. If I forsake an opportunity to do good will, I deny others its outcome."

SOPHIA no longer felt the cold that had created convulsive shivers throughout their conversation. The intensity of his conviction was compelling. She removed her hand from his chest to gaze at the fingers that had felt his heartbeat. She knew she could have loved him in that moment, but of course that was silly. She didn't need another lecture from yet another man, regardless that he held his faith convictions.

A man of the cloth, a priest, but at this tender moment he seemed no more than a hero whose righteous purpose was to help people. He had helped her and his actions had saved her soul from damnation. How could she ever recompense? Would he want her to?

"Father Mathias, I don't know what God's purpose holds for me." Sophia sighed. "But I can see that I must give myself time to discover it. I promise you, I won't take such a risk again."

"Should you ever face such a quandary, will you come to me?"

"And release my poorer intentions upon your spirit?"

"Yes," he said simply, pondering her whimsical expression. "I'd be delighted for the opportunity."

"Then you give me little choice but to agree."

A wistful smile shone on his face. He had sacrificed his comfort without thought or consequence for his person. She didn't remember when anyone had attempted such a risk for her, for Lady Sophia of Baldemar Manor.

He stepped closer. She stood still, perfectly motionless and quietly numb. So near now, that she could see the golden flecks in his amber eyes. In a slow lazy movement, he made the sign of the cross on her forehead.

She sucked in a breath, seeing the innocent passion in his eyes. As if in a trance, she could not look away from the tenderness.

"You are marked for God, Lady Sophia. Our praises be to the Lord, Hallelujah. How very pleased I am that you have chosen life."

"I've certainly been baptized anew." She smiled slightly, tilting her head to the side, very much in awe. "It's a powerful light you walk in, Father. I'm grateful to have found care within your sensible words."

He laughed softly, observing the cerulean blue sky. "For so powerful of a radiance, my clothing clings most uncomfortably to my skin," he said with a frown, glancing downward at his wet robe. "I suggest we depart for our residences, soon."

Sophia considered her own fragile state, frowning miserably, stepping slightly away. "Yes, the situation is grave. I cannot go home only wearing a cloak. My gown is soaked through. What am I to do?"

"It seems to me that it would harm no one if you joined me for the midday meal while your clothes dried by the fire."

"I accept your proposal," she said with a grin, then followed him as he led her back to Maraclese. She wrapped her cloak more securely around herself, hurrying to match his longer stride.

CHAPTER 6

*M*athias stood in the hallway inside his house; separated from a way of living he once had thought would be his own. Had he made a mistake by agreeing to his mother's wishes all those years ago?

He studied Sophia's daydream expression. She relaxed inside his parlor, lounging in an armchair by the fire, her feet tucked under her legs, holding a steaming mug of cider in her hands. A woolen blanket encircled her shoulders, and lay against her middle and across her legs. She suddenly stretched, pointing her bare feet to the warmth of the embers in the hearth, closing her eyes.

Sophia, she was perfect in every way and he liked her taking up space in his life.

Mathias watched as she sipped the nectar, swallowing when she licked a stray droplet that had spilled to her bottom lip. It was sinful to study her beauty. Blasphemous. But was it really wrong? Understanding the conflict didn't make it easier to dispel his growing awareness. She touched her lips, and he knew her kiss would be pleasant. He didn't delude himself; he wanted to kiss her.

Moments ago, he had been prepared to walk into the room. He didn't know what held him back. Surely it was wrong to stand in the shadows, *watching*, studying Sophia in her half-dressed immodesty. Guilt furrowed his forehead. Yet, he felt defenseless to stop the maelstrom of awareness that compelled him to silence, rendering himself helplessly still.

So he continued his appreciation, clenching and unclenching his hand in a massaging motion. Compelled, he observed Lady Sophia where she sat. In his favorite chair, absorbing the heat from the fire in his hearth.

Reclining into a relaxed position, she stretched comfortably backwards, exposing the creamy softness of her neck. He followed the columnar trail of pink skin that led to the base of her neck and downward to the indentation that separated her breasts. As if the depiction burned, he forced his gaze away, but her captivation drew him shamefully back.

Closing his eyes briefly, he leaned against the wall to support limbs that suddenly felt weak. He related the fervid enigma to adolescence and a student's developing sensuality. In those days, the frolicking gazes of a forthright girl brought foolish boy replies and sometimes not so boy-like meandering. Teasing had earned a few sweet kisses, which could have surmounted to much more.

Times were different then. Life was different when Marcos, *his brother*, had been the chosen one. Sometimes, Mathias hated his sibling for his weakness. Even for his death.

At this juncture in his life, thirty years on, he understood his perusing and man-like thoughts courted devil's sin by eyeing a female form. He realized the foolishness, and the disaster that could devastate his vocation through such sights. Sex was a sin for a priest. And yet he wondered, why such a vision of innocence, of veiled beauty, should be deemed such a threat?

His scrutiny strayed to the innocence of her relaxed expression, of cheeks reddened by the warmth of the fire and lips turned blood red, upturned into the slightest whimsical smile.

God forgive me, but she is beautiful, and as precious as the feathered wings of a dove and as pure as the hallowed cloak of an angel's wing.

But her embrace would be as damning as the devil himself. He couldn't have her. Not without leaving the priesthood, and if he decided to do such a thing, he'd not only disappoint his mother, he'd also hurt his parish community. Promises had been made. It was too late to change the past. Marcos—

Still, doubt grew as he leaned to a natural yearning, his eyes perusing her soft curves. The swell of her chest rising upward, then down, followed by the slightest exhalation of air from her rosebud lips.

Mathias was sure an infusion of color must have washed over his face at that moment. Followed by the quickening canter of his heart, the labored breathing of his lungs, and the shameful reckoning of his manhood. Even his hands seemed to perspire from the scene he silently witnessed.

As if she sensed his presence, Sophia turned her head to where he stood and welcomed him warmly with bright eyes and a soft smile. Mathias took a deep breath, and then wiped his perspiring hands against his black woolen robe. Following that, he entered the room.

She should have been embarrassed to be in his presence in little more than a blanket and a servant's thin nightdress. But he could tell that Lady Sophia was comfortable. He cleared his voice and sat in an adjacent chair.

"I see that my housemaid has seen to your comfort. Is there anything else you require, Lady Sophia?"

She smiled affectionately, and then pulled the blankets more firmly around her shoulders, drawing her knees to her chest. The satiny look only puzzled him more.

"Edda has seen to everything. She has spared some clothing and a blanket, as well as soothed my appetite through a delicious cup of cider. Alone in this quaint little room, before the embers of the fire, I hardly remember when I have felt so cared for, or at peace."

"Are you closer then to accepting the trials which have caused havoc in your life? Have you come to terms with what your life-path may hold?"

Her smile vanished. He almost wished he had not asked, but the subject could not be avoided. Not with the choices that had been made earlier today.

"Father, surely by now you understand my struggle. Of course I've accepted the nasty business, but it's most difficult to seek a promising future within that change."

"Indeed, there's no debating the difficulty." The haunted look returned to her eyes, alarming him. "But don't underestimate your prowess as a woman. You have many advantages, virtues which may not have been fully considered."

Curiosity rose among her brow line. "Franz told me that no other man would want me with my name sullied," she declared, taking a sip of cider. "I almost believed him when he told me the position of mistress was the best I could hope for."

"Did you consider it?"

"Did I what?"

"Did you consider his offer, to become his mistress?"

She turned away, refusing to look at him. "Would it have been so terrible if I had?"

Mathias followed the cup to where it touched her lips. "Yes. To court sin is always wrong."

"Why?"

"Surely a man of the cloth doesn't need to educate a lady on matters of adultery."

"Love knows no bounds, Father, but you being a priest, wouldn't understand that."

The comment angered him. "I assure you, I'm not a eunuch; I understand a great many things." He swallowed, courting sin himself. "I wasn't always a man of the cloth."

"I'm sorry, I didn't mean to offend," she said with some seriousness. "But perhaps I thought better of lowering myself to such a poor standard. I dug within my soul, scraping up my pride. I won't settle for second best. I won't be called worse than a bastard, namely, a whore."

"But you think of him still, a man who betrayed you? Your faith would be better placed in the teachings of Jesu."

"I believe in the doctrine, but religion won't warm my bed at night, nor will it gain me children. I shall never succumb to the affair of a mistress, so hope is lost."

Mathias shook his head. To live the life of a woman would indeed be hard. They lived in a state of constant worry and reflection.

"Lady Sophia, if it's love you seek, then love you shall find. It may not be within the arms of a noble man, but would the devotion of a lesser human being embrace you any less?"

"I suppose not," she mumbled, nibbling at her lower lip. "But sleeping in some crofter's dwelling with chickens and pigs to tend to in the yard, and me wearing some scratchy-thick woolen, doesn't paint a pretty picture."

He raked his hands through his hair. "If God's purpose is that you should wed, there will be a man. His occupation matters naught. Hold to some faith."

"Faith," she whispered, tasting the word on her tongue. "That's a tall order, but I suppose that devotion should always encourage thought. Perhaps you're right, perhaps there is a man in the world who is worthy of my love."

She paused then, staring at him. Her daydream expression returned, a vision that relaxed Mathias and put his mind at ease. Perhaps now with renewed hope, she would no longer consider disastrous deeds.

Hearing Edda's approach, he turned to the open doorway. She bustled into the parlor with a serving tray, filled with the aroma of freshly made buns, and layers of meat and cheese. She placed the tray on a small table, harrumphed loudly, and then addressed Lady Sophia as if Mathias were not in the room.

"Lady Sophia," Edda ground out, "I have found a dress from a cotter's lass. Although its quality is inferior to your fine muslin, it will suit your purposes."

Mathias wondered why she felt the need for forceful speech? But he realized her tact, protection of himself. Yet she didn't look his way.

"I know you'll want to take your leave," Edda continued, "as soon as your lunch is finished. Of course, I shall see to your fine gown and have it delivered to the manor."

He should have said something, Mathias realized. But he understood that Edda was only trying to protect him from a beautiful woman's temptation. And rightfully, they shouldn't be sitting together like this. He would make a mental reminder to thank his housemaid for her intervention.

He watched Sophia tap her index finger against her cup. "Very kind of you to make such arrangements. I appreciate the effort and I'm sure the dress will be suitable."

"Very good, I'll have it ready for you shortly, you'll find it in the kitchen. I hope it's not too, scratchy!" After the curt comment, Edda left the room.

"I'm sorry. My housekeeper only means to remind me of the impropriety of our situation. It's not common to entertain a woman in regular street wear, much less bedroom attire."

Her face flushed red. "I suppose it's unthinkable to be in your private chambers, given that you're a priest."

"Let's not think about that right now. Let us give thanks, instead."

"Is there something you wish to say, Father?" she asked when he grew quiet.

"Yes," he said as he clasped his hands in prayer, looking pointedly at Sophia. "Grace. Thank you for this food that we have received and thank you for this woman's soul whom we have saved together."

"Amen," Sophia whispered, "and thank you."

AFTER THEY FINISHED THEIR MEAL, Sophia rose from her chair, pulling the blankets with her. "I think it's time I took my leave."

His observance was no less intense. "Should I see you to your home?"

She wanted to say yes, but knew their time together must end.

"I'd rather not go, if truth be told, but I suppose I must. I can find my way. If you'll excuse me…"

She left the room, promptly stumbling over an imaginary object. Recovering herself, she made her way to the kitchen where she expected the housemaid would be waiting, but the room was unoccupied, with a simple peasant dress tossed over a chair. Changing quickly, she left the priest's house, and walked to the enclosure where Maraclese waited with her ears raised.

Mathias's voice drifted from the doorway.

She turned to him, her heart pounding, smiling. "I'll expect your presence at Mass this Sunday, Lady Sophia. Do not disappoint me."

"I wouldn't miss it," she called out, and then mounted Maraclese. Soon after, she was cantering away from the sanctuary of his religious world. As she rode, she tried to dispel the memories that came to mind, but she could not dispel the worry.

Sophia was sure she had witnessed a powerful passion in the Father's eyes. It was likely no more than the passionate telling of the word. Perhaps the underlying currents that had heated her face were only imaginary.

Mathias…

She wondered as she trotted closer to home, had he witnessed the very same need in her eyes?

A choir of young boys stood in the choral loft wearing robes of indigo blue. Singing, their angelic voices resonated throughout the noisy din of the chapel, echoing off its limestone walls.

Our Father, who dwells in heaven, bid us to dwell in love—[1]

A heavy song for young souls to sing, Sophia ignored the music to study the sculptures instead. Located high above her, if the statues of the saints had been real, they'd have been impressed with the boys. Indeed, the Saxon congregation seemed in awe. Finally quiet, they sat on their private benches in order of societal status, row upon row in an elongated procession; not one piece of unwarranted gossip slipped from their mouths.

But before the boys had taken up their song, the conversation among the churchgoers had been loud with proper gossip. However, no one permitted a fallen angel to be privy to their discussions, which could only mean that she didn't mean anything to them. The obvious shun was made more obvious by set expressions that perused her way in rolling disapproval, hurting her. She almost cried for the pain endured, indeed the tears threatened to fall, but pride had kept her emotions intact.

The abandonment by a community and friends was a hard lesson to overcome. Not even Lady Emilie, usually the most thoughtful friend in the community, would welcome her friendship now.

As Jacob Hermann's soprano voice soared over the choir, Sophia eyed her stepsister cynically. Alisz seemed to enjoy the mess of her life. Though her stepsister attempted to show society that she sympathized with her plight, Sophia knew these displays to be nothing more than a false ploy. Her actions of the previous week indicated as much.

She cringed when their eyes met. Lady Alisz's lips, though raised in a smile, pressed tight into a thin sneer. She fingered the ruby pendant she wore about her neck possessively, her eyes never faltering from her quarry. Sophia glanced away, not amused by the quiet laughter that followed her eye's retreat.

It had been a difficult week and Sophia reflected sadly on the events that had transpired. Alisz had played a part in her discomfort, seeming to confront her every move.

It had begun with the loss of the miniature portrait of Franz. His painted image had rested on her bureau, only to be pilfered to lie in Alisz's hands. She wondered *why*, even as she recalled her sister's bitter words.

"Such a lovely miniature, would you not agree, Sophia? A fine gift to provide one's betrothed before the wedding day. I'm sure Franz would want me to have it."

She took it! Sophia wondered why the loss of the picture had not garnered more pain? Perhaps she was beginning to recover from the loss of Franz and the painting no longer held its prior importance. However, if the portrait had mattered, she could have snatched it back, instead of allowing her sister to keep it.

The game should have ended with that slight, but Alisz's schemes continued. Not a day had passed before she was confronted again with thievery. This time in the music room with the ruby pendant adorned around her neck, sinking low to lie between her breasts.

Sophia chastised herself for the weakness that had transpired. Her ill feelings had almost led her to remove the ruddy jewel in a less than lady-like fashion. Indeed, she had held her fisted hands in check by her sides to ward off the action. Hoping that she wouldn't strike the woman who had obviously invaded her bedchamber to steal a gemstone that didn't belong to her.

Alisz's voice came back to haunt. "I knew you would want me to have this, Sophia," she had cunningly whispered, while fingering the brilliance of the ruby. "I took it so as to save you the trouble of gifting it yourself. Do you think the beauty of the stone, so well positioned between my breasts, will inspire passion?"

Sophia's face flamed anew at the remembrance. The boldness. The cold clarity; a sister should never be so cruel. She had turned on her kid heels, stealing into her room, taking the jewels that Franz had given her. Cruel laughter had raked up her hearing.

Just a trinket, Sophia had told herself, and as such was not worth her disappointment.

There was no denying, however, that these escapades had a way of downing one's mental wellbeing. The gifting of Franz's material treasures, once given in representation of their love, seemed like the answer to the problem.

Sophia had taken a small package that contained a few small, yet priceless pieces of jewelry. She had laid them at the foot of Alisz's door, not wanting to venture into the lion's den. Hoping that this act would end the petty pain, but her sister was a strong opponent. Recalling the conversation of this morning in the company of Lady Wendeline, Sophia flushed with anger.

"It is a shame, Mama, that Sophia has been forced to walk away from a marriage match with Franz. I would step aside from the commitment we've made to his family, if only to save Sophia further embarrassment." Sighing heavily, she had continued. "But of course that would be impossible. I must proceed bravely, however moved I am by my sister's plight."

Sophia rolled her eyes, waiting for more of the charade. Alisz was indeed a good actress. "It's appropriate that Sophia take a small role on my wedding day. You know, Mama, to feel a part of the merriment. As well as to show unity within our family, in that we are not bothered by the fact that she is, excuse my words here, illegitimate. I was thinking, it would be practical if she were my maid of honor."

A rush of air exploded from Sophia's lungs. "Never!" she had bellowed. "I shall not escort your damnable presence down the aisle. Not now, not ever!"

Alisz was not deterred from her speech. "Please do not interrupt, Sophia. This is between Mama and me. As I was saying, she is my sister. Though a half-sister only, it seems right for her to take a natural place by my side."

Sophia was brought back to the present reality when Father Mathias walked down the long aisle, swinging the smoking censer as he approached the pulpit. The boys' voices filled the sanctuary with sound, even as the purifying fragrance sanctified the air. Everyone waited for the ending of the hymn:

From evil, Lord, deliver us. The times and days are perilous...[2]

Sophia watched Father Mathias where he stood at the pulpit, cloaked in white, a cloth halo inset with gold about his head. His presence in white encouraged the congregation to watch only him. After a short prayer, he began to preach.

He raised his hands in a grand gesture to the ceiling of the church. "For God so loved the world, that he gave his only begotten Son, our Lord Jesus Christ. Through our Blessed Virgin Mary, a child was born in a manger, and humankind was promised a future within his faith. For those that believeth in him will be blessed with an eternal life."

He lowered one hand, motioning it to the parishioners in the front row. "Some of you will say the obvious. I was born to age and die, and within that death there should be nothing more. But I say to you that death need not be the ending, if we only believe in our Savior. For as the scripture reading reveals, when we believeth in him, we shall have everlasting life. Our souls will surpass our bodies."

Father Mathias continued in this vein for a time, and Sophia found herself entranced by his sermon, and the compelling nature of his voice. When the style of the Mass changed, she was surprised at the strength and intensity of the man that changed with it.

He looked at her often, seeking her attention. The intensity of each perusal washed over her fervently, lighting a fire within her chest as heated as the speech he pursued. She realized his purposeful words were offered to the congregation that he wished to save from their evils and not a lure to passion.

"Though we are promised eternal life through our beliefs, we must respect the Ten Commandments that God revealed to Moses. They were intended to govern a better people. Failing to respect these rules, and sinning against them, will result in the sinner's judgment at his time of death. The devil's wrath and eternal damnation to the fiery pits of Hell, could be the sinner's final resting place, regardless of their belief in Jesus Christ."

Sophia felt the hair on the back of her neck rise as she pictured the horrid scene of fire and brimstone. Alisz was deep in thought, not affected by his words, which suddenly became merciful.

"But we are fortunate, *you and I*, for our Heavenly Father is as compassionate as Lord Jesus is forgiving. He cried out on the cross: 'Forgive them, Father, they know not what they do.' Even during the last moments of our Savior's life, he relayed a vital message of forgiveness. This message is one we must learn from and obey, in order to reap the rewards of heaven and eternal life."

Everyone watched, waiting for him to speak again. "I ask of you, can the sacrifice of our Savior be found here among us? Have each of you led an honest life this past week, free from the pillages of sin? And if some of you have succumbed to iniquity, favored others poorly and behaved improperly, have you requested forgiveness and penance for your actions?"

Mathias's voice grew louder. "We are told that Jesus died for our sins, but I tell you, he perished because of our sins. We must learn from his sacrifice in order to prevent further destruction of our souls. In hopes of such a travesty never occurring again."

He took a breath before continuing. Raising his right hand, he curled his fingers into a fist, and then pounded on the pulpit. Though the sound was minimal; the crowd barely breathed, suspended by the impact. A child's startled cry the only timbre to break the din.

"I command you now and always to keep free from sin, for sin will affect the devastation of man. But wherein sin occurs, seek penance and forgiveness from those that would be hurt by you in order to cleanse your souls. As Jesus is forgiving so must we be repentant."

His voice abated somewhat. "Finally," he breathed deeply. "Allow myself as your priest to grant absolution for your sins, so that you might begin anew and not be burdened by their weight. With this in mind, let us pray."

After prayers, Mathias urged his parishioners to be a compassionate people throughout the course of the next week. He urged each congregant to do one kind gesture for another. This act of thoughtfulness would put a gold star on their halos and keep them on a righteous path. He also reminded them of the community picnic the following week after Mass, celebrating the betrothal of Lord Franz Altbusser and Lady Alisz Baldemar.

Sophia groaned, attempting to conceal her emotions. But the idea of Franz and Alisz marrying was an eventuality that still caused her pain.

The choir began to sing as Mathias took his exit to the back of the church. She watched him walk down the aisle to stand at the entrance of the church. Congregants were soon shaking his hand and wishing him well. Thanking him for his effectual words that some would heed, but most would ignore.

She allowed Alisz and Lady Wendeline to leave without her, telling them quietly she could find her own way home. Only after the last person had shaken Mathias's hand, did she rise to approach him. As she walked down the aisle, nearing him, he closed the heavy oak doors, locking them within the church, quite alone.

She realized that she should have been alarmed by the impropriety of his action. What would people think who stood beyond the door, still gathered and conversing about the sermon? Did they realize that Sophia of Baldemar Manor, a fallen angel, was still inside the church, alone with their priest? Would his action damage her reputation further, his own perhaps as well?

What unsettled her further was his grin. She glanced away, supposing that the joviality she witnessed grew from the victory of his impassioned speech.

"Excellent service, Father Mathias. Surely, potential souls have been saved."

He calmly approached. Sophia took an uneasy step backwards, but she could not escape his purposeful voice. "I'm happy to hear I've paid proper homage. The threat of the devil is a heavy burden to set free on a fearful people. Yet I hope my sermon has encouraged those that wrongly judge, to change their ways and act in good conscience of each other."

"Opinions are not altered so quickly, and some toss their coins into your basket only to indulge their sins. But are you saying that your service was intended for me?"

He took a step closer and grasped her hand as if this act was natural, possessing her with his eyes in his happiness. She blushed, felt the heartbeat fluttering in her chest. His touch was innocent, but her response was a burden of guilt too heavy to bear, for he was a priest. The rising sensations afflicted her as a man's caress might and she stepped closer, leaning to the flame that glistened in the furthest corner of his eyes.

It was wrong, she realized forlornly. And her point was made clearer through the sanctity of the church she stood within. She could almost feel the weighted eyes of God on her, chastising her for a wanton behavior that she was weaving on his steward. But she couldn't help the scrutiny. Despite the fact that the man was a priest, he was handsome.

His expression changed as if he realized her pondering. He released her hand and stepped to a safer proximity before he spoke again.

"I'm saying that my service was indeed for you, for you and others that are affected by careless sins. Some people never beg forgiveness; they take and never give back. Somehow," he confided, "I never seem to reach the darkness that destroys their souls, try as I might."

"I'm stunned, Father," she whispered solemnly, her eyelids fluttering downward. "No one has ever done such a thing for me before."

She chanced to look up, unable to hide from his gaze. He was thoughtful in his expression, quiet, considering. He stepped to her again and reached for her shoulder, grasping her hand again. The world's motion seemed to slow, possibly coming to a noticeable stop as an electric current swept through her.

"You," he whispered confidently, "are worthy of God and welcome within his embrace."

Sophia searched his eyes. "That's kind of you to say."

"Sophia…"

In the moments that passed, it was Mathias's grasp and perusal, which brought an unforgivable yearning. Heaven help her, she could care for this man. "Father—I should leave."

She stepped to his side to escape his gaze, but he didn't release her hand, which forced her right shoulder and bosom to graze his arm. She peered at him in wonder and he released his hold, stepping away.

"I suppose that would be wise. I have hours of reading ahead of me."

"I wouldn't want to keep you from it," Sophia breathed, standing so close to him that she could hear his uneven breathing. She saw the emotion that banked within his heady stare, but she couldn't add kindling to the fire, no matter how much she might want to.

She attempted to walk past Mathias once more, only to have her hip brush against his thigh. Every muscle breathed awareness.

"I believe I should take my leave, Father," Sophia faltered, noting his weighted breath. She pretended not to notice his tension; perhaps this sense of passion was an illusion as well. If she turned her head, seeing his eyes again, the trueness of her thoughts might be revealed.

"I hardly know what to say." His voice was valiant. Soft, quiet, compassionate. "After sharing so much with the congregation, I find myself at a loss for words."

"Don't burden your soul. It's not uncommon for a man to appreciate a woman."

"Is that what this is then, an appreciation?"

"What more could it be? You're my spiritual advisor. Nothing more."

She knew it was a lie. Gazing quizzically at him for a moment, Sophia turned on her heel to approach the oak doors. He didn't deny the emotions and his last words to her indicated that he too, had felt their passion. She held her hand to the knob and pulled it open slightly, then closed it again, looking back at him.

She held his amber gaze intently within her own for a moment longer, before she spoke to him.

"Mathias," she barely whispered. "Words perhaps cannot properly convey the message, but I wish to impart my gratitude. Two minor words gifted from my heart. Thank you."

With his nod of understanding, she turned and fled the church.

AFTER SOPHIA'S DEPARTURE, Mathias considered the reverberation of the door. The resounding noise was almost as loud as his heartbeat, which threatened to run out of control. He took a deep breath in his attempt to dispel the conflicting emotions that had risen to engulf him.

What has happened? My heart is racing.

In ten years of ministry, a woman had never affected him like this. He had responded in an eager manner that might be pleasant for the average male, but was terribly embarrassing for a priest.

He tried to reason why the emotions had come into play and several thoughts occurred to him. She was weak, a lost lamb among a pack of wolves. It was natural for him to take pity on her plight and attempt to save her.

But having her in the church with him, *alone*, and then touching her? Most unwise!

Likewise, it was his responsibility to give her the strength to break the chains that bound her heart. Show her the necessary tools to lead a constructive and normal life. He was her priest. It was his duty to help. *Not hinder.*

Mathias sighed as he left the sanctuary to move to the relative privacy of his house. Later as he removed the white robe, laying the fine garment on his bed, he wondered if there was more? Was he attempting to save Sophia's soul for God, *or for himself?*

Even as he considered her name, her image came unbidden to his mind. In the privacy of his room, his fingers lingered over the flesh that had touched the softness of her breasts.

He couldn't allow the situation to grow out of control. Not only had he offended a woman whose life was unsettled, he had also brought disfavor on the church. His only excuse was the excitement of a service that had gone well.

In that moment, he had discovered an emotion never experienced before, a woman's gift of love, passion, and old-fashioned desire. Fragile feminine qualities shaped the warmth of a flesh and blood woman. Surely, they were meant to be.

He approached the wardrobe wearing only his linen tunic, soon retrieving a clean robe. Moving back to his bed, he sat down, holding the black cloth loosely in his fingers, shaking his head.

What could he do? Was there any way out of this situation? Should he consider leaving the priesthood? But he'd made his promises. He'd hurt people if he broke his sacred vow.

Still, he could love her. This woman, whose soul required deliverance from her past would be easy to protect. He would be lying to himself if he didn't admit that he wanted to protect her from the evils of the world.

It was a sinful thought, blasphemous, a notion that could destroy his vocation as a priest. He rubbed his arm, remembering the blessed sensation of his skin brushing against her—

"I will save you," he whispered, believing his own convictions. "But only for God."

CHAPTER 8

*S*ophia stood apart from the other guests speculating why Alisz had bullied her into coming to the celebration. She hated being at the Altbusser Estate. The betrothal party could only make a difficult situation worse, and she feared the conflicts that could arise.

Sighing, Sophia sipped from a goblet of red wine while contemplating a cerulean sky, trying to enjoy the sun's warmth on her fair skin. Admittedly, it was a pleasant summer day, but fetching her horse and galloping across the low-lying hills would have been more appealing. Giving her the opportunity to reflect on the man who had been in her thoughts these past days. Instead, she'd endure a man's cast-off hurt, the scorn of society peers, and the real object of the game, her sister's drama.

Sophia watched Alisz conversing with her newly acquired admirers. Yawning out of boredom, she recalled that the women had once been her companions. Not anymore. Felines didn't make good friends; they were too fickle for such bonds. But Alisz's rise to a new and better last name had attracted elitists,

74

and of course, the riff raff wanted to be acquainted with the next Lady Altbusser.

They laughed in obvious amusement, their body language posturing in her direction. Lady Emilie, gowned in fashionable blue silk, had the temerity to point her finger, glancing her way. Alisz merely smiled, then giggled, adoring the attention.

Anger constricted Sophia's chest and her face surely reddened. She knew they were talking about her, but she willed herself to disregard the taunts. Let them talk and point their fingers. They thought themselves high-classed ladies with their societal ways, but they were no better than the lowest of the peasant class. Only a vile person would turn on a peer who they had once called a friend. She could do without that type of spit-in-your-face loyalty.

Without thinking, she searched the perimeter for Franz, scrutinizing the assembled guests scattered in various places across the back lawn. She saw him standing near the fire-pit, conversing with the hired help who basted and turned the mutton on a spit. The aroma drifted to her, reminding her of the hunger that stirred within. Not only for cuisine, but also for a love she had once known. But that was finished now, dead and buried.

When Franz caught her staring, the intensity of his scrutiny caused her to turn away. She should leave. This was not a place to heal. Thinking she'd take a walk, she passed across the lawn, but she felt his greedy stare with every step. She thought she'd escape and walk along the river, but Alisz wouldn't permit her to leave just yet.

"Sophia…" she called out merrily, "many have gifted me with their presence, offering their congratulations for a long and happy marriage. I have yet to hear from you?"

Sophia stepped nearer to the clutch of men and women. "I shouldn't think it necessary. So many guests have propped up your chest already."

She moved decidedly too close to Lady Emilie and stumbled, instigating the spill of wine on the lady's dress.

"You clumsy fool—" Lady Emilie gasped in horror, gesturing at the stain. "Look what you have done!"

"Oh my," Sophia muttered, nibbling at her lip as red crimson seeped through the silken fabric. "How clumsy of me."

"You did this on purpose!" She fumed angrily while Lord Finster endeavored to sop up the wetness. She didn't push his hands away.

"So sorry, Lady Emilie, please forgive my slight." Sophia tried to control the emotion that threatened to bubble forth in laughter. After all, it was all in good fun, pointing fingers and the like.

Removing the lord's hand herself and not caring about the embarrassment that Lady Emilie would suffer, Sophia presented her former friend with a handkerchief. "Perhaps this will help to claim some of the spill."

"It's just like you to act like this," she raged, accepting the offering. "Look at me, look at what you've done."

Lady Emilie allowed herself to be led away by the lord. Although no longer in his prime, he still held the handsome qualities that made him appealing to the opposite gender. No doubt he'd enjoy the fruit of her efforts.

Sophia glanced at her stepsister after their departure. Alisz's face flamed with barely concealed anger, but a smirk hid just beneath the surface, too. "That was a dirty trick, Sophia. But one I'd expect from you."

"Accidents happen, and I don't care what you think," she bit back, paying her no mind or the other ladies who rebuked her with clandestine looks. "But before I leave your suffocating presence, I have a gift for you. 'Tis why I interrupted your reverie." Sophia reached for a small wooden box that was hidden inside the folds of her skirt.

"You surprise me. I didn't expect a gift."

"It's not much," Sophia whispered, soon pressing the box into her sister's hand. "It doesn't in any way congratulate your success, but it is appropriate."

She watched Alisz lift the lid, and then peer inside the empty box lined with red silk.

"Tell me," Alisz whispered, grasping her wrist. "What does this non-gift mean?"

"'Tis simple," Sophia breathed icily, removing her hand. "A simple box, free of carvings or etchings, represents your humble beginnings. The red silk portrays the manner in which you captured my betrothed, with deceit and trickery."

Alisz laughed gaily, not wanting to appear offended, as Lady Richelle and Lady Lisbeth approached where they stood, perhaps keen to overhear the tête-à-tête.

"Clever," Alisz said, stepping closer, whispering in her ear, "but the box is empty. Why?"

The smell of jasmine perfume suffused the air and penetrated Sophia's nose. Satiny skin grazed the side of her face. "You've taken everything that should have been mine; I have nothing more to give you."

"I've only taken what was mine to receive."

"One day, you'll pay the price for your thievery. Your soul is as empty as that box."

Alisz stepped slightly away, her face heated a shade of scarlet and she fanned herself vigorously as if the sun was the culprit for her unease.

"Let me help you, sister," she emphasized bitterly. "It's time for you to move on. There's nothing more to discuss. Get over it. Franz is mine and I've come to know him in an intimate way."

"You can't possibly have done such a thing."

"Listen. I've given myself to your former fiancé," she snickered, licking her lips. "I've lain within his arms and claimed him, a *babe* could rest within my womb. Let me tell you, he was, delicious!"

"You lie!"

"You think so?" she hissed, throwing the box to the ground. "Why should I lie?"

Sophia turned angrily on her heel, her sense of calm gone. She wouldn't break. She attempted to leave her stepsister's company, but couldn't stop herself from turning back.

"Congratulations," she retorted angrily. "You've earned yourself a spot in Hell. May God take pity on your soul."

"Worry about your own divinity," Alisz said with a curt nod, "your halo is slipping."

Sophia ignored the parting comment, but her former friends were equally cruel: "What a little fool. How rude! Not a nice way to manage a sister!"

Breathe easy, she told herself. *Words can't hurt me.* Walk slowly, patiently, steadily. They watch for any slip you care to make, waiting for your pride to land about your feet.

Sophia rubbed her aching temples, managing a tight smile. Taking a deep breath, she glanced at her nemesis. She was sipping her drink, smiling, unperturbed by the turn of events. In fact, it appeared as if she had enjoyed the scene.

Why?

Sighing heavily, Sophia left the celebrants. Passing some distance across the lawn, she soon stood by the river's edge. It was peaceful here. The sunlight glistened on the water in shimmering ripples, and the water flowed smoothly downstream. The birds, unhindered by human activity, sang joyful tunes, hidden within the leafy branches of deciduous trees. She shielded her eyes from the sun and watched their flight among the branches.

The beauty of the scenery calmed her, eased her breathing, and helped her gain some control. Looking over the water again, she thought of Father Mathias who had saved her life a bit further upstream.

How could I have attempted it? Was my despair that great?

Funny, but Father Mathias hadn't made an appearance at the party just yet. Perhaps she'd see him later, she missed him after all. He'd become a friend in this difficulty. Leaning downward, she picked up a rounded stone. Warming it in her palm, she tossed it into the water and watched it land with a plop.

Hearing a sound, Sophia pivoted, soon realizing that she wasn't alone. She smiled at first, thinking it might be Mathias, but then frowned, seeing that it wasn't her supportive friend. Instead, Franz stared at her in an unnatural way.

"If I were the stone held in your hand," he called out, gesturing with his fingers, then grabbing a stone, skipped it across the water. "Would you carelessly toss me away? Wouldn't you hold me for a moment, permitting the slightest warmth to show your appreciation of my character?"

Sophia stepped backward, worried by the tension she saw in his eyes. He was visibly changed from their last encounter. The unshorn face and untrimmed hair were gone; days of uncared-for growth had been expertly trimmed into a tasteful beard, presenting a handsome portrait.

It suited him, gaining him a masculine appearance that would delight many a woman. Had once delighted her. But it didn't encourage her care now, nor did it increase her heart's pace. He had deceived her by agreeing to marry Alisz, and now he thrust a knife into her gut by going to her bed. If indeed, he had done so.

Sophia sighed, finding the courage to speak. "A stone is a mineral of nature, Franz. I don't own it, but I do appreciate its natural purpose. If I were to commit to its ownership, I would hold it tenderly, like a precious jewel, never deceiving its worth."

He stepped closer, so close she could smell the liquid spirits on his breath. "We're back to that, are we," he rallied, "your presumed deception of the heart."

"Your definition of deception apparently differs from mine," she said in exasperation. "There's nothing presumed in my treatment by you, Franz Altbusser. I ask you, do we celebrate our marriage betrothal this day? Or do you take another to the altar?"

He grabbed her around the waist, shocking the breath from her lungs. "I want you by my side. Have you no care for me any longer?"

"Please…" she cried out, attempting to wrestle his hands from her waist. "This is not right."

"But of course it is," he wailed, pulling her to his chest. Grasping her hair in his hands, he nestled his head into the crook of her neck. "I've missed you," he breathed deeply, "don't be unkind. I'm a man starved."

"This is not my day. Alisz has stolen everything."

He wound his fingers into the tresses of her unbound hair. "It should have been our day. You should be the bride at the altar. I still want you there."

"You've made your decision. It's too late to turn back." Sophia tried once more to remove herself from Franz, but he wouldn't let her go. The strength of his grip almost hurt. "You cannot have us both!"

"If only you would agree, I could have you still! Why would you be so unkind?"

Relenting somewhat, she rested her hands on his chest and stared blatantly into his eyes. "You say you want me at the altar and yet we shall never meet there. You're too weak to marry the woman you deem so nobly to love. And though you speak of not wanting your intended, already you have tasted her lust-filled fruit!"

Anger darkened his eyes, making Sophia wonder if perhaps she should have been more cautious with her telling, but it was too late to take back the words.

Franz grasped her derriere roughly and pulled her against the spot that bulged with longing. "I assure you, Sophia, that although I have an acquired taste, my appetite only burns for one woman. Alisz has never been to my bed, but should she ever find herself beneath my sheets, her purpose there is to beget my heirs."

Sophia reeled with frustration. "I can never accept this. The man I once loved, making babies with someone else?" She punched him in the chest. "A future together is impossible.

Can't you see that? Please…" she begged, softening her voice, "let me go."

He only pulled her closer, suffocating her in his embrace. "I won't release you. You reside within my heart, a tempest that threatens to overcome me. I can withstand it no more."

Darkness suffused his hazel eyes. Suddenly, she was afraid of his motives, and the liberties that he might seek. His lips crashed down on hers, beginning an onslaught of touch that shocked and hurt.

Where was the kind and considerate man who once wooed her with effectual charm and grace? What had become of the cavalier boy who had sworn his love, at one time vowing to protect. He hurt her now.

Sophia gasped for breath as his lips laid siege upon her mouth. She pleaded for him to stop as his hips thrust against her abdomen. Cried out in embarrassment, when he ripped the fragile laces that held her bodice together, to reveal the ivory chemise that lay beneath.

Abruptly, he released her lips to kiss the delicate skin of her neck as his left hand fumbled with the fabric of her bodice. The first tear slid from her eye. "Please, Franz," she cried out desperately. "If you've ever loved me, I beg of you to stop."

"I've waited long enough," he moaned hoarsely, nibbling at her earlobe. "I shall have you. On this rocky bed, I will make you mine."

He swept her into his arms and carried her to the veiled cover of tree branches, far away from the river's edge. Sophia squirmed, attempting to break free from his hold, but his strong arms held tight. Soon enough, he laid her against the forest floor.

"No!" Sophia shouted, scuttling backward. "You cannot do this…"

The tears didn't deter his actions. In his demented state, she supposed he didn't see or feel her emotional struggle. In one quick motion, he ripped her chemise apart revealing her bosom.

"Mein liebling," he muttered, grasping her, his breathing coming faster, "your breasts are beautiful."

"How dare you!" Sophia shouted, slapping him across his face, leaving the red imprint of her hand on his cheek.

"What's the matter?" he asked, raising his hand, making a move to hit her, but then his expression turned predatory. "You're a crazy woman. Accept your fate and let me pleasure you."

He grasped her hands, pinioning them high above her head. "I won't. It's wrong."

"You have little say in the matter."

He was hasty now in his actions. He pressed his face against her breast and suckled, while bringing his free hand up under her skirt, his fingers sliding along her leg until he reached the juncture of her thighs. She attempted to move backward, gasping when his finger touched her most intimate spot.

"Please," she begged, "stop…"

"Stop squirming," he yelled, forcing her legs apart. He positioned himself, and then loosened his breeches, exposing his shaft. Sophia squeezed her eyes shut tight, hoping for an intervention. She was able to break free of his hold momentarily. Scratching his face, she attempted to nudge him in the groin with her knee before he pinioned her hands again.

"In a few more moments," he gasped, breathing heavily, wiping blood from his face, "you will be mine. Not my wife, mind you, but my mistress. Marked by this my blood and soon your own red liquid taken from your maidenhead."

"Ah," Sophia wailed, trying to buck him off, but his shaft soon prodded near her entrance. "Franz," she pleaded, squirming to no avail. "No—please—don't destroy us. Franz, stop—"

But he was beyond hearing, beyond communication. He closed his eyes and his mind to her pleas. Though Sophia risked the embarrassment of the town, she screamed.

FROM THE MOMENT Mathias arrived at the celebration, he searched for Lady Sophia. Scanning the crowd, he looked for her willowy frame, but her presence eluded him.

Different countrymen attempted to gain him in conversation, children cavorted at his feet, yet he could not keep his thoughts from the one woman he wished to converse with. Giving up the futility of speaking to the guests, he searched for her.

Seeing Lady Alisz apart from the rest of the celebrants, and returning from across the yard to a group of ladies, he approached her.

"A good day to you, Lady Alisz." He paused, scrutinizing the green. "Have you seen your sister?"

"Oh dear," she said with a sigh, staring in the direction she had just walked. "Yes, I've seen her," she sniffed, wiping a tear from the corner of her eye, "but she's busy at the moment, and I don't think she'd welcome your company."

"You're upset. Why? Is she with someone?"

"Yes, with someone she knows quite well." Alisz's lower lip quivered; she stared at him knowingly. "She has deceived me, Father, and on a day that should have been mine to enjoy."

"How has Lady Sophia deceived her sister?" he asked, taking her hand. She pouted, she pursed her lips; a tear trickled across her cheek, but the display of emotion didn't concern him. Something she didn't say did. "Explain yourself, my Lady."

"She's taken something that doesn't belong to her," she barked, releasing his hand and pointing to a location far beneath the lawn where the shrubbery merged with the river's edge and taller deciduous trees. Sniffling, for effect, Mathias assumed, she looked at him, dropping her hand in despair, then again, gazing back to the distant edge.

"She is down there," Alisz said, staring far below the lawn at the river. "I saw her," she attempted, her voice breaking. "Beyond the trees, embraced beneath Franz."

"What were they doing?" Her grabbed her shoulders without thinking. "You must tell me."

"He was, was—" She paused, inhaling deeply. A horrid look contorted her face. Placing her hands on her cheeks, she began to cry. She escaped his hold and turned away.

However moved by Alisz's display of hurt, Mathias needed to find Sophia. Had she lost her head, choosing to do something sinful? She knew a future with Franz was impossible, but would this man she had once loved be as honorable?

He left Alisz, and walked in the direction that she had indicated. His footsteps quickened, he was soon running to the river's edge.

A scream alerted him to the possible location and he ran along the river's edge until he found them. The sight that met his eyes, a man wedged between her knees, her hands pinioned above her head, the sound of terrified screams, brought a bout of anger that could not be contained.

"My Lord," he yelled, marching forward. "You go too far!"

"Mind your own bloody business," Franz yelled, his full weight on Sophia who struggled beneath him.

"Get off of her, you bastard," Mathias warned, hating the man suddenly, then reaching for his coat. "The Lord judge you for your horrid actions, the devil take you for the crime you commit."

Mathias grabbed Franz by his coat and by the roots of his hair, pulling him from Sophia. Anger consumed him and he slammed Franz forcefully into a tree. He held him by the collar against the rough bark, pausing to look at her face.

"You bastard. How could you?" Her beautiful face was swollen with fright, eyes full of tears, tortured from her struggles. She attempted to right the fabric of her skirt, but not fast enough to conceal her nudity.

"Father, didn't you see that we were busy? How dare you interrupt!"

"How dare you, sir, take such liberties. Have you lost your head? You think to rut like a common animal? Who gave you the right?"

"God gave me the right, when he stole a rib and made a woman."

"You don't own this lady. May I remind you, you're not her husband?" Her bodice lay open, revealing her bosom. She struggled to pull the fabric together. Her beauty only made him angrier.

"She was betrothed to be my wife. I would have her still!"

"As a mistress? Such is not an honorable vocation for any woman." Mathias had never struck a man in his life and though he prayed for patience, the pain he witnessed in her eyes was his undoing. Raising his fist, he was sorely tempted to strike. "Forgive me if I don't understand. I thought this celebration was for you, and Lady Alisz? How dare you take sinful liberties with another woman!"

"I take what is rightfully mine, and with no regrets."

He heard Sophia wince as if the comment pained her. "You can't have two women, but regardless, you force yourself on this lady."

"She's no lady. She's my whore."

Mathias pulled back his arm, ready to strike. "You will apologize or suffer the consequences."

"All bite and no muscle. You won't do it. You're a man of the cloth."

But as Mathias watched Sophia, struggling still to cover herself, pulling torn silk together, tying laces to hide her breasts, his anger only ignited further. "Don't test me, my Lord. I wasn't always a priest and remember well what it feels like to be a man."

Franz guffawed, laughing. "She begged for it, or I wouldn't have lain between her legs. As I said, I had the right of it."

"Your dishonesty can't hide. I see the red scratches on your face. What you sought to do to Lady Sophia, forcing yourself on her, it's a mortal sin."

Huffing and puffing, he spat at the ground. "Big holy man, you've stopped me this time, but who will prevent the next coupling? You—A village priest? I think not! I will have this woman."

"Bastard!" Mathias spat, forgetting himself. In one swift blow, he slapped Franz across the face.

"Father," he begged, chortling. "Have mercy for the sins I commit, forgive me for I have acted on a poor conscience and forced myself on the woman I love." He stopped to catch his breath. "I will pay you an indulgence on Sunday to purge myself of my sin, but for now, release me. I will not rut with her again. At least not today."

Mathias gazed at Sophia while holding the man who had committed the worst type of crime. She leaned her head in dejection, not three steps from where he stood, clutching her abdomen with her hands. Fresh tears slipped from her eyes. He could not think for the rage. How dare this man?

"Let me go, you imbecile," Franz said, attempting to free himself. The need to avenge consumed him, something snapped and anger took control.

"You need to learn a lesson." Mathias hit him, once, twice, perhaps three times his knuckles connected with Franz's jaw. In his anger, it was hard to tell how many times his fist struck bone.

Someone grasped his hand. "Please, Mathias. Stop. Let him go."

Releasing this vile man was the last thing he wanted to do, but he forced the tension in his muscles to relax. "All right," he spoke, throwing Franz against the tree and stepping away.

"Go. Apologize to your fiancée for betraying your promise. She witnessed your crime. If you value your life, never come near Lady Sophia again."

"I do love her." Franz attempted to reach Sophia, but his approach was blocked when Mathias placed a hand on his chest.

"Leave us be, Franz," she cried out. "Your actions have proven the depth of your love. Do as the Father says: and don't bother me again. Go to your Alisz, she will welcome your embrace, so eager is she."

"Sophia..." he mumbled, appealing, trying to reach her. "I'm sorry..."

"Don't come near me," she shouted, "not ever again."

Franz harrumphed, then left their company.

Sophia took Father Mathias's hand into her own, searching for any sign of injury. He let her massage his knuckles, rubbing the reddening flesh. When he pulled her slowly into his arms, she came willingly, laying her head on his shoulder.

"I'm sorry that I must ask you this, but did he, was he able to…"

She sighed heavily. "No, you came in time. Once more, you save me."

Mathias breathed a sigh of relief and held her closer. "What could he have been thinking to act in such a violent manner?"

"I don't know him anymore. It feels like the man I fell in love with has died, perished."

"The situation must be equally difficult for Franz, but to act in such a manner speaks ill of him. Best to avoid him."

"Indeed, but we won't speak of it any longer. It's over."

"I hope so," Mathias said with a grimace. "But I saw the way he looked at you. You best be on your guard."

CHAPTER 9

"Sophia," Mathias murmured, expressing concern. "I should have known that Franz could hurt you. Had I counseled him, I could have prevented this."

"Father, don't blame yourself. Not even I knew he could be so cruel."

"Hmm," he breathed, shaking his head. "Everyone has the ability to make mistakes, wrong-doing lies within us all. I strive to teach the doctrine, fight the darkness. I speak of faith, of hope," he said with a sigh, prevailing on her with his eyes, holding her shoulders firmly. "And love of mankind."

"It makes no difference what you preach. Discourse cannot change the evil that lies within a man's heart, especially if he refuses to hear the message." She squeezed his hand in reassurance. "You're blameless when a poorer soul, for whatever reason, rebuffs your homily."

"One soul lost is one too many," he beseeched, his brow furrowing with concern. "One broken soul has almost cost you a heavy price." He squeezed her hand firmly, as if to make his point clearer. "This fate shouldn't have befallen an innocent. If I could have reached the pain that motivated his action, you might have been spared."

Sophia didn't know where the conflicting emotions came from. He had wanted to save her completely, she realized. Yes, she had suffered, but if not for his timely interference— Frankly, his worry over the aggressor caused her further irritation.

"How could you think about Franz, of saving him, after what he did?"

"As horrible as this is, we must have mercy."

"Mercy?" A tear welled up within her emerald depths, collected on her lashes and rolled down her cheek. "It's too soon for forgiveness. Franz has hurt me. I must impress upon you, that you have saved me from a much worse fate."

She breathed deeply, the tears continuing. "My virtue is intact," she entreated, looking away. "Had you not come, had you arrived moments later, he would have taken everything. He would have violated me."

Mathias released his hold on her shoulders and cupped her cheek with his hand. She closed her eyes; her head nestled against the warmth of his palm. She felt his thumb-pad slide across her cheek to wipe away her tears. She opened her eyes to peer into his furtive expression, only to experience a sentiment she had not perceived before.

A certainty, a new devotion warmed the depths of his eyes, encouraging her to pause in awe. But the frown that appeared suddenly thereafter, clouding his happiness and flattening his expression, gave her reason to pause.

"I would never let anyone hurt you," he said with a grimace, further encouraging her worry. "Maybe God has a plan, for he ensures that I watch over you, protect you. And I won't let anyone—ever—hurt you again."

A slim smile broke through the barriers of depression, but changed just as quickly to a portrait of absolute misery. He released her hands, rending the bond that had held them together. In agitation, he wiped her tears on his robe.

"What is it?" Sophia asked, worrying. "What's wrong?"

"It's nothing," he replied, but she saw that his hand visibly shook. To her surprise, he turned away, hiding his sentiment.

"Look at me," she beckoned, grabbing him, placing her hand on his back. "Father, what is it? How can I help you?"

"I'd rather you called me by my real name. It's just the two of us. I'm not your father."

"If that's what you want."

"It is."

"Mathias?" she mumbled, tasting his name on her lips. "Tell me where your thoughts lie?"

"Don't concern yourself," he breathed. "I'm a sentimental fool caught in a tangle of my own doing."

"Because you touched me? It seems to me that every now and then you must allow yourself to be human. To welcome the emotions that mark us as human beings, and not feel guilty by showing compassion."

"Your courage knows no bounds." He smiled simply, turning back.

"Yes, well, if I may be so bold as to borrow a page from your own holy book, our Deity has a formula for everyone, as you have shared so wisely and often from the pulpit."

"I do try. I agonize over every sermon. Words sometimes don't come easy."

She sucked in a breath, denying the emotions that swept through her, hoping for the strength to continue. "My thanks be to you, a soldier of *The Word*, for assisting me in the rebuilding of my life. And I'm sure you need no further reminders, that he has a plan for you, too."

"I fear my responsibility some days, but we're never given more than we can bear."

"If only that were true," she said with a wince, remembering. "I for one don't believe that burdens are handed to us."

"Wherever they come from, it seems our troubles are not over yet. The guests are gathering further up the lawn."

"Huh," Sophia proclaimed, a whoosh of air coming from her lungs. "I don't know if I'm ready for more conflict. Given the angry expressions, a quick prayer might be in order."

"I see that you'll require my support. Take my arm, Sophia, I'll escort you safely through the crowd."

She took a deep breath, puzzling, scrutinizing the people who gathered at the edge of the wood. Lady Wendeline stood among them, daughter in hand. The looks pressed her way promised an ugly confrontation.

"That's all right, Father. It would appear unseemly for you to escort me. I'm damned in their eyes and I don't want you to be harmed by the association."

A change occurred in him then, as if the man he had become moments before had vanished. A religious servant emerged, seemingly unscathed. His voice was the only reminder of the man he had been moments before.

"I care not what people think. God will judge, not a misled flock of sinners."

Sophia raised a quizzical brow. "That may be so, but God offers understanding and love. These people will show no such mercy."

LADY WENDELINE CAME CLOSER with Alisz by her side. Already anxious, Sophia tried to dismiss the pair, but she could see that their anger would not be ignored.

"How rude of you to spoil my daughter's day!" Lady Wendeline barked. "A lover's tryst, and with your sister's betrothed? How dare you ruin her special day!"

"Appearances can be deceiving," Sophia protested, giving her stepmother a quelling look.

"You were seen with your sister's fiancé. Do you deny it? I realize you were hurt by the loss of Franz; this whole situation has been disconcerting, but it's unpardonable to lure the man into your arms by a sensual means."

"Lady Wendeline," Mathias interrupted, "you have misunderstood the situation. If we could withdraw to a more private place and discuss this matter calmly, and in private, it will be apparent that your accusations are incorrect."

"There's no misunderstanding," Alisz shrieked, her voice elevated to an intolerable pitch. "I saw them," she shouted, stepping forward, stabbing her finger into Sophia's chest, and expressing tears for effect. "I saw them beneath a tree. She was willing, moaning, laughing!"

Sophia knew that Alisz could be cruel, but this turn of events was shocking. "If you press your finger into my chest one more time…"

"You desired his affection; you wanted to lie with my fiancé."

Proper ladies stood near, listening, displaying shocked expressions, not speaking. But why did Alisz feel the need to lie? Hatred raged within the depths of her ice-blue eyes, fueling her deception. Sophia would have none of it.

"Tell them you're lying," Sophia shouted, delivering a slap to her cheek. "Tell them the truth, that Franz took liberties. Tell them!"

But her sister the actress only coiled within herself and fell against her mother, crying. Her grief-ridden display left a real impression on those who watched, surprising Sophia.

"Why this display of nonsense? Can't you see she's putting on a show? It's not true," Sophia pleaded, attempting to make eye contact with her peers, her former friends. But they shunned her, refusing to hear what she had to say.

"Poor Alisz," Lady Richelle said with a grimace.

"Poor Alisz?" Sophia scowled, her anger threatening to reign out of control. "Why will no one listen to me? Look at this man. Look at his face! Do those scratches not say something about the situation he placed me in?"

Franz stood apart from the crowd, coolly aloof. She sought him out. "Franz, tell these people the truth. As God is your witness, choose your words carefully."

"Remember," Father Mathias pleaded, attempting to help, "face your crime and beg forgiveness for your actions. Tell the truth, or be damned for your sin."

The scrutiny didn't convince Franz to submit, even though he seemed to shrink before the onlookers. He was nothing more than a rogue dressed in fine clothes and she should have known he would hide from the truth. He turned from them, departing their company.

"My conscience is clear," he threw back, "I succumbed to the teasing. It's not my fault that this woman," he said, gesturing with his hand, "seduced me with the expertise of a woman born to such a life. She got so excited that she, well, scratched me."

Even as his words reached her, a stab of grief gripped her more firmly than his hands that had held her. "You've deceived me in every way, destroying everything we've ever shared together. You've gutted me, to the very core."

"Aw darling, put on a show."

"I have my pride, Franz. Still," she attempted, scrounging for patience. "Say what you will, as God is my witness, I have done no wrong and I'll see this sufferable trial through, come what may."

Sophia stepped closer to Lady Wendeline who held a quivering Alisz to her bosom, crying like a child. "You're smarter than this. I don't care what you think you saw, your fiancé is lying. Regardless of our struggles, I would never do this to you, or to myself!"

Walking among the guests, her former friends, Sophia eyed every person that shuffled away as she passed them by. "I'm innocent of the accusations," she pleaded.

"Cruel," Lady Emilie sniffed, "I don't know you anymore."

"I didn't flaunt myself in an inappropriate manner." Sophie begged them to believe her. "I'm telling the truth."

Sophia forced her gaze on Alisz. "There's foul play afoot here and make no mistake, I mean to get to the bottom of it."

She could have been mistaken, but her words seemed to create a fear in her stepsister's eyes. Perhaps it was time she investigated the mess of her shattered life instead of relying on the word of others.

Sophia made to leave the Altbusser estate. Lady Richelle, Lady Emilie and Lady Lisbeth entered into a lively discussion, about her no doubt. It was only when her footpath had taken her a fair distance down the road, did she realize that Mathias followed behind her at a slower pace. His voice surprised her. She turned around to meet him.

"I'm proud of you, for standing up for your honor. You faced your peers bravely, managing them with a swift hand."

"I didn't feel the least bit brave. I don't suppose you might escort me home?"

A conspiratorial smile came over his face. "We've come this far together. Let us journey a bit further."

She took his hand without asking, smiling. The motion seemed natural and he flinched for only a moment, before he allowed the embrace to continue. She cared for this man and holding his hand gave her comfort. He was her strength and she had faith in his convictions. Mathias would help her get through the trying times that lay ahead.

Alisz was merely a symptom of something more devious and someone had to get to the bottom of her duplicity. The truth was built on a much firmer foundation than the lies that had been twisted into believable rubbish. How deep did her deception go?

Sophia could not even imagine, but she decided it was time, long past time, that she stopped discovering her fate through the words and actions of others. Alisz was up to some dastardly scheme, and it was up to her to unearth the truth before it was too late.

CHAPTER 10

*M*athias tried to relax inside the confessional booth, but a burden weighed heavily on his heart and mind. He sat on the bench, bracing his foot against the closed door—overwhelmed—holding his head in his hands.

The confessional was not only a sinner's spot to redemption, but also a sanctuary to find solace from life's difficulties. He often came here to dismiss his grief by considering the sins or problems of others. Now, he faced his own.

Sophia's beautiful face filled his thoughts. He cared for her, desired her, too. Given the vows he had made, he knew such emotions were wrong.

He ran trembling fingers through his hair, holding his aching head, praying: "Forgive me, for I have sinned. I have grown too close to a woman. I am aware that by helping her through her tribulations, holding her in moments of stress, I have betrayed my faith. I succumbed to her sweetness and encouraged a behavior that tested our boundaries."

I dreamt of her, only I was the man between her legs, not that sinner...

A memory of Bishop Eberhardt came to him, urging him not to meet the same fate. He had decisions to make. He'd taken a vow of celibacy.

He drummed his fingers on the sides of the wall. The commitment of celibacy was something else entirely. At the time of his ordination, he had wondered if he could live with the sacrifice. Now, he wasn't so sure.

He was a fool for not acknowledging that he wanted to save Sophia, but not for God, for himself. What in Christ's nails was he going to do about these feelings?

"Forgive me, Father, for I have sinned. I would sacrifice everything for love, *for her love*, but I've made a promise to you, to my family, to my brother, and I don't want to disappoint anyone. Can I undo the damage? How do I arrest the care that tempts my heart?"

Mathias lifted his head when he heard soft footsteps. The opposite door adjoining the confessional booth opened to a swish of skirts. He couldn't tell for sure, but he assumed a woman had entered the confessional booth.

Once the door closed, Mathias slid the window open, surprised to discover that the penitent was standing. She didn't kneel before the wooden screen, as was the custom.

"My child?" he asked, "what is your confession?"

"Forgive me, Father," she whispered, tapping her foot impatiently, "for I have sinned. It's been two years since my last confession."

An extended silence encouraged him to ask the next question. "Tell me, child," he coaxed, "tell me about the sin that has brought you here."

She laughed then, a cynical laugh. Mathias wondered if she'd come to the confessional to plead forgiveness? He saw the shadow of her hand pass over the screen. "I have succeeded in blackening a name, and ruining the life of my sister. Surprisingly, it took little effort. But I've received little comfort from the effort."

Mathias's brow wrinkled in concern. "But why? Why would you seek to dishonor your sister?"

Her voice changed from one of passive laughter to controlled anger. She pushed roughly on the mesh screen with both hands. Surprised by the intensity of her onslaught, Mathias reacted by leaning away from the opening. "Because," she fumed, huffing, "she's not really my sister."

"What?" Mathias scratched his head, uncomprehending. "Perhaps I heard you wrong, when you said you blackened the name of your sister."

She was quiet for a moment, but then pushed away from the screen and presented her back to him. "What I intended to say, Father, is that she is my half-sister."

"Half-sister," he stated. "What then, has motivated you to hurt your half-sister?"

"It's rather simple," she said, raising her voice. "I hate her!"

Mathias was shocked at the outrageous display of heated emotion, and he pitied the woman who had suffered from this woman's vicious actions. Suddenly, the similarities of Sophia's situation occurred to him. Could it be the same woman? Could the woman standing on the other side of the barrier be none other than Lady Alisz of Baldemar Manor?

"My dear, this hate will do you harm. Whatever she has done to earn your disfavor has blackened your soul just as dark. The only path to redemption is to forgive her and reveal the truth of your actions."

She came close to the screen, and pressed her face against the wooden slats so that she could peer inside. A chill came over him at the thought that this woman was studying him with little regard for manners or respect. But the hostile behavior and icy voice that followed unnerved him.

"Forgiveness, repentance, is that why you think I'm here?" She laughed cruelly. "The only reason I've come to this place is to ensure that my plans don't fall to ruin because of the meddling of a lusting priest."

"Lady Alisz?" Mathias winced, shifting on his seat. "Since your motive is not to repent, why do you come to the confessional with accusations? Surely you realize the risk you take by revealing your duplicity."

She broke away from the wall then, clicking her heels on the floor. "So you know who I am, good for you. But the game is not over yet. I have much more to say. Shall we stop playing and get serious?"

"Poor Sophia."

"Poor Sophia, poor sweet Sophia," mouthed Alisz. "A slender girl, born to the culture of riches and ribbons, and with massive curls. A vision of loveliness," she went on. "My sister received every kind of bloody reward from our father. He spoiled her with material baubles, forgetting about me. Selfish, completely selfish."

"Hmm," Mathias sighed. "Jealousy has led many souls on journeys of self-destruction. Even you must realize that your sins will harm you in time. God has the last say in everything and justice will be done. He will be the victor, not you."

"No powers in Heaven or Hell are strong enough to overthrow my rightful destiny. I will go to whatever means to protect what should come to me naturally. This is not a game, nor a power struggle in which we play. I will have that which is due to me, owed to me, and I care little what happens to the people who get in my way."

He extended his arm to the window, wondering if there was a way that he could destroy the darkness that threatened her soul. Was there something he could say that would help her see the futility of her actions?

But perhaps attempting to help this woman was futile. She seemed to have no moral conscience. A disease had blackened her heart and unless she came to believe that her actions were wrong, he couldn't help her. Vengeance was a strong motive and he suspected that Alisz might have succumbed to this rage. He had to confide this.

"Threatening people, Lady Alisz, is no deterrent to the deception that you weave. If you came here thinking that you could convince me to fall prey to your schemes, you have misjudged me."

"You can call it whatever you wish, Father, I prefer to call it a warning. Stay away from Sophia."

"She is a congregant in need of my guidance," he called out defiantly. "If she requests my help, I shall not refuse."

"She's a woman, you hypocrite!" Laughter erupted from her voice, but turned just as quickly to a cruel tone. "I know the tender guidance you wish to share with Sophia. I have watched the two of you. You took an oath, and yet you allowed Sophia, a common harlot, to hug you longer than was proper."

"The action was innocent, and not at all inappropriate."

"Ah hah," she wailed. "To tell an untruth is a sin. How fortunate that you reside within these gloomy walls, for after I leave, you can beg forgiveness from the Creator for your lie. One Hail Mary for redemption, but perhaps say the prayer twice?" She suggested, whistling. "In truth, I don't believe that the prayer will assist in ridding yourself of the sexuality I saw burning within your eyes."

"How dare you," Mathias yelled, losing control. "How dare you speak to me in such an offending manner, and with such a lack of respect."

"Hail Mary, full of grace, the Lord is with thee…"

"If you choose to say the prayer," Mathias breathed, seeking calm, "say it with real intent."

"I'll be attentive all right," Alisz snickered, lowering her voice. "Hail Mary," she whispered, "Mother of God, pray for this sinner. I witnessed the longing that flared to life beneath his robes. Sophia is far too simple and naïve to have discerned his pressing needs, but I understood. Perhaps, God did, too?"

"Get out," Mathias yelled. "Leave me in peace."

"I will leave only when you have given your word to stay away from Sophia. Otherwise, like her name has been blackened, yours will suffer the same fate. Do we understand each other, Father Mathias?"

"I will not make such a promise. I will not be held hostage to evil."

She opened the door to leave. "Stay away from the bastard child, Father. Men have danced with the devil for greater cause then you so freely court. I promise you, if you get in my way, you will burn within the eyes of the people you are meant to serve. I will send you to the pits of Hell without batting an eye. Even if I have to tell a tale or two."

The swish of Lady Alisz's skirt was the last sound he heard as the woman fled the confessional, closing the door behind her. But her presence was with him long after she had departed. Running his fingers through his hair, he placed his head into the palms of his hands. This situation with Sophia was becoming complicated and God help him, for the first time in his life, he faced a crisis.

But he wouldn't turn his back on Sophia when she faced the greatest crisis of her life. She needed someone to depend on, and he told himself firmly, she needed him. Especially now that he had learned of the purposeful evil of her half-sister.

Mathias rose from the confessional and hurried to the kitchen inside his house. Packing a luncheon of meat, cheese, and freshly made bread, he left for his kinfolk's home. It had been a long time since he had visited. Perhaps the time had come to confront the burdens that conflicted his heart.

CHAPTER 11

*C*onsumed with anxiety, Mathias stood at the threshold of his parents' door holding the brass handle. He knew he should press the lever and open the door, to greet a life he'd once known. But he hesitated—worrying that he wouldn't be accepted after sharing his truth.

Perhaps, he shouldn't have come home. His mother would criticize his choices; being judged by God would be far easier to accept.

The aroma of fresh bread and an evening meal wafted on the breeze, causing his mouth to water and his stomach to clench. He imagined his mother hard at work, her age-worn hands stirring garden-fresh vegetables and fowl in an earthenware pot. She'd always kept him well fed. Hungry more for her love and acceptance, Mathias worried he'd be a disappointment after the disclosure, so he lounged on the stoop, uneasy, unable to enter. Releasing the door handle, he stepped away from the potential conflict, shaking his head.

What am I doing here?

Whack! Mathias heard the recognizable sound of an axe striking wood, and he realized that his father must be working in the yard. Delaying the cottage visit, he decided to place his conscience in the confidence of his father instead. It didn't take long to reach the woodshed, and he soon saw an older man in the midst of the forest, hewing a log.

Beneath the leafy branches of a beech tree, Mathias watched Lars Rohland methodically chopping notches into the bark. A carpenter by trade, his father had aged, his hair threading silver, but his arms still bulging with strength. He had to be strong; squaring a log was hard work.

"Gonna stand there all day watching, or make your presence known?"

"I'm sorry," Mathias said with a grimace, leaving the shadows. "I didn't think you knew I was here."

Whack!

"My hearing isn't as great as it used to be," he remarked, pausing to stare, "but I can still see plain as day. What took you so long to come home? Did you forget you had a family? A mother and father who care for you?"

"I," Mathias said, swallowing, searching for an excuse, staring at his father's bare chest, "could never forget the parents who have loved me."

"Then why?" Lars Rohland asked, holding the axe against the tree. "The years have passed us by. You're hurting your mother by staying away."

"The demands of the parish are great." Mathias sighed, taking a step closer. He had known this discussion wouldn't be easy. "It's not often that I can leave."

"Is that the truth?" his father asked. "Or are you making excuses for yourself."

"Look, Father, I'm here now. I meant to come home sooner, the days pass and…"

"We all get older, Son." Lars Rohland finished for him. He leaned the axe against the log and wiped a sweat-ridden brow with the back of his dirt-stained hand, assessing Mathias in a way that made him uncomfortable. Proud, his father couldn't hide the displeasure from his expression.

"What are you thinking, Father?"

"It's good to see you, looking so well," he said with a choked voice, stepping nearer. Soon grasping Mathias's arm, he pulled him close, hugging tightly. "I've missed you, Son."

"I've missed you, too."

It almost undid Mathias that his father appeared as if he would cry. He watched him take a deep inhalation of air, gaining his composure. "Shall we retreat to the house? Your mother has the evening meal cooking."

"Actually, I'd like to have a word with you first, if you don't mind. Just you for now."

"Sounds serious," Lars said, placing his hand on his shoulder. "Let's go inside the woodshed then."

"Okay," Mathias said with a sigh, and then followed his father inside.

"Take a seat. No pews here, just a few tree stumps, but they work."

Mathias did as requested. He watched his father retrieve an age-worn tunic from a hook and put it on, and then he reached for a jug hiding in the woodpile. Pulling the cork, he poured aqua vitae into two pewter mugs.

"I don't drink that stuff anymore," Mathias blurted.

"Any son of mine drinks," Lars replied, passing the cup over. "Here you go, Son, my blood poured for you."

Mathias ignored the comment, but accepted the cup, staring at the liquid spirits. "I've not had a drink, other than the Holy Eucharist, since…"

"Since your brother died."

"Yes," Mathias said simply. His stomach lurched and forlorn memories came to mind.

"You wouldn't talk about the accident when it happened. Perhaps it's time to share your truth. A confession, if you will."

"After all these years," Mathias said sadly, "I can still see the boar coming at us. Sometimes at night, I relive the horror of that day."

"What do you see in your memories?"

"My arrow shot true, and I thought I hit the mark. Marcos and I guffawed thinking we'd killed the beast. But as Marcos approached where it lay on the ground, it suddenly reared, catching him in the chest."

"It was an accident."

"Perhaps if we'd not over-indulged beforehand, if we'd never gone hunting, if my arrow had hit its mark—"

"If I've learned anything in my years, it's that we can't live our lives by wondering what might have happened if we'd chosen a different path. The boar reared its ugly head," Lars said with a sigh, "you couldn't have known that your brother would die."

"But…"

"Is this why you've stayed away? Because you blame yourself for that day?"

"In part."

"You can't change the past." Lars took a drink. Mathias stared at the liquid.

"It was supposed to be a final hurrah before Marcos joined the priesthood. It was his desire, his calling. My actions robbed him of his life, and spoiled his vocation."

"Did you suddenly grow a horn then? For the way I see it, the boar took your brother's life, not you."

"Yes, but I'm still responsible."

"Not the way I see it. Mathias, you need to forgive yourself. Is this not the doctrine that you preach to your parish?"

"Yes, Father, it is."

"Then why can't you accept forgiveness for yourself?"

"Because, I don't deserve it."

Lars took a swig from his cup. "Are you less human than your congregants?"

"I killed my brother. It's my fault that he died. Nothing I do can ever redeem his death."

"Well, good for you, you've finally said it. Do you think Marcos would want you to suffer this way?"

"I don't know, he seemed pleased enough when I said I'd live out his dreams for him."

"And you've tried. How has that worked for you?"

"I've found comfort in helping others."

Mathias watched his father's eyes draw together. He squirmed under the weight of his father's scrutiny. "Why are you really here, Mathias? There's something different about you. If I didn't know better…"

"What are you insinuating?"

"Just what type of comfort have you been providing, because a father knows when his son is in love. Why have you really come home, and is a woman to blame for your current woes?"

Mathias stared at the cup, finally taking a sip. "Yes," he admitted, looking at his father uneasily.

Lars smiled, clanked his cup. "Well, I'll be damned," he chuckled, a sour expression turning into a grin. "I never thought I'd see the day. But I won't lie, I hoped for it. Prayed for it, even."

"I know your feelings on the subject. You never wanted me to take my vows."

"Damn straight, and if truth be known, I never wanted Marcos to enter the priesthood either."

"Why is it so terrible?"

"It isn't, not anymore."

"Why are you smiling, Father?"

"I thought my only living son would die, my name dying with him. But now, you've given me hope, maybe the blessing of grandchildren?"

"Not so fast," Mathias entreated, taking another sip. "I've a lot to consider. Nothing has come of our friendship and I made a promise to my brother."

"Oh son," Lars Rohland said with a grin. "Why did you wait so long to come home?"

Mathias took another sip of the drink. "Guilt has a way of eroding one's confidence. I suppose that's why. I'm not sure Mother will understand."

"I'll take care of your mother. It's time for dinner. I can hear her calling."

INSIDE HIS PARENTS' cottage, Mathias stood near the kitchen table, not sure what to say or do. His mother stood on the opposite side, spooning pieces of chicken, vegetables, and broth onto three pewter plates. Surprised to see him, she couldn't seem to look his way, or find the words to enter into a conversation, and appeared as if she'd break into tears at any moment.

Mathias...

She'd cried out his name moments before, squeezing his shoulders, and searching his expression. But then she'd turned away to go about her work in the kitchen, just the way he remembered.

"Take your seat," his mother said with a woebegone expression. "Supper is ready."

"You can talk to your son," Lars threw out, taking control. "Our boy has come home and we will make him welcome. He has news to share."

"Is that so?" she said simply, taking a seat, gazing at her plate. "Do tell."

"I," Mathias said, sitting as well, not knowing where to begin.

She calmly placed her fork beside her plate, and then looked directly at him. "Why, Mathias? Why have you waited so long to come home?"

He took a deep cleansing breath. "I didn't want to disappoint you, Mother."

"The only disappointment I've faced was the missing plate at the table. I thought you'd come home and share the good news of your work. But the years passed without a word. I was so proud of you when you left, accepting your brother's position, taking up his calling."

"Speak for yourself," Lars Rohland said. "One son given up to God is one too many; two sons, a heavy weight in coin to pay."

"It's okay, Father. I was happy to do it for Marcos. Mostly."

She stared at him directly. "Your father told me about your discussion in the woodshed. You might be surprised to hear my thoughts on the subject."

"I daresay; I'm afraid to know what you think."

"You shouldn't be," she replied, placing her hand on his. "In my heart, two sons died the day the boar charged. Not one. My soul has been barren since you left. And while I was proud of your sacrifice, when you chose to stay away from home, from your parents, it felt like my heart stopped beating."

"I'm sorry to have caused you sorrow, Mother. I should have come home sooner."

"You're home now. And you have news to tell?"

He was quiet as he gazed at his mother, hoping she'd understand, but he had to share his truth or he'd bear this cross for the rest of his life.

"I've met someone," he appealed, gazing downward. "I may not be able to keep the promise that I made to my brother, the promise that I made to you, and to my God. I don't want to disappoint, but…"

"So the news your father shared with me is true. You've met a young lady."

"I have."

"Does she love my son?"

"I don't know for sure. But I love her and knowing that I love her, compromises the vow that I've made to the church, and to God."

"What will you do?"

"I don't know. Leave the church? Build houses and furniture with my father? Jesus was a carpenter first, would he mind if I returned to my roots?"

The first hint of smile played on her face. "Your father won't mind," she mused, squeezing his fingers. "You have my love and support, whichever path you choose to take."

"Our support." Lars Rohland confirmed. "We will pray on this, Mathias."

"Mother, did you hear me? I have come to love a woman."

"I heard you well enough, Mathias Rohland, and what I have to say on the subject might surprise you. We all must make our sacrifices, but *a sacrifice for love* is not such a terrible thing."

"Do you mean that, Mother?" Mathias said with a gasp, filled with emotion.

Lars Rohland took hold of his wife's hand and then his son's. "Hold your son's hand, Ilsa, the meal is getting cold. Let's give proper homage for this meal and ask of God's assistance in this matter." He glanced at Mathias, appearing faithful. "Have an open heart, Son. The right answer will be known, when the time is right. Will you give a blessing over this meal, and this family?"

"I will."

Mathias closed his eyes, feeling his mother's hand take hold of his own. A warmth consumed him then; he felt loved as he prepared to say grace.

"Heavenly Father," he prayed, sighing, letting the tensions go, "we give thanks…"

CHAPTER 12

*M*athias had to make a decision. He weighed *the left and the right* sides of each viewpoint, knowing that either choice, to stay or to leave, was not easily achieved. In every respect, not only a woman had to be considered, but also a congregation. Conflicted, he admitted that the constant worry, doubt and fear of the unknown, weighed heavily on his soul.

A new life—could he leave the church?

Hmm. He'd come to love Sophia; he acknowledged his truth. He was starting to believe that their emotional connection was shared, an exciting and terrifying state of affairs. He didn't want to hurt her or anyone else.

He'd come to the White Elster River to meditate, but as he approached his haven, the unexpected sight of Sophia, *resting*, unnerved him.

She lay upon the ground, sleeping, relaxed and smiling as if she didn't have a care in the world. He crept to her, not wanting to disturb. He should leave her to her privacy, but something captivated him, drawing him inexplicably closer. He sat nearby, to watch her breathing, her chest rising and falling.

Captivated, smiling, he took in her beauty.

SOPHIA SLEPT PEACEFULLY on a carpet of flowering sedge, her fingers cupped beneath her cheek, supporting her head. A bird sang sweetly, scampering from branch to branch, high above her in a canopy of green. And the swash of river water lapping against the bank eased her into further relaxation, lending her mind to dream.

The vision was much too sweet and compelling to release Sophia from its hold, so she enjoyed the drama, and succumbed to its fantasy. *Strangely*, Mathias filled her thoughts. Sitting nearby, he didn't wear a neck-cloth and his silver cross was absent, too. His fingers feathered across her arm and she welcomed the touch, but the contact could also have been the wind blowing against her skin. She shivered in reaction to the stroke, her cheek twitching in response. Confused, she raised a quizzical brow, questioning the reverie. *Was this a dream?*

Suddenly, someone pressed feather-light kisses to the crook of her neck. Smiling, Sophia turned her head to the ardor, giggling as a man plied delicious games on her skin. She thought she heard Mathias whisper in a passion-induced state, the three little words that every woman longed to hear.

I love you.

Such a telling was impossible; yet she giggled when he kissed her again, understanding he could not give her his heart and frankly, she didn't expect him to. Sophia knew where his responsibilities lay without question, even as she was alerted to more than kisses.

The love-play was scandalous. Mathias drew her earlobe between his teeth and nibbled gently, caressing her, encouraging her need, soon licking the ridge of her ear, his hand sliding into her curls.

In his apparent need, he couldn't seem to stop himself and slid his fingers down the incline of her neck, stopping only to rest his palm above her breasts.

It was then that he rose above her, beseeching with his amber eyes and seeking approval for the quest he wished to continue. All she felt was need. That and the urgency for him to touch her, explore her, everywhere.

"Mathias—" she breathed, calling out. "Kiss me."

The dream changed—firm lips pressed against her mouth—a hand feathered across her cheek. His lips lazily caressed her mouth, but she was greedy for more, and he was far too modest. Reaching for his head, she captured him. Twining her fingers in his sandy strands, pulling him closer, bridging the gap he seemed hesitant to cross.

She was forced to become the aggressor, and kissed him firmly. With increasing intensity, she continued, refusing to stop the passion that bound her in tranquility. She didn't want the embrace to stop, the kiss was pleasant, but he broke free of the embrace and called her name.

"Sophia, Lady Sophia, please wake up..."

She opened her eyes and her hands clung to the back of his neck. Her lips so close to his mouth, she considered kissing him again.

"Oh dear," she whispered, blushing. "What have I awakened to?"

He rose above her, blocking out the sun. "I don't know what to tell you," he said, touching his mouth. "I'm no better than Franz. Taking advantage of a good woman. God forgive me."

"Please, Mathias," she urged, "don't feel any shame." She smiled then, overcome by emotion and the surprising happiness bursting inside. "It was only a kiss."

"Oh Sophia," he whispered brokenly, searching her eyes. "It was far more than a kiss. What will we do?"

"Come to me, lie down beside me," Sophia murmured, reaching for Mathias and pulling him close, cradling his head on her shoulder, and soon running her free hand through the strands of his hair. Much the same as a mother would console a child, but he was a man and she was aware of this fact.

"It's our secret. No one will know, no one will find out."

"I will know," he whispered with regret. "God will know."

"So be it," Sophia breathed, sliding her cheek across his forehead. "Three of us will conceal this indiscretion. But tell me, how can a touch that feels right, be wrong?"

He pulled away from the embrace and rose upward to peer into her eyes. She swore she'd never seen a man's eyes shadowed with so much guilt.

"Two of us shall feel the sting of God's wrath for this sin and make no mistake, this is a sin. We will be punished."

"But Mathias, why should a kiss be considered a sin?" she questioned, touching his lips. "I understand that you took a sacred vow to bind yourself closer to God. Help me understand why kissing a woman would hurt your role as a priest?"

"Sophia," he sighed, shaking his head, "you're a woman of the world. You understand the ways of the church. You know that I made a commitment, and I take my pledge seriously. I understood the problems that could eventually come. I prayed I might overcome them."

"Did you? Did you pray for truth?" She wouldn't make this easy on him. "Then why did you touch me?"

"Because, I wanted to. You were beautiful in your sleep and when you asked me to kiss you, I couldn't help myself. I wanted to tempt fate, to know what it felt like to touch you."

"Kissing a woman won't lead you on a path of destruction. Even a priest must love the parishioners he oversees." She paused. "Though I realize that our relationship should be visited from a place of purity, I wonder if you should question the religious burden that weighs heavily on your heart."

He sighed, closed his eyes, and attempted to move away, but she held him close, not allowing him to leave. "It wasn't a burden, at least not until I met you."

"Would you have it otherwise?"

"Yes, no!"

"So what will you do about it then, pray some more?"

"Prayer," he growled, his forehead furrowing with frustration, "I've done little else. You're a beautiful woman and I've come to have feelings for you. A man would be a fool not to notice your curves. But I fear how God might judge me, perhaps damning me for caring for you."

She forced him to look at her. "Truly, do you care for me, Mathias?"

"I won't deny it."

"Then don't speak of such foolishness. We will not be damned for sharing a natural human emotion."

"But I'm still a priest. I made a vow of chastity, a commitment to bring me closer to God, to be whole, Christ-like."

Sophia sighed, frustrated. "Mathias, unless something happened that I'm unaware of, we only kissed. But even if we had coupled, surely God created man in his image. He also shaped the masculine nature of a man with procreation in mind. Loving a woman shouldn't be a sin."

"You're a convincing woman," he remarked, scrutinizing her expression. "Perhaps the devil has bested your head because surely you know that a priest should not be kissing one of his parishioners."

"Look, I respect our faith, but if men were created to love women, surely our God wouldn't discriminate between a priest and other men?"

He rose upward onto his elbows, tore his gaze away from her sight, and for the first time, made no mistake that he was studying her breasts beneath her gown.

"The words you speak are true," he said in resignation, "still, I took a vow of chastity. It's not easily swept aside."

"A dilemma I can't help you with."

"Sweet woman, what will I do? I've kissed you, touched you. Compromised you while you were sleeping."

"I don't imagine that your intentions went quite that far, but of course, I was dreaming. I will accept," she said, "that you indulged my fantasies without my knowledge."

"The mind is honest in its sleep." He rose from the ground to a sitting position, grasping a blade of grass and twisting it between his fingers. "But you should take care in where you lie down. It could have been Franz taking advantage of your beauty."

"That's ridiculous."

"You barely understand the selfish urgency that awakened your appetite," he said, staring at her in a most uncomfortable way. "I cannot give the required price to satisfy it. At least not yet."

"Of course, I understand. Such attention could only come from my husband and…"

"We can never marry," he finished. "Unless I leave the priesthood."

"Would you do that, Mathias, would you do that for me?"

He pulled away from her then, rose from the ground to stand on his feet, turning his back. Sophia slowly came to a standing position, too, tears threatening.

"I might. If I knew your feelings were the same as mine."

"I think I might be in love with you, Mathias," she admitted, shaking. "But my emotion is not complicated by wickedness. Love is a powerful elixir, all-reaching and full of purpose. My love is not selfish, nor is it unkind. I have faith that the feelings that have grown between us are as God encouraged them to be."

He stepped to her then, reaching for her hand. "Sophia, the love you feel is normal," he said, brushing her lips with his thumb-pad. "But as of now, I can't satisfy the feelings between us. We have much to consider. I need time to reflect on what I need to do to set this situation right."

"You're saying goodbye."

"I'm doing no such thing."

Could Sophia trust in his words? They stood close together, but an emotional distance grew between them. "I shall never forget this day," she said, "the day I found my best friend and lost him again, and all because of a kiss."

Sophia saw the pain that gave his amber eyes a downcast look. She witnessed the emotion that existed between them, a seed suppressed, but also saw the faith he had in Christ. She believed then, that he would never betray his beliefs. Not even for her.

He clutched her face gently. "Sophia, your sweetness and innocence beckon to me; I have much to weigh," he said with a grimace. "Please give me time."

"Oh Mathias," she replied, crumbling to the ground, clinging to his black robe. "I'm so sorry. How could I have done this to you? I see the situation that I've placed you in."

He knelt down, gently released her fingers from his clothing then pulled her to his chest, holding tight to her hand, to behold his passionate regard. "Stand tall. You have acted out of love. There's no gift more beautiful. My only regret is that I'm not free to receive it."

"What are you saying?"

He hesitated, but his amber gaze didn't waver from her eyes. "Please, don't make me say it."

"I have to know, have I played myself for a fool, or could you love me?"

Mathias wrapped his arm around her waist and held her close, threading his fingers through the strands of her hair. "I most certainly could. I do love you."

He grasped her buttocks, groaning as her abdomen came in contact with his swell. She could sense how he battled with the desire to conquer her passions and his own will.

"You have no idea how much I want to lie with you," he moaned, his mouth plundering her lips, kissing her for several moments. When they finally parted, Sophia was left reeling, feeling shaken and breathless.

"Do you see what I mean?" Mathias said. "If I were free to take what I desire, I would demand far more than kisses. I would want everything you have to give!"

He visibly shook now, turning from her, he motioned with his hands while stepping a slight distance away. "But I made a commitment. I'm not free to love you though I may wish the outcome to be different. You have not played the part of a fool. I have compromised you and I will pay the price for my indiscretion."

"Mathias..." She raised her arm, reaching to him in vain.

"Sophia, you're stronger than you realize. You will recover from this circumstance."

"Will, will I see you again?"

He turned to face her. "I don't want to hurt you, but it would be unwise to continue on this path of destruction. We must remain apart while I think this through. If you require further counseling, you should seek out another priest."

"I don't want another priest. I want the friend who has helped me; Mathias," she said, beckoning as he turned to leave her. "I love you..."

"I will hold that knowledge dear in the days ahead. Please don't worry, Sophia. If there's a way, we'll find it. We'll work this out."

He looked at her, sighed, shook his head, then walked away, passing through the trees and finally out of her sight. It was then that she found her way back to the beech tree.

She touched the bark, just as Mathias had indicated for her to do. Rough, like the difficulties of life, she could only hope that the love she had found, would find a way to overcome.

"My Father who art in Heaven," she prayed, "help us…"

CHAPTER 13

*C*hrist's bones! What had he done? Kneeling down and kissing her like that? Mathias flushed with guilt, recalling the softness of her bosom. The touch, *it was wrong*.

He drew a quivering hand across his heated brow, wiping at the perspiration that beaded on his forehead and trickled down his cheek, knowing he was ill. Perhaps he was consumed with a loving flux. An innocent touch, *a loving kiss*, brought him to this impasse.

But he must *find his way* home.

Sophia inspired his passion. A picture of innocence, she toyed with his emotions and warred with his senses. Even now, his heart beat at an unusual rhythm, linked by irregular breathing and heated longing. His shaft was still hard! It was as if his masculinity had forced blood to every vessel, filling his muscles with tension, affecting his organs to throb painfully alive.

Looking downward, Mathias attempted to draw the conflict of smoldering love within. But one glance at a masculine projection drawing proudly upward shattered his goal. This and the painful reality, that he could not control the steadfast reaction of his desires.

He was a man, strong by nature, and determined by the spirit of the Lord. Why should it be so difficult to prevent the shameful ascension of his manhood? Held in a state of physical frustration, the heat burned within him, causing his face to color the shade of scarlet. And though he had walked at a leisurely pace, his breathing rampaged as if he had run a great distance.

He attempted to dispel the reflections, his tortured thoughts returning to the pleasure of her invited kiss. So shockingly tender, innocent, and blissfully soft against his mouth. He rubbed his lips.

Why had he done it? Why had he kissed her? How could something so beautiful be so wrong? He hung his head in shame.

Pain twisted within his gut, creating knots of tension. Holding his abdomen, he walked to the nearest tree, nearly doubling over. He was sick.

He had wanted to draw Sophia intimately closer. God help him, he wanted to break through the barriers of virgin love unheeded. Discovering together, the awakenings and skin tingling yearnings of the rapture. He, *the man*, had wanted to trace every sensitive ridge of her skin, drawing each of them closer to a final and joyful climax.

Was he doomed to leave the church, then?

Mathias refrained, as another crippling pain stabbed at his gut. He covered his mouth with his hand, falling against the tree, allowing the bark to hold his weight. He realized he should accept his fate, that her love could never be his. But that part of him that was inquisitive by nature searched for answers.

"My God, why? Where did this celibate business come from? Who made this rule?"

The only reply was the gentle brush of the wind, whispering through the trees.

"Why did it change? Surely, you wouldn't design such a dictum. To love is the most important assurance, isn't it?"

Bishop Eberhardt's words came back to haunt as if his risen form walked across the earth to resurrect a begotten love, or more likely to ensure that he made the right choice and took the necessary risk.

Rejoice in love should you find it. His ramblings seemed to carry on the breeze, a forceful murmur brushing across his face. It would be sorely tempting to lose himself and act on Bishop Eberhardt's advice. After all, the clergyman had always been blessed with a keen intuitive sense.

Likewise, if he were to respect the Pope's narrative, there was only one answer, to reject Sophia's love and hold fast to the celibate rule. God help him, he couldn't do it. He couldn't deny her love.

Yet as Mathias searched for answers to his dilemma, he understood that only one being could help him with the trial he battled with. Only one entity held the necessary power to challenge man's authority. It was God's doctrine priests followed and his commandments that they preached by. Where was it written that celibacy was a firm conviction of God's rule?

For the first time in his life, he doubted the dictum. He knew it was blasphemous to question a vow that he himself had agreed to live by, but perhaps it was time for someone to examine the covenant more closely. Why must he make this supreme sacrifice —denying Sophia's love, rejecting his love—forgoing their pure affection for each other?

Why must loving a woman be a sin to a priest? As Sophia had said: he was a man, chiseled in the likeness of his creator. God had made him what he was and therefore His Heavenly Father should understand the awakenings. Would God think it wrong? Would he despise him for natural inclinations?

Would he be able to guide other men any less if he adopted a more compassionate love? Did His Heavenly Father expect such a sacrifice from him? He had to know. He had to understand, because he wanted to serve his Creator and fulfill a commitment he had made a long time ago.

For himself *and for his brother, but the heavens were quiet…*

Mathias fell to the ground, fighting a wave of nausea. He was going to be sick.

Staggering on bent knee, he stood, beads of perspiration collecting on his forehead. Spreading his arms wide to the sky, he raised his voice in sorrow.

"My God, my God," he breathed. "Why do you serve me with this cross? Would loving Sophia corrupt my ambition? Would my cup of compassion, my goals of preaching, be poisoned by her touch? Or would I be like other men, accepted as other men, but respected for my duty as a priest?"

His strength weakened, his spirit like his body collapsed to the grass.

"My God, my Savior," he moaned, wiping the tears from his eyes. "A job, like other jobs. I'm a man, yet also a priest. Why must I be punished and denied the love of a good woman? Why?"

He paused, curling like a child on the ground, clutching his abdomen as a pain so rife knifed inside of him. He curled his hand into a fist, breathing the musty soil that rested beneath his head. Dust mixed with his tears. Clouds hid the sun and the winds shifted and blew stronger across the landscape.

"Is this your wish, Heavenly Father?" Mathias winced, his voice a whisper. "Believing in you, I've always tried to follow your doctrine. I will follow your path—*for myself, for Marcos*—only tell me that this sacrifice is your desire, your precept and my destiny."

He cringed, curling further into a fetal ball, pulling his knees to his chest. The wind blighted his eyes, inducing tears. "Or is this some trick that you play, providing a woman to test my faith. My God," his voice broke slightly, "your scheme threatens my future, the promises that I have made." Mathias breathed, attempting to calm. "But in your wisdom and infinite knowledge, do you want such a sacrifice?"

"You hold the power, the commandments—what do I do now that I've tasted her lips?"

Mathias's voice broke and the pain that he had carried, that he had buried within the reaches of his soul, spewed forth. He emptied the contents of his stomach on the ground. After his stomach stopped heaving, he wiped his mouth, and then rolled onto his back. The tears fell, slowly trailing a winding path across his cheeks, slipping to the ground. The tension seemed to lessen with each drop of moisture but the question remained, like a persistent knoll.

Could he give Sophia his heart, his love?

"My God," he shouted, the tears streaming down his face. "Please help me."

Mathias held his head in his hands, disregarding the whistle in the wind. He didn't have the strength to rise; how would he ever find his way home?

But somehow, he found the strength to rise from the ground and walk. When the church and his home came into sight, there was no conscious memory of the footpath he had traveled. He felt tired, his bones ached, his head burned with fever. The warmth of his bed was the only thought on his mind as he reached for the doorknob.

He entered his house, smelling the aroma of food cooking, which only made him feel nauseous.

"Father," Edda called from the kitchen, "I've kept your dinner warm. Sit down and I will—"

He stumbled into the room and clutched at the wall for support. Edda turned, and promptly dropped her pewter ladle to the floor. Before he could speak, she was at his side.

"Mathias, you're so pale." She rested her hand on his forehead. "You're burning with fever, we must get you to bed."

"Yes, bed," he muttered, staggering. "Warmth, I'm so cold."

She took him by the arm and led him down the corridor. When he stumbled, when his knees buckled, she bore his weight. Somehow, she moved him to his bedchamber, pulled back the covers and sat him on the bed.

"Should I stay the night?"

"No, leave me in peace."

"Father," she remarked, scrutinizing him. "Your robe, it's completely saturated."

He didn't want to listen to her, his pillow called. He reclined to the mattress, soon closing his eyes.

He heard Edda open the bottom drawer of his wardrobe. She seemed to mutter something as she sorted through his belongings. The heavy lull of sleep beckoned to him, and drew him away, but the sound of the drawer closing brought him quickly back to alertness.

"Forgive me for disrobing thee, but if you weren't so ill, I'd not contemplate such action. The good Lord will forgive me. 'Tis sure of that I am."

After much maneuvering, he felt a rush of cold air as Edda removed the robe, and then his linen undergarment.

"You won't feel any embarrassment," she griped, "I've tended to my brothers many a time."

Once he was wearing a lighter cotton, she urged him to lie down. He gladly succumbed, pressing his weight on the pillow.

"I'll watch over you. Rest now. Sleep will help heal whatever ails."

EDDA SHOOK HER HEAD, brushing aside the long gray strands that had escaped her chignon. She left Father Mathias's room to find a basin of water to mop his heated brow. Though sickness pervaded, she knew what ailed the good Father, had witnessed the same signals years before. So sad, she muttered, walking down the corridor, remembering.

She knew the coming trials that he must face and she felt sorry for him.

Aye, sorry for the lass as well.

She would say a prayer for them when she finally took herself home and to bed. It would be a long night, she sighed, a very long night.

CHAPTER 14

*S*ophia nestled into the soft down of her quilt and pulled the coverlets around her shoulders, not wanting to wake up. But something didn't feel right. She squinted, scrunching up her face, soon opening her eyes. Someone rested near her on the bed.

"You whispered his name three times." Alisz was mocking her, raising a curious brow, and calmly preening her nails. "Three times, with nary a sign of guilt."

Sophia wiped the sleep from her eyes, and then shifted on the bed, raising herself onto her elbows. "What did I say? I don't recall saying anything."

"I assure you," Alisz chided, appearing serious, "you whispered a man's name quite seductively. Sister dear, I'm surprised."

Smiling, Alisz tilted her head back, bringing her hand to her chest, tittering with amusement. Just as quick, she calmed, staring at her sister.

"Out with it," Sophia barked, her brows drawing downward in anger. "Reveal the man's name and hoist your weapon. For I'm certain, knowing you as I do, that there's an advantage to this game you play."

"Very well," Alisz chortled. "Let's have some fun, shall we?"

Tapping her finger on her lip in contemplation, she rose from the bed, suddenly giddy. Then her booted feet calmly clicked across the floorboards. Strange footwear, Sophia mused, for a woman dressed in lavender finery.

"Riddle me this. He chose a role as a father, but you didn't utter our father's name. For shame, dear sister, you can't have this man, for he's committed to the Almighty."

"You won't rest until I confirm that your theory is true. Well, all right, damn you. You will have the name..."

She bounded onto the bed in the same way an excited child would leap. "Christ's nails," Sophia screeched, falling back against the headboard in surprise.

"Oh, calm down, there's no need to swear. I already know the answer to the riddle."

The silence was impenetrable as her eyes narrowed in doubt. She stared into the ice-blue crevices of Alisz's eyes. Waiting, she mulled the announcement that was forthcoming in her mind. So too did her sister, quiet in her anticipation.

"Mathias, I must have said Mathias."

"Ah, yes," Alisz drawled, reclining again, this time at the foot of the bed. "That is the priestly cleric you spoke of with sensual ease. Yet curiously, you didn't mention his forename. Interesting, is it not?"

It could have been her imagination, but Sophia wondered if she had been drawn into a trap. It seemed Alisz wanted far more information than a name. Sophia brought her hand to her lips, and then giggled into her hand, aware of the true nature of the game that was afoot. "Imagine that, that I wouldn't call him Father. Quite interesting, actually."

"Yes," Alisz echoed. Her laughter now muted. "Interesting, indeed. Why do you suppose you forgot his title?"

"I don't know, as I do not recall saying his name. Why do you assume such an interest in my dreams?"

"Sisterly concern, Sophia, 'tis no more than that."

"Since when have you shown affection or concern for me? There's no love between us."

Alisz rolled her eyes, pouting petulantly, batting her eyelashes, then rolling to her side and bracing her hand on her hip. "Well yes, perhaps we share more conflict than love," she said, smiling brightly. "But you must admit; the two emotions resemble each other to the degree of satisfaction one gains from each."

Sophia threw back the covers with a rush, shaped her nightdress around herself then slid off the edge of the bed. She was accustomed to seeing that baneful look in Alisz's eyes. She wished she'd just leave, leave her in peace.

"What do you want? What is the true reason that begs you to disturb my bedchamber this morning? A place you were not invited to enter."

"One objective gave me cause to enter your room, but three words spoken out of turn, might have gained me two."

Sophia braced her hands on her hips, scrutinizing her sister's twisted expression. The wooden slats on the floor were cold beneath her feet and she longed for the warmth she had left behind. But she wouldn't venture back to the bed where Alisz now sat.

"Well, will you confide the information, or do we continue to play charades?"

"Very well," Alisz drawled, throwing back her blond strands, and removing herself from the bed. "I long to leave this pretty-girl place anyhow."

Sophia watched as she sauntered across the room, pulling a letter from her pocket and holding it boldly in her hand. She hesitated, rubbing the parchment between her fingers as if she fought with the nobility of the act. Finally, she passed the message to Sophia.

Receiving the letter, Sophia contemplated the neatly written script, not recognizing the handwriting or the seal. "The seal is broken?" she said with a grimace. "You had the audacity to open my mail? How dare you?"

Sophia tapped her foot while waiting for a response. "Complicity interests me, and frankly, because it annoys you."

Sophia narrowed her eyes, her anger affecting her to press the letter too tightly between her fingers. "Leave. Obviously, you know the contents of this letter, so you need not stay to watch me read the message."

Alisz sauntered across the room, swinging her hips, finally settling herself on the settee. Breathing easily, resting comfortably on the patterned tapestry adorned with a rosy hue, she caressed the dark wood grain of the hand-rest with her fingers.

"I'm not leaving, not until you have realized the full intent of the message written on the parchment. I suggest you read."

Sophia walked to the window, turning her back on her stepsister. She was not about to allow her to study the impressions on her face as she discovered the import of the message.

She opened the packet, withdrawing the parchment scented with rose water. Rose water? A distant memory, long buried from her childhood came to her. Alisz forgotten, she held the letter to her nose and breathed the scent of the paper. She knew who had sent the letter before she began to read the neat script.

Dearest Sophia, my darling niece,

Though the years have passed, I've thought of you often. I remember holding your tiny fingers and pressing them to my lips, just before you entertained us with a tune on the pianoforte. I can still hear the music of yesteryear, a child's first notes, a mother's proud visage, a father's love, and myself about to wed. Do you recall it, Sophia? You were so young.

I have missed a great portion of your life. The child I remember fondly has grown into a woman and this woman soon to become a bride. You should not be alone at this time of your life. During this transition, I'm your only living relative. I should be with you.

I have thought this situation over carefully and I believe it is my duty to prepare you for your coming nuptials. You need a hand to guide you through the final wedding preparations and help prepare for the wifely duties that lie ahead in the marriage bed.

This is the last errand I can attend for your dearly departed mother and my sister. May God rest her soul; she would have wanted to share this day with you.

With your father departed, too, you will require my help. I fear you shall find no assistance from your stepmother, but we will not speak of unpleasantness.

With your approval, I shall come. Please write and convey your thoughts to this end. Say the word and I shall set forth as quickly as I'm able.

Waiting for your reply—

"Aunt Lovisa," she muttered. "I had forgotten about my mother's sister. It will pain me to write, shattering her illusions to reveal the truth. And of course, I would have enjoyed a visit, it has been a long time."

Sophia turned around to face Alisz, still holding the open letter in her hand. Alisz sat on the settee, quiet, staring at the flooring, twisting a golden band, round and round her finger. "Surely you will not reveal the sordid tale of your ancestry to your aunt."

"She deserves the truth. I will tell her everything."

"I read the letter. Your aunt thinks you're an innocent babe, grown to a luxurious woman and about to become a fairy-tale bride. Though she must be told that the wedding has been called off, do you really want to shatter her sweet picture of you?"

"Why should you care?" Sophia asked, stepping shrewdly forward. "You have never shown common courtesy to anyone. What is your true ambition? What do you have to gain by my silence?"

Alisz's hand flew to her mouth, feigned hurt and surprise registered in her eyes. "Sophia," she began, "how could you think so low of me. I offer my advice with the best of intentions."

"That's my point," she acknowledged. "You have never offered sisterly counsel before. You openly admit your dislike, and yet you'd have me believe you assume my best interests? I'm sorry, but I will not buy into your deception."

"Fine," she managed, standing abruptly. "I attempted niceties, but if you won't do as requested, perhaps you need a little urging."

Sophia was not about to be fall prey to the antics of this wicked child. Though she only wore a cotton nightdress, she faced her sister squarely. "I'm not afraid of anything you have to say. I shall do as I please. I cannot imagine why you should care if my aunt should learn that her niece is a bastard. I would think the revealing of this information would give you pleasure. This only proves that something I might say will hurt you. What could that be?"

Sophia knew she had struck a deadly mark with unerring accuracy. Alisz's breathing came fast, encouraging the veins in her neck to bulge and her face to turn bright red. Anger furrowed her brows, light sparked within her blue eyes, and she balled both of her hands into fists.

"The choice is yours to make," she all but spat. "Write to your aunt. Tell her your fate if you must, but be careful about what you divulge. If any information, and I mean the smallest details should arise to hurt me, I will let the demons out of your closet."

"I do not fear you."

She stepped ominously closer. "You should!" she quipped. "I'm warning you. Be careful, very careful."

Sophia laughed in the face of her threat, whirled her finger in the air and coughed in her face. "Get out of my room."

Turning in anger, Alisz walked to the door and opened it, thrusting it against the wall in a loud bang that reverberated throughout the room. The look of hatred, of intense dislike should have warned Sophia, but she believed her stepsister to be full of empty threats, and so she paid no heed to the voice that rose out of control.

"Three little words, three little words whispered while you slept will be your undoing."

"Just words, little sister, nothing more."

"I'm not naïve. I see what happens around me and when I cannot, I ensure that someone else is taking up the cause. I know of your sinful dalliance with the dutiful priest."

Sophia stepped back as if she'd been slapped. "There is nothing sinful or shameful about my friendship with Father Mathias."

Alisz stepped back into the room, crossing the floor space like a predator, howling with laughter. She was on the hunt again. "You love him, you spoiling idiot. In the eyes of God, that is a sin, *a crime*, a breach of everything holy."

Sophia turned around to face the window once more. Facing her sister was impossible. She would read the blatant lie written on her features. "He's a friend, nothing more."

"Lie if it eases your conscience, but I have seen the two of you together. You, my sister, are embroiled in a love affair that will destroy you—an unnatural passion that will dig a grave for a lusting Father—and for yourself. Frankly," she sighed, releasing some of the pent-up anger, "I couldn't care less whether he takes your virginity or another's, as long as you don't make your bed with Franz, and you've teased my fiancé quite enough. I warn you, stay out of my way or the knowledge that I hold will be revealed to everyone who will listen. And you realize, sister darling, the hotter the gossip, the further it travels."

Sophia turned to her; the tears full in her eyes, already slipping down her face. "No one will believe you."

Alisz grinned, *winning*, moving back to the door. "Everyone will believe me. Look in the mirror. People will see what I see when I look in your eyes—a burning lust, a common love."

She would have the last word, Sophia reflected sadly. As Alisz left the room, she heard her call. "Tell your aunt the wedding is off, or the man you have come to love will suffer. Mores the pity, you will bear more of society's taunts, too."

Long after the confrontation, Sophia sat at her writing desk, holding her Aunt Lovisa's letter in her hands, reflecting on the conversation. She had not even bothered to dress. She faced a dilemma, a problem that represented itself in the form of a nasty stepsister.

She had given her two options and each preference held no merit, as each seemed to only benefit Alisz. But what did she have to fear by revealing the honest truth to her aunt. The truth, or so it seemed to her, could not hurt any more or less than it already had.

Alisz, on the other hand, must have a great deal to yield if she was adamant that Aunt Lovisa be given no knowledge as to her change in societal status. Could that be it? Sophia wondered, drawing her brows together in consternation and tapping her finger at the side of her face. Could Alisz's master plan be so bold? And if it were true, how on earth had she managed to carry it off with no one the wiser?

It certainly led her to an important query that she herself had never questioned before. She sprang from her desk, turned and ran to her doorway, ready to break through the arches of her bedchamber, eager to find Alisz and set to wring the truth from her evilly plotted mind.

But reason stopped her at the doorway, purpose and a plan. Sophia realized instantly what must be done. She would get to the bottom of Alisz's deception, and God help the woman if she had managed the scheme that Sophia now suspected.

Returning to the desk, Sophia reached for parchment, took up a quill and began relating the events that had shattered her life. She didn't skip a detail, no matter how small or inconsequential each point seemed. The only information she kept to herself was the affection she had come to realize for Mathias. This news could hurt him if the truth came out, and she was not about to harm the man she cared for.

The letter grew and grew and in some parts, the ink smudged where her tears had fallen during more painful recollections. When she finished, she signed the letter regretfully. Revealing to her aunt how she would love to make her acquaintance again. A friendly face and a soft shoulder to cry on would be welcome in her time of strife.

She didn't mention her suspicions, for if her assumptions were correct, her aunt would be on the next carriage from Paris. And this, she told herself, smiling in conspiracy, is what she believed so frightened Alisz.

But in the event that her stepsister should guess the strategy that she was about to play, she fashioned a second letter, much shorter than the first. One that would satisfy her curiosity, should she choose to view the contents without permission.

This should keep her evil counterpart more concerned with her coming nuptials. But if she played her cards right, she might be able to forestall this farce of a wedding to Franz, if not stop it all together. She didn't want him for herself as he had proven himself a weak and shallow man who was beholden to his parents. But neither did he deserve Alisz. If her suspicions were proven true, perhaps he would thank her for saving him from his fate.

Folding each of the two letters carefully, and placing each in their separate packets, and sealing them with her seal of a knight-errant, she hid them in her desk.

Then she rang for Adeline, her personal maid, to come aid her in dressing and then to deliver the letters. The one bound for her aunt, the other to be discarded in a heap of trash.

It would be weeks before she heard from her aunt, but the hope that she would foil her stepsister's evils gave her cause to smile. When the time came, she would relish the moment when Aunt Lovisa charged the steps of Baldemar Manor.

In her mind's eye, she saw her aunt avenging a wrong done to her person for the sake of hatred and greed. "Come soon, Aunt Lovisa," she whispered.

CHAPTER 15

Sophia waited for Adeline to come to her bedchamber. Standing in front of her wardrobe perusing an assortment of fine gowns, she fingered each creation not sure which one to select. Finally, in her anticipation, she chose a fine linen dress of yellow saffron. A color matching the radiance of the sun that presently reflected her optimism.

Taking off her nightdress, she threw it atop her rumpled bed, and then reached for a chemise of fine cotton lawn. Just as she finished adjusting the garment around her shoulders, she heard a knock at the door.

"Mistress Sophia, it's Adeline. May I enter?"

"Yes," Sophia called out in greeting. "Come in, please do come in."

The door opened, and Adeline entered. With her back straight, she stiffly carried a serving tray laden with breakfast breads and a porcelain pot of freshly brewed tea. In a quick maneuver, her leather-covered foot efficiently propelled the door shut.

Adeline was dressed in a long-sleeved shift of serviceable muslin with a wheat overskirt and white apron, and her smile brightened the room. Walking to a side trestle table, she deposited her tray, and then rearranged the muffin cap that hid her long golden braid. A hint of exhaustion underscored her soft blue eyes.

"Good morning, my Lady Sophia," she remarked, her face uncertain. "How do ye fair on this fine fresh morning?"

"Very well," she said, clapping her hands and smiling, "very well indeed. And you?"

She watched Adeline approach the wardrobe. She seemed tired and out of sorts, her expression pinched and strained as she leaned into the wardrobe to withdraw a satin corset. Her movements were shaky, unbalanced.

"Is something wrong?" Sophia asked, stepping away from the bed.

"'Twas a long night." Adeline sighed, splaying her hands on her back. "My young'un took ill. I bathed his brow most of the night."

"What of your child today?" she asked, as Adeline molded the corset to her figure. "Is he better?"

"Some," she whispered, pulling the dress fabric together; adjusting here and there, she soon tied the laces.

"Will he recover?"

"He's a strong lad. I imagine he won't be down for long."

She kept to her work, helping Sophia into her petticoat, then fashioning the overskirt over top. Finally, a kirtle was placed over top of the chemise and laced only halfway up.

Although she didn't have children of her own, Sophia understood that a mother's duty should come first. "Is there anything I can do?"

"Very kind of you to offer your concern, Mistress. But the only thing I'm lacking, I reckon, is sleep. Much to be done today, I'm afraid, I can't take my leave early."

Sophia smiled conspiratorially at her servant as she began to brush her unruly locks. "Maybe you'll be freed of your duties earlier than planned. If you agree to an errand that I need attended to most urgently—by one I can trust."

"I would do anything for you, Lady Sophia." She stopped fighting with the knots momentarily. "'Tis my responsibility."

"I need a letter delivered, Adeline, and I will pay well if you follow my wishes to the exact detail. If you would attend to this errand first thing this morning, not only would I give you the rest of the day off, but I would also ensure your family dines on the finest mutton this evening."

"I would be happy to have the day off, my Lady, to tend to my son and rest. It'll spare my husband to undertake his own duties. But you need not bother with reward. 'Tis my duty to serve thee."

The knots gone, she began to braid Sophia's hair. "I don't know what I'd do without your loyalty. The errand is not simple. It involves deceiving my stepsister. This alone could make this task more dangerous. I will not see you hurt."

"I see," she whispered, suppressing a grin. "I shall do it then, and gladly. I have never fancied your stepsister."

Once Sophia was dressed and her hair was braided, she recovered the letters from the dresser. "Take these two letters," she requested, handing the packets over. "But hide the thicker packet where Alisz is sure not to look should she become suspicious of our plan. Then after you leave my room, seek her out and explain you are required to attend a task for Lady Sophia."

"If she questions the chore, what should I tell her?"

"Tell her the truth, that you are delivering a letter for your mistress and that after you have achieved the task, you have been given the day off for your efforts. She will fume about the lack of help, but she will be more interested in the contents of the letter."

"Seems easy enough."

"I wager she will want to view the contents and will likely bully you into allowing her to read it," Sophia said, pacing across the room. "Pull the thinner packet from your pocket, and hold it beneath her nose where her curiosity will be aroused. But do not place it in her hands, toy with her a bit."

"Mistress," she said, grinning with amusement, giggling, reaching for her lower back again. "I had no idea you could be so sly."

Sophia smiled too now, joining Adeline in laughter and reflecting on the brilliance of her plan. "Now we must not become too loud, I'm sure she has her spies."

"Not me. As you said before, I'm loyal. Are there any other instructions?"

"Yes, tell her what you just said, that you are loyal to your dear lady. But then share your difficult times, in fact you have a sickly child, and if she were to grace your hand with a silver thaler or two, mayhap you will turn your head and pay no mind. Knowing Alisz, she will take the bait and pay you for your efforts, hopefully none the wiser to our ploy."

"When she lets you on your way, be very discreet about keeping the letter I intend to mail hidden, until you are at the depot. As you make your way home to your family, you may destroy our decoy letter, burning it within your own chimney. If you are successful with this venture, I will be beholden to you."

Adeline winked conspiratorially. "You, my Lady, will never be beholden to the likes of me. This is important to thee I wager, and as such, it's important to me, too. I will do thee proud, I will. And just for thee, I'll fleece a few more silver coins from your stepsister's coffers. I have never liked the way that girl manages you."

"Well, yes, she can be disagreeable, and terribly unkind. Anyway, shall we celebrate the coming scheme we'll weave together? Will you share my breakfast feast?"

"I must not, it wouldn't be proper."

"Oh, come now," Sophia chided, taking her arm. "Fellow conspirators always toast their campaign. I have an extra teacup in the sideboard. Join me, Adeline. If not to celebrate Alisz's lightened purse, then to gain strength to support your coming errand and after that to care for your ailing child."

"If it will please, I will join you."

"It will gratify my heart, you have no idea how much. Sit down then, allow me to serve you for a change."

Sophia led Adeline to the settee, and then urged her weary servant to rest while she collected the extra cup. Returning to the tray, she reached for the porcelain teapot, then poured the contents into two dainty cups. After offering a breakfast bun, she joined Adeline on the settee.

"To success," she grinned, toasting.

"Aye, my Lady," Adeline joined, raising her cup as well. "To success."

Sophia contemplated her victory, while savoring the tea as it infused her taste buds. Though she was sure her plan would reap victory, she calculated the scheming mind of her stepsister carefully. She wouldn't be easily fooled.

Realizing this, she would have to play the part of the loser, until the time came when her Aunt Lovisa could come to her aid. That would be the moment, a golden moment, to celebrate her victory!

But until that pretty picture came true, she wouldn't forget the task her loyal servant was about to undertake. She must be compensated properly for her efforts.

"Adeline, in my gratitude, I will ensure that a full slab of mutton is delivered to your residence."

"The offer is most kind, but if you want to help my family, there's something we need more."

"What is it? You shall have it."

"I don't like to ask, being as you are so kind. I would help without the offering of payment, but with my son ill, well, milk is what we need."

Sophia clapped her hands. "Done! You shall have milk and the mutton as well. I will direct a field hand to choose a nanny goat immediately. The doe will be waiting when you arrive home."

"What about Lady Wendeline? Will it not upset her?"

Sophia sighed, and then grasped her chambermaid's hand. "She'll never know, for we shall not tell her."

Adeline rose from the settee and placed her teacup on the serving tray. A grateful expression and a fresh teardrop glistened on her cheek. Sophia sat up also, leaned forward and gave her servant a hug. "Thank you, Lady Sophia. I hardly know what to say."

"It is you that deserve the thanks," Sophia stated, patting her shoulder. "You do realize that presently you are more a friend to me than a servant. Whenever your family needs help, you only need ask."

Adeline got teary then, could barely talk.

"You're a kind woman," she whispered. "You don't deserve the family that's been placed on your doorstep. They're a shadow of darkness."

"I assure you, not forever. In time, I will take proper care of them, as they have taken care of me."

Adeline retreated to the door, but as she grasped the handle, she stopped and looked back. Reaching inside her pocket, she withdrew a letter of her own.

"I'm sorry. I almost forgot. This letter came for you early this morning. A lad working in the fields gave it to me as I made my way to work. No one has laid eyes on it but me."

Curious, Sophia took the letter. She didn't recognize the handwriting.

"Thank you, Adeline. Once again you do me a service in handling this missile discreetly."

"You're welcome, my Lady. I will attend to your errand now. I will apprise you of the outcome tomorrow morning."

"Only if your son is well enough. If he's no better, stay at home and attend to your first responsibility."

"You are kind. Thank you."

After Adeline left, Sophia returned to the settee. She poured herself a second cup of tea, and then settled herself to read the message.

My Lady Sophia,

Please come. Father Mathias fights a terrible ague. I wouldn't write, considering your station, but I know aught else to do. On his sick bed he calls your name. His situation is grave... I fear the worst if his fever lingers much longer. Though he might not believe it, he needs you.

"Edda," Sophia whispered, folding the parchment in her hands. She nibbled at her lip, picturing a pale image, gray from the ravages of sickness.

She realized the futility of worrying, understood the need to remain strong and in control for his sake. Yet the visions that came unbidden to her mind, spelling havoc and possible death, elicited a cry of fear. Her arms fell aimlessly to her side. The note between her fingertips was slowly crushed to a small ball. She barely felt the rush of cold air that penetrated the tissues of her back, sweeping across her spinal column, rendering her cold.

The note slipped through her fingers and fell to the floor. Shivering, she reached for the teacup in an attempt to fill herself with the content's warmth. But she shook so badly that she knocked the cup over, spilling the liquid onto the saucer, the side table, and further to the carpeted floor.

"Oh no," she cried in bewilderment. "He is sick, deathly ill. I must go to him. He needs me."

She rushed to the clothing stand and retrieved her black cloak. Not bothering to put it on, she held the folds loosely over her arm. Opening the door, she rushed down the hallway, her feet a dull thud as she rushed across the carpeted opulence.

Reaching the stairs, she almost collided with Alisz in her haste to get to Mathias. Gripping the handrail, she attempted to move past her stepsister.

"Slow down, Sophia. What matter has tempered your clumsy flight?"

"Leave me alone," she bit back, gripping the whitewashed railing. "Please, for once have a care, move aside and let me pass."

Her brows drew together with interest; Alisz stepped down one stair. "You're upset," she speculated, drawing a partial smile. "Am I the source of your misery?"

"Get out of my way," Sophia growled, trying to avoid her. "Or I swear, I will strike you."

"Sophia, it pains me that you're so weak. I wish God had granted a better adversary so that our moments of strategy could bring about a better outcome. Winning our minor skirmishes is compelling, but just this once, you could display a backbone."

Sophia pushed Alisz, sending her sprawling against the wall. She went halfway down the staircase, moving at a leisurely pace.

"Is that backbone enough for you? Really Alisz, I don't have time for your games."

Putting on her cape, with the woolen fibers swirling around her feet, she rushed to the door, opened it and fled into the sunlight. She hurried to the stable where Hans quickly saddled Maraclese. She thanked him for his quick efforts. But in her haste to be on her way, she didn't notice that her rival had followed her outside.

Alisz leaned against the backdrop of the door, rubbing her shoulder with an indifferent gaze. The action betrayed the pain that affected anger to turn her pale blue eyes to a cauldron of fire. Her gaze followed the trail that Sophia's horse favored at a full gallop.

When her sister was out of sight, Alisz left her post at the door and walked across the lawn to the stable. She found the stable-master and had him saddle her beau gelding. She was soon on the horse's back commanding the reins.

With a flick of her wrist, she turned the horse and fled from the yard. Sophia was plotting and the chambermaid might have some useful information. She would pay the servant a visit and see if she could bully the truth from her lips. The knowledge that her child was sickly might expedite her tongue to wag.

If threats didn't work, money would. She was certain from the gleam in Sophia's eyes that she was plotting, and she must get to the bottom of her schemes.

Above all, she wouldn't allow her stepsister to get the better of her. She'd worked too hard to bury the past. It wouldn't serve her to have the truth uncovered now.

CHAPTER 16

"Where am I?" Mathias mumbled, recognizing that he was no longer confined to his bed. Freed from his body; his weightless soul floated on a highway of blue with thick puffy clouds swirling about his legs.

He reached forward, trying to part the vapors, but the thick haze wouldn't yield. A beacon of light flickered in the distance, but though he tried to reach the nimbus, he was thwarted. Each step forward, the radiance seemed to drift further away and appeared just beyond his reach.

He supposed his soundless footsteps walked on clouds divine, somehow supporting his weight. Unafraid, Mathias stepped toward the light, reaching, searching for the wisdom that could end his suffering.

"'Tis not your time," a familiar soul affirmed. "Stay away from the light."

Mathias paused in his pursuit, surprised to hear the husky timbre. He turned to the sound only to see Bishop Eberhardt's apparition.

"You shouldn't be here," the Bishop tittered, his voice unusually shrill.

"But Your Grace," Mathias beckoned, reaching. "I'm tired, weak. I yearn for peace."

"You're young, strong, free to enjoy a satisfied life. Turn away from the light, reach for the living."

"I'm not free to pursue what I desire most," Mathias emphasized, his voice breaking. "I'm committed to serve the church. I must banish all else. Regardless of my past, I chose this path. Let me serve the Almighty in the holy realm where a woman's lips cannot tempt."

"It's not your time," he said with a sigh. "Serve the Heavenly Father within the parish, or other places where the Holy Spirit is strong. Go back. Face your burdens. This is God's ruling."

"I can't accept this."

"Ah, Mathias, have you discarded your faith so easily? Faith, hope, love abide, these three; but the greatest of these is love? Make love your aim, and earnestly desire the spiritual gifts, especially the gift to help others."

Mathias tried to touch Bishop Eberhardt, but like rays of sunshine, his presence seemed illusive. Just like his sermons in the sanctuary, his discourse commanded attention, so much so that Mathias's spirit contemplated the safe return to his body.

And to her love... Yet he fought against the pull; just now he wasn't ready to return to humanity.

"What are you saying? Love may be a gift, but when it's gained through a woman's advance, it's a sin. I'm a priest."

"You were born a man, Mathias," the Bishop stated, his voice firm, loud, certain. "Remember what I once told you. *Rejoice in love should you find it.* Love is an assurance and a blessing from our Creator. The greatest gift—a couple shall ever know. Turn away from the light."

"Go home," a brotherly voice whispered. "This life was never your calling. It was mine."

"Marcos?" Mathias gasped, swallowing his surprise.

A vision of his brother materialized before him. Wearing a long white robe, Marcos appeared much younger and more youthful than the sibling he remembered. A rosy hue colored his cheeks.

"But I promised you. I said I'd take your place at the altar?"

"You have a good soul, Mathias, you're so brave to bear the burdens of our people. But if you desire a woman's love, then seek her affection."

"I don't understand."

"You know all you need to," Marcos entreated, reaching with his palm extended. "Go back. Learn. Embrace what you have found. This is God's will, and my blessing."

"Are you certain, Marcos?"

"Make lots of babies, brother. Give our mother something to hold. Bless the world with your compassion and teach your children well. I know you'll do good and kind works."

"Marcos, I'm sorry."

"You've nothing to be sorry for; I've found my vocation. Bury the guilt, reach for the heart. Live."

The mist subsided then, spiraling to a central vortex that grabbed hold of him, pulling him into its apex. He fell, his hands reaching, legs kicking, searching for something solid to brace his fall. He landed safely, back inside his body.

He could not see the Bishop or his brother any longer. His eyelids felt heavy, too heavy to open, but still a voice whispered. "Tell her I love her. Do this for me."

"Who, tell who?" Mathias breathed, wheezing, longing for sleep. A throbbing pain stabbed at his chest.

"My fair Edda. Tell her I'm watching, waiting, here in the light."

"I will do as you ask," Mathias inhaled, succumbing to the infirmities of painful breathing once more.

SOPHIA HAD NEVER PUSHED her horse so hard. She thundered across the countryside giving Maraclese the full rein to run, digging her feet into the animal's flanks, stampeding toward the parish church. Pulling on the lead, she was sliding off the horse's back even before she stopped near the corral. She didn't bother to take her horse inside the pen, instead, tied her to the post and ran to the house. Not bothering to knock, she stepped inside and closed the door.

Removing her riding gloves, she walked through the archway into the scullery, sighing in dismay at the presentation. Unwashed pots littered the trestle table, earthenware plates, pewter utensils, and a frightful silence lacking of Mathias's presence.

She tossed her gloves on the table and removed her riding cloak too, folding and placing the cloak on the back of an armchair. Taking a deep breath to calm her worry, she walked to his bedchamber. She was just about to enter the room when the door opened.

"There you are, my Lady," Edda said with a frown. "I thought I heard you."

"I came as quickly as I could. How is he?"

"He's weak. I thought the good Lord came and took him for a time, but he fights on."

"I'm sorry," Sophia mumbled, wiping a tear from her cheek. "Is he doomed then? Is there no hope?"

"He needs a reason to live, a will to fight. Truthfully, he needs you."

She was shocked that the housekeeper would say such a thing, but she let the comment pass. "I will do what I can. I—"

"I know, my dear," Edda said with a kind regard, grasping her hand, squeezing her fingers. "You care for him."

"How did you know?" Sophia sighed, glancing away guiltily.

"A woman understands matters of the heart."

"Presently, the truth doesn't matter." Sophia paused to collect herself. "May I see him?"

"Of course, my dear," she replied, releasing the embrace. "I'll take my leave while you're visiting. I've not slept much the last few days. If he should wake, I've placed a tincture of horehound and sage on the side table. Give him a half-teaspoon."

Sophia nodded, then took a deep breath and moved to his door. She laid her hand on the oak-grain, and then gazed back at the housemaid.

"Have faith, child, all will be well."

"I hope so."

With the parting comment, Sophia pushed the door open and stepped inside the sick room. Shutting the door softly, she leaned against the frame, allowing the door to support her weight. Ghostly white, Mathias lay on the bed, all too still.

She was afraid to approach him where he lay for fear he had already breathed his last. Her heart beat rapidly, and she felt certain the appendage could rend from her chest, seeing the man she had come to care for so ill. She feared he'd die.

"Oh, Mathias," she whispered, rushing forward, bending down to listen to his breath rattling from his lungs. She trembled as she knelt by his side, before his pallid form, soon touching his inflamed head.

So hot, too hot...

Fearing that she would lose him, she traced the heated lines of his forehead, drawing her fingertips along the edge of his whiskered cheek. She grasped his hand that lay at his side and squeezed his fingers. Leaning closer, she breathed his manly smell. He didn't even know that she lingered at his side.

"You have to live," Sophia attempted. "A community depends on you, needs you. I need you."

Placing his hand back at his side, she moved close to his hearing. "I'm here," she whispered, gently nuzzling his earlobe with her lips as if the act were common. "I will take care of you, I'll see you well."

Sophia hovered close to his cheek, hoping he might speak, praying he might find the strength to return to the living. To whom did she wish him to return, the people, or her own selfish needs? Who was she kidding, she longed for his embrace, even in sickness. It didn't matter that her touch was not reciprocated. She yearned to kiss his cheek, but she dared not take advantage.

Instead, pushing away from the bed, she gazed about the room. There was much to be done, a war of sorts to be waged. The situation was dire. Rolling up her sleeves and reaching for a pitcher, she opened the door and fled from the room. Allowing herself the release of a few tears, she hurried to the scullery to fetch a jug, and then rushed through the back door, making her way to the well.

Placing the pitcher on a bench beside the brick surround, she grasped the bucket that hung from a wood frame on a length of

168

hemp. Turning the lever, she lowered the bucket into the dark recesses to the water far below. When she heard the splash at the bottom, she waited but a moment for the bucket to fill. Then wound the rope back to the top, procured the bucket, and poured the ice-cold water into the pitcher. Returning to the house, she fetched a scrap of cloth from the cupboards in the scullery, and then returned to the sick room.

Mathias was too hot and bathing him with cold water was the only way she knew to cool his burning flesh. She collected the basin from the side table and threw its contents out the kitchen door into the yard. Then returning to Mathias's bedchamber, she placed the cold water from the well into the basin.

"I don't like seeing you this way," she said, squeezing the water from the cotton, hardly sensing the cold temperature as she drew the cloth across his forehead. He moaned in response.

"So hot," she murmured, sliding the wet cloth across his cheek, along his jawbone, following the curve that led along his neck to the indentation between his ribs. She wet the cloth again, and then pulled the blanket lower to his abdomen.

Sophia blushed. She'd never seen Mathias without his robe. She understood without looking at his naked chest, or the masculinity that hid beneath the lowest edge of the blankets, that her fingers travelled in dangerous territory. "*Sweet Jesu*," she said, surely blushing. *Damn*, she was intrigued by the possibilities. She shook her head, attempting to dispel the dangerous thoughts, her breathing quickening.

Squeezing the cloth above his chest, Sophia watched the water droplets collect on coarse sandy hairs spiraling about his chest.

He shuddered, shivering as the liquid collected between his ribcage, slowly trailing lower to his belly and further still to the blanket's scandalous edge.

She couldn't help herself. She cared for him, and wanted to love him in the manner that a woman expressed her desires. She wanted to touch, wanted to explore, and find the hidden treasure beneath the sheets.

Tentative fingers drew the cloth along the center of his chest, beside the outer edge of the blanket, more fingers than fabric. She closed her eyes, succumbing to the motion of her hand, her fingers becoming one with the cloth, massaging his lower abdomen. The moisture evaporated in the time it took to place the fabric back in the basin.

"Sophia..." Mathias moaned.

She turned to the sound of his voice, scarcely believing that he had spoken. She squeezed the water from the cloth and placed it on his forehead, then moved to him, cupping his cheek with her hand, grasping his hand with her other.

"I know, Mathias," she said, hoping his moan was a positive sign, coming close to his ear, her lips grazing his earlobe. "You're ill, but I'm bathing you. Don't despair, I will see you well, see you healed from this misery."

She willed him to open his eyes, praying he would regain consciousness. She watched, waited.

"I'm sorry," he rasped, coughing. "My God, my—"

"Yes, of course. You must serve your God as you do it so well," she confirmed. "But surely our Heavenly Father wouldn't mind so much, if you cared for a woman, too?"

"Marcos…"

"I'm here for you," she replied, reaching for the tincture. "Not to tempt you."

"Please," he inhaled, wheezing, "I can't breathe."

"Don't talk, Mathias. I have something that will ease your breathing."

He grimaced when she placed a half-spoon of tincture inside his mouth. "Foul."

"Perhaps," she said, bathing his forehead. "But the horehound and sage will help heal the bad humors."

Although Sophia continued her administrations, Mathias didn't speak again. Finally, when he didn't feel so hot, she leaned against his side and rested. After a time, she must have fallen asleep, for someone's fingers gently nudging her shoulder, awakened her.

"My Lady," Edda whispered, her hand on her back. "He's better. Still hot, but not nearly so."

Sophia rubbed at her eyes, then stretched, resting against the armchair, rubbing her aching back.

"He was awake for a time," she said with a yawn, then stood, moving aside so Edda could come closer. "Well, not really awake, more as if he spoke through his delirium. He never opened his eyes."

"A good sign," the housemaid mused, taking up Sophia's spot on the chair to spoon a poultice of assorted herbs on his chest. "With a little care and God's grace, he will rebound."

"I'm not sure I should be here. Friendship with the Father has become a problem," Sophia admitted, despair written on her face. "I fear my care of him might have the opposite effect. Destroying a man I could see myself loving."

Edda stopped administering the poultice and peered into her eyes as if she held the wisdom earned from a lifetime of experience. Smiling, she departed the chair, grasped Sophia's hands, and urged her to sit.

"This poultice will help. It's not fun to look at, nor is the scent sweet, but if you rub this mixture against his chest he will breathe easier. Touch is love. Care is not measured by words, my Lady. It happens through sacrifice and kind deeds."

"I could lose him," Sophia moaned, taking up the task.

"Aye, you could. 'Tis true enough."

"I fear I want more than he can give. I want more than his spirit will allow. I want..."

"Marriage, physical love," Edda said with a nod, understanding, sighing. "Aye, I once yearned for such a proposal myself. But what I'd give now in my advanced years, just to know the man loved me."

"You talk as if you've suffered your own losses."

"I have, Lady Sophia, but we won't speak of it. Time has passed me by and my youth with it."

Sophia washed her hands in the basin, and then grasped the aged woman's hands. "I'm sorry, so sorry."

Edda brushed her hands away, her face wrinkling with unspoken emotion. She wouldn't pry, but it was in her nature to question.

"Who was he? Surely not a man of the cloth?"

"Aye," she answered, gazing into space as if his image lingered. "A priest when I met him. 'Tis why I understand your situation."

They both sighed in unison. "There's no hope?" Sophia asked, afraid of what the housemaid might say. She glanced away from the woman whose history mirrored her own conflict. Gazing at Mathias, she wondered if the devastating resolution that had afflicted Edda years before might become her own sad reality. At this moment, she could not imagine a promising resolution.

"He's a different man, but he's made a promise. Can't rightly say how that vow can be rectified."

"I'm compromising him, just by being here."

Guilt consumed Sophia as she watched his chest rising and falling, too sharply. Perhaps his ailment was a sign that their love was forbidden. Mathias was destined for something greater than a woman's love. Perhaps it was time to end the suffering, to set the man free.

She reached to him, rested her palm on his cheek and closed her eyes. This was the only solution. An honorable exit freeing the man she loved of the conflict she raised in his life.

"Take a moment. There's a pot of stew on the cook-stove if you're hungry. I will tend to Father Mathias while you sup."

"Yes," Sophia whispered, rising from her post. "I do need a break."

She left the bedchamber without saying another word, considering the decision she must make for herself, and for Mathias.

She thought about her future while sitting at a small wooden table, holding a pewter spoon in her hand, stirring her stew, prodding rutabagas on her plate. They had come to a crook in the road. She only had one choice to make. There could be no other alternative. She dropped the spoon suddenly and rose from the table, pushing back the chair, leaving the remaining stew to grow cold in the bowl.

She needed a place of sanctuary, of comfort. She left the house and walked across the yard to the church, a place of worship where she had first met Mathias.

Soon inside the sanctuary, she stepped along the center aisle, walking past the darkened pews, approaching the front altar. Standing there, she retrieved two waxen candles.

"This illumination," Sophia said, lighting the first candle, "casts light on the difficult decision that I must make. I pray, my Lord, that you will accept my sacrifice; comfort me, and help me during this time of struggle, holding me steadfast in your love."

"This candle," she prayed, tears pooling in her eyes, lighting the second taper on behalf of Mathias. "This sacred light is for the priest I love. Make him well. Let him live. He is worthy of your grace. I release him to serve you, giving him back to the righteous life he has chosen."

A tear swelled within her sight, then slipped from her emerald eyes as she blew out the wick that represented her life. Embers of smoke drifted upward, melding into the darkening shadows, leaving a barren and lonely wick. Anguish squeezed at her heart, seeped into every vital organ and poured forth from her eyes, staining the limestone floor.

Not attempting to wipe the tears away, she allowed her pain to suffuse through her, permitting herself to grieve the decision, and then retraced her steps back down the aisle. Unable to seek her peace in this sanctuary any longer, she knew it was time to leave. Everywhere she looked, she saw Mathias.

Approaching the door, she hesitated, feeling some sense of recognition. She turned and gazed at the Madonna while embracing the door handle. Her sacrifice flickered on the solitary candle left burning. The flame was high on the wick; strong and brilliant like the man she loved.

"I set you free, Mathias. Free, my love."

She then escaped the chapel, leaving the sanctuary to its reflective silence.

CHAPTER 17

Sophia didn't know whether her promise could be kept. More than a week had passed since ending her relationship with Mathias, but the grief had not lessened. She missed his friendship and advice, the only anchor to console her wellbeing during these turbulent days. Having collected Maraclese from the stable, she galloped across the lower hills, but emotional distress and memories overwhelmed the chase.

She felt conflicted, even ambivalent at the decision of discharging a close friendship. On this morning when the wind blew cold, rending tears from her eyes, and the sun barely risen, she wondered what consequences would be met by worshipping at the parish church this Sunday? He'd be there.

She urged her mare to a canter in pursuit of her favorite waterway, trotting across honey-scented fields of emerald green with roe deer feeding several paces away. The life of a deer was simpler, and more natural. The animals ran as she came closer.

The situation's impossible. Why can't I stop thinking about him?

It didn't matter that he was a priest. She loved him, dreamt of him, and longed to be held in his arms. If there was anything to take comfort in, it was the fact that Alisz had minded to her own affairs, preparing for her wedding.

The nuptials were less than a fortnight away. The invitations had been delivered, the menu planned, dress fittings and the like a daily distraction. Sophia had not heard from her aunt on the subject, but she hoped a message might arrive before the wedding day, so her suspicions could be proven correct. The truth was another affair altogether and it didn't matter when it was acknowledged. Though she longed to know her true paternity, the news wouldn't gain what was yearned for most—Mathias.

Franz might even be saved from his future wife, throwing preparations into turmoil. But then again, perhaps the brute deserved to be padlocked to a cold-hearted woman after courting their former relationship with shame and humiliation.

Swaying with the motion of her horse, Sophia ambled closer to the river's edge. Swinging her leg over the horse and sliding to the ground, she soon walked a dirt-packed trail, leading Maraclese to the water's edge, grateful for one outcome. Mathias's health had returned. Edda had sent news that Mathias had returned to his parish. Though he was weak, she had heard he'd managed to conduct Mass this past Sunday. Not wanting to intrude on his conscience, she hadn't attended the service, feigning illness herself.

Maraclese's ears picked up suddenly, sniffing the air, alerting Sophia that they were not alone. She dropped the lead and stepped closer to the water, walking through the brief foliage and trees, coming closer to the embankment.

The sight took her breath away. Mathias on bent knee, hunched over the rocks, picking up stones and tossing them into the river. Watching, not daring to breathe, she didn't want to disturb his peace. Stepping backward hesitantly, she attempted to leave without him knowing. And though her footfall seemed loud sliding across the rocks, it was her horse's neigh that betrayed her presence.

Mathias turned, looked at her, and then rose to his full height.

She could not bear to see his anguish or intrude on his private thoughts. This spot offered Mathias as much security as it gained her peace. Leaving the way she had come seemed the only option, rather than letting him see how his discomfort affected her own suffering.

"Sophia..."

She pivoted to the sound of her name, watching Mathias as he strode nearer. "I must look a terrible sight," she said with a sigh, hoping to keep her emotions in check.

"You're beautiful as always." He reached for her face, soon drawing his index finger over the puffy rings that underscored her eyes. "You've been crying."

"Yes," she replied, shuddering a breath, "but you need not worry."

He closed his eyes, quiet, struggling with an unseen burden, then cupped her cheek and gently massaged her skin with his thumb pad. When he opened his eyes, his sight held a roguish purpose.

"Oh, Sophia, my sweet lady," he moaned, pulling her to the wall of his chest. "How I love you. God might find disfavor for feeling this emotion, but I cannot hide the truth from you any longer. What am I to do? *I love you*. There, I've said it."

He descended upon her, his lips kissing her, his hand wandering into thick tresses, urging her closer. She likened him to a starved man, denied affection too long. At first she stood limp, her lips unmoving, unresponsive. Then the full magnitude of his words struck.

He loves me...

"I love you, too," she breathed, returning his kisses. "Oh, my darling, so much."

But even as she greedily accepted his caresses, guilt consumed her for not being strong enough to reject the advance. A promise made before candlelight burned in her mind. Each kiss seemed wrong, unselfishly she knew: this affection could hurt and destroy.

He broke their contact for a moment, pressing against her forehead.

"Come with me. I have something to tell you."

Fearing what he might say, Sophia didn't say anything. She grasped her horse's reins, and walked beside him to a large beech tree.

"Let me help," he said, taking the reins from her hands and tying Maraclese to a tree, several paces away. Nervous, Sophia watched him as he returned to her side.

"Come," he said, taking her hand. "Don't look so worried. Join me on the ground."

She went willingly. He laid her on a woolen blanket, beside a carpet of sweet sedge, and beneath a canopy of emerald leaves. He joined her there and her head soon lay on his shoulder. It seemed natural to embrace, to place her hand on his chest. Yet, she was hesitant.

"Let me kiss you with the kisses of my mouth," he said, caressing her lips again. "I've felt uncomfortable loving you, desiring you, wanting you. But when I saw you standing there, and saw how this emotion was hurting you, *hurting me*, I couldn't deny our love any longer. Surely," he whispered, closing his eyes, threading his fingers through her auburn layers, "love should not hurt."

"I thought I had freed you from my life." She nestled closer to him. "You were sick, almost beyond help. I believed if I ended our relationship, you would recover. Free to pursue your life as a priest."

His fingers slid beneath her chin and she tingled with awareness, shivering in response. "It's complicated, but I'd perish without your affection. I want to serve God; I want to know your love, and perhaps someday I can be assured of both."

"What is it, Mathias?" she asked, hearing him sigh, watching him frown. "Where do your thoughts lie?"

"With you," he admitted. "I've never lain with a woman. Never touched a woman intimately, the way I desire to touch you now."

"That's quite a confession, Father."

"Please, don't call me that. Let me be a man—your man—desiring your fancy. Just now, not a priest."

Sophia swallowed, seeing he was serious. "I want you, too, but what of the implications? How will your soul fare if I agree? I will not be a party to your damnation."

"God will not damn me for this care, of that I'm certain."

"How can you be sure?" She wanted him as much as he wanted her. She told him so, reaching, touching the side of his whiskered face.

"I have reason to believe that love should find its way." He released the clasp of her midnight cape, allowing the folds to fall open, making a blanket for them on the ground. Beneath she wore a russet vest and a simple white peasant blouse and a long gray skirt. She gasped when his fingers slid up and down her clothing, touching a row of bronze buttons.

"May I see you? Touch you?"

"Mathias," she said, sucking in a breath. "I'm shocked that you'd ask such a question, have you forgotten your vocation?"

He kissed her forehead. "Will you deny my discovery?"

"Yes," she nodded, sighing, closing her eyes.

"I'm sorry," he breathed, his fingers beneath her breasts, roaming. "What am I attempting? And you, a lady."

"Perhaps you wondered why God borrowed a man's rib, fashioned the bone into a woman, and where he placed it?"

"Of course," he mused, gazing at her. "A scientific discovery. Perhaps I kiss your lips then, instead, and rejoice in the pleasure."

"I'd like that." She grasped his head and pulled him close to her mouth. She gasped when his hand grasped her breast.

"Mathias…"

"Do you keep me from touch now, too?"

She stared into his heated expression for several seconds. She swallowed, seeing the desire. "No," she whispered, placing her hand on his. "I won't prevent anything that happens now."

They kissed for several moments; she was soon begging him to tackle her buttons. He rose above her, opening her vest slowly, one button at a time, until her garment lay open, only a bodice and chemise barred his view. He looked his full, but his uncertainty was apparent.

"We are equal, my darling. You can touch me as long as you promise to protect."

"With my life, Sophia."

She knew she held the power to prevent this affair from going any further, but she wanted his exploration, desired his love, so she unlaced the white blouse, then parted the folds of her chemise, baring her breasts to his view.

"So beautiful," he mumbled, rising onto his elbow. "Thou art fair and God has made you, perfectly."

"Just like other women whom he fashioned, too," Sophia giggled, placing his hand on her flesh, "I suppose."

She thought she might die from the tingling sensations that rose to consume her. Though timid and uncertain, she realized that she wanted more of this glorious heat. His fingers gingerly stroked her breasts, his roughened thumb pad stroking taut nipples.

"I think only of you," Mathias mused, perusing her beauty. "I behold only you. Soft, lovely, and beautiful."

He did something strange then. He rose to remove his silver cross, placing it at his side. The Roman collar at his neck was removed next, followed by his robe. Before Sophia realized his full intent, he sat beside her fully naked, unashamed of his glory.

"I want to worship you as a man, not as a priest. Do you understand?"

"The way God made you?" she asked, lying on her back, reveling at the sight of his masculinity. A well-formed chest, strong arms and a heart full of caring. Reaching for him, she pulled him to her embrace.

The weight of his inner thigh draped against her leg, the tip of his shaft pressed against her thigh. She wanted to touch the need pulsing against her, but could not bring herself to ask. An ache reacted deep inside her core from the contact and she grew warm. A flush reddened her face and consumed in the nether region of her abdomen, settling slick between her legs.

"Oh my," she cried out, grasping him around his neck as he took her nipple into his mouth, suckling gently. The other bud, he kneaded with his fingers. She moaned, attempting to rise, but his leg held her still.

She released the hold on his neck and drew her fingers along his pectoral muscles, down the length of his arms, feeling every ridge of his muscles. The fever inside intensified; the pull to touch the twitch of his manhood grew stronger. Though she didn't consciously think about it, her fingers traced his back, tentatively discovering bare buttocks, then slowly, oh how slowly, to the top of the bony ridge of his pelvis.

Should I touch him?

She made tiny circles in his pelvic hair. He pressed tighter to her in response, and she could feel a pulsing urgency, wet against her leg. The desire to touch that need urged her fingers to creep lower. But when she finally touched the length of his shaft, then brazenly grasping him, he jerked, pulling away so suddenly she released him.

Mathias pulled away from her breast, breathing hard, one hand shaking, his other hand wandering freely.

"It's all right," he whispered. "It's just that touching me... there," he took a breath. "You have no idea how it makes me feel."

"Was it painful?" she smiled teasingly.

He kissed her lips, grinning. "Torture," he laughed. "I aim to have it released."

"How?" Sophia asked in wonder, licking her lips, giggling.

"I'll show you, my Lady." He pulled the layers of her skirt up around her abdomen, revealing to his hungry gaze long and slender legs. She shivered in response to his scrutiny, barely feeling the caress of wind that wafted across her bare flesh. Then he ran his fingers along the flesh of her inner thigh, kissing her neck. When he embraced the bridge at the top, she placed her hand over his, preventing him from further exploration.

"Should I stop?" he asked, seeming like a petulant boy.

"We can't return from this exploration. I'll be a virgin, no more."

"You'll be mine," he said, coaxing her hand away, "forever—"

She gasped when he stroked the slick wetness between her legs. A convulsive shiver caused her to pull slightly away. Gently leading her back to his desire, Mathias stroked her folds until she quivered from the need of his massaging fingers. Moaning, she grasped his fingers and pressed them tighter to her. Surprised at the sensations that he awoke, shocked that she allowed him to touch her in this way.

He rose up slightly, his need apparent, then he shifted her knees apart and fitted himself between her thighs. He kissed her mouth once more before suckling her breast, still fingering her soft petal folds.

"Mathias..." she called his name as he stroked her femininity, then sliding inside, inducing a flare that sparked a sensation that garnered an intense wanton need.

"I need you," she begged, grasping his hips, raking her nails along his back. He responded by kissing her lips and kissing them firmly while still sliding his finger in and out.

"Oh, my," she cried out, arching her hips upward, knowing that a wonder was soon to overwhelm her, when she felt a different stirring. He removed his finger and positioned his shaft at her entrance.

"I have to have you," he whispered, staring into her eyes. "Please forgive me, I need to make you mine."

"Yes," she breathed, not quite sure what she was agreeing to, only knowing that she had to have him, too.

Gently, he pushed, entering her slightly. Some of the desire diminished as pain intruded. "It hurts, why does it hurt?"

"Your maidenhead blocks the way, but never mind my love, the pain will vanish once..."

"How do you know these things; have you done this before?"

"I have not... I'm a virgin, too."

"Christ's nails," she cried as he thrust, filling her completely. Her muscles clenched, folding around him, holding him tightly.

"Oh, my sweet Lord," he said, holding still. "The pleasure..."

"Is it pleasurable?" she asked, clutching him; the discomfort was surely written on her face.

He began to move, sliding in and out. She held him tightly to her, matching his rhythm instinctively, arching with each thrust. Soon, the pain lessened and a tingling sensation replaced the hurt; excitement grew, rising from the depths of her being.

Then suddenly, she moaned, nearly screaming as an orgasm overwhelmed her, catapulting her to an astounding height. She rejoiced in the bliss, her soul free of anguish, succumbing to a precipice to land in a pool of tranquility. Sweet heaven. She wanted to be quiet, but couldn't help the moan that burst from her lips.

Soon after, Mathias stopped thrusting, holding firm and buried to the hilt, groaning.

"What has happened?" she asked.

"Something astounding."

Mathias reached for her hand and held it tightly, searching her expression. "I love you. You know that, right?"

"I love you, too," she whispered, still feeling him there. "But?"

"I won't forsake you. You can trust in me."

"I hope so, Mathias. Because you have just thoroughly deflowered me."

He withdrew and rolled to his back, pulling her close to his chest, his mouth brushing her ear.

But he became so quiet after the second admission that Sophia began to fear they had made a terrible mistake. He broke from her arms and silently dressed.

She followed his example, putting on her chemise while lacing her bodice and buttoning her vest. Rising from the ground, she rearranged her skirt. He turned to face her, with that look of guilt, and shame wrinkling the lines of his forehead.

"Don't do this, Mathias," she said, quickening to anger. "Not now. What could I say? I'm sorry I showed you how much I love you? No, I'm not sorry about our love."

But standing beside him, she was deeply aware that she had pained him once more. It wasn't her fault that he had forsaken a sacred commitment and broken his vow of celibacy. She knew the dangers faced by loving him completely, physically. His quiet countenance suggested he was struggling with the same dilemma, but he had to come to terms with his actions.

"Does it show so clearly?"

"Yes."

"Loving you will be easy, making amends with my vocation won't."

"Would you rather we'd left your commitment intact? I can never go back. A virgin's folds can never be put back together."

"I made my bed."

"Perhaps you think you've been challenged by devilish schemes."

He grasped her shoulders. "I know which rod encountered you," he said with a grin, bringing her close. "I enjoyed our lovemaking and greedily yearn for more."

"But you're unhappy. Guilt is written on your face."

"I'll accept whatever fate God deems necessary."

"For this mistake?"

"My darling," he said, kissing her lips. "Love is never a mistake."

He had taken a gigantic leap forward in making love to her. Hopefully, her affectionate offering wouldn't lead Mathias further astray.

HE COULD HAVE LAIN among the leaves, naked in the sight of God until the sun chose to give way to darkness. The contentment, peace and tremendous joy realized from uniting his heart, mind, and body with Sophia, had been earth shattering.

He couldn't recall a moment in his life where any single event had affected him so boldly. Little could compare to the lovemaking that had culminated into the most compelling climax he had ever experienced.

Sitting upright, he crossed his arms at his knees; he wanted to turn and face Sophia. A woman newly ordained into sensuality. Mathias viewed the evidence of the desire he had provoked, written in a satisfied flush on her face.

But he couldn't turn around and look on the wonder of her loving. If he took such a chance, she would gaze into his eyes and sense his inner struggle, suspecting the negative connotations that their love-play had aroused. Sophia would question, as he questioned, if sharing their bodies in a physical manner had been wrong.

She touched the side of his robed chest, massaging the skin that lay beneath the folds of black fabric. He closed his eyes against the feelings that her fingers ignited. He wanted her again.

"Mathias?" she questioned. "Are you all right?"

He didn't turn around, instead stared silently, watching the meandering river.

"Fine," he muttered. "Just fine."

She grabbed his arm, forcing him to face her. "You're not fine. I can see the turmoil written on your face. By loving you physically, I have harmed you, have I not?"

He reached forward and stroked her sloped cheek, noticing how her forehead furrowed with concern. "I can see what you're thinking," Mathias said. "I'm not sorry and I feel no shame for sharing myself with the woman I love."

She grasped his hand intimately, sliding it to her lips, kissing his palm. "But you are sorry, are you not?" she prompted. "Perhaps shame is not an issue, but what about guilt? Mathias, you have this look about you. An expression that warns a mother that her son's hand has wandered where it shouldn't go, and yet the deed is done and you're helpless to restore what is lost."

He turned more fully to her, pulling her into his arms, kissing her forehead. "Nothing is lost, but I won't deny the truth. I do feel some guilt for betraying my vows. And yet, had I the opportunity to experience our affections again, I would do it."

He realized she should have smiled at his admission, but she was wise, much too wise. Leaning against a tree, he cradled her head on his chest while she mulled over his words.

"The act of loving another human being is not difficult," Sophia said with a sigh. "However, after the deed is achieved, fortunate souls find promise from their hearts beating together as one. Where does your heart lie?"

He was taken aback. He knew the nature of the query. Where did his responsibility lie—their future? The answer was wedged between the commitment of a parish church, *God*, and the woman he loved. He stood at the dividing point of two paths, unable to decide which road to travel, yearning to have both, knowing he had to make a choice. Sacrifices must be made and it pained him to think that the woman he loved might be made to suffer for his love-play.

A baby…

The thought made him uneasy, but also filled him with hope. If his near-death experience had really happened, Marcos had blessed this result. His father would approve, too. *Something for a mother to hold?*

"Where does my heart lie?" he whispered, massaging the nape of her neck. He prodded her with his fingers to raise her head. "Although I love you, I don't know if matrimony is possible for us. I'm so sorry, I cannot make a promise that I might not be able to keep. Our relationship might end up as stained as the one you considered with Franz."

It pained him to say it, when she presented such a brave front. He tried to wrap his arms tightly around her, holding her closer, but already there was a distance.

"It's all right," her voice cracked. "I knew the risk when I welcomed you. I will not force a decision that you cannot live with."

He brushed her hair away from her eyes; emerald eyes that glistened with unshed tears. "You say that as if you believe that I would forsake you. I understand what has taken place between us. I know that I must come to terms with the future, for both of our sakes."

"You must do more than consider the future. I need a commitment from you."

"I understand that, but I'm not free to give you one, at least not yet."

"When then?" Sophia asked. "When will you make a commitment? You have lain with me, Mathias."

"Have I made a mistake, entertaining our love too soon?"

She sniffed, wiping away an escaping tear. "What is love, Mathias? The Bible describes this emotion as patient and kind. Love is not jealous, or boastful, or rude, or arrogant. You cannot touch its source or insist on its way, and yet I believe that *feeling* is a definitive part of its meaning. A trifle brittle, it will break if not embraced by couples yearning to experience its mystery. So how can I know your love, if your decision is to deny these things?"

He reached for her hand and held it tightly. "You must have faith that all will be set right. I have not denied anything. Ancient words also state that love bears all things, believes all things, hopes and endures. Love will not break, no matter how brittle it might seem. But I do require some time to set things right."

"Are you suggesting that I love you from a distance?" she questioned, wiping away another tear.

"Yes," he whispered, sharing her anguish. "I must come to terms with leaving the priesthood. To be with you, there is no other option."

Her eyes bored into his soul. "And may I visit you during this period?"

He rested his head on hers, sighing. "I don't think that would be wise. I'd only take you into my arms again, take you into my bed."

He wiped the tear away. "What am I to do during this hiatus? I will miss you."

"Proceed with your life until such time that you can share it with me."

Taking a deep breath, she kissed his hand, squeezing it tightly. "The church is a strong force. I fear you'll reach for the priesthood and deny our love, deny me."

"I could never deny loving you. It's taken some time, but this truth won't be buried like some dirty secret any longer."

Sighing, Sophia rose from the ground, turned away and walked to her horse. Grasping the reins, she hesitated momentarily, but then placed her foot in the stirrup. "I will respect your decision, but understand. Though I'm trying really hard to have faith, to cling to a hope that our relationship might stand a chance; without our love, I'm nothing."

He wanted to shout across the prairie that her sentiments were wrong. She was everything that mattered to him. The sun that kissed his face, the perfume that scented his soul. Pure, innocent, and beautiful, how would he set this right?

"Sophia, you must not reveal the nature of our relationship to anyone."

She sniffed, perhaps shocked by his statement, and then rose upward onto her horse's back. "How could you ever question my loyalty? Are you so blind that you cannot see the sacred trust between us? Our secret is safe."

"I trust you, Sophia."

He knew that three little words wouldn't suffice, would never be enough to satisfy the hope she required and so he remained silent. Quiet, high atop her horse, she waited for him to offer some sort of reassurance. Finally, he watched her nudge her horse in the side. Watched her maneuver the mare and leave him. He could not remember a moment when he had felt so alone.

"I will come to you when the time is right," he murmured, but she was already gone, and out of earshot.

Even God, who had always been a comfort, didn't provide the peace he sought. The choice, which path to travel, was up to him. He required time to study the problem, to understand the obstacles faced in each direction. Time to believe that when the choice was made, it would be the right one.

How would he see this through, when every moment away from Sophia foretold that there was really only one answer; he had to leave the church, but without the financial benefits of his vocation, how would he support his wife?

CHAPTER 18

Sophia frowned as she rode toward Baldemar Manor. Her life had changed forever since lying with Mathias. Curiously enlightened by the experience, every instinct warned that their intimacy had been a dreadful mistake.

No longer a virginal maid, now, she was a fallen woman. Was it terrible? His touch lingered inside her nether region and the sensations were pleasant. If truth be known, she desired to have him touch her again.

She dismounted Maraclese, leading the mare across the short distance to the stable where Hans mucked about the stalls. "Ah, my Lady Sophia," he said with a wince. "Finally, you've returned."

He leaned a pitchfork against the wall, withdrew a straw hat from his head, and wiped the perspiration from his brow.

"Yes," she replied, considering his apprehension. "Have you been waiting for me then?"

"Ah Mistress," he breathed, replacing the hat. "The whole household's been waiting on your return. A war is about to erupt."

Sophia scratched her head, unaware of the misplaced strands. When she'd left, the house had been peaceful. Everyone had been sleeping, with the exception of the scullery maids who had awoken early to do their baking in the kitchen. But if there was a problem, she knew who'd be at the root.

"What has Alisz done now?"

Han's face lit up, his expression lifting into a humorous smile. "It's not so much your stepsister, as it is the lady visitor who has come to call. She's a whirlwind, a high-spirited filly who's quickly become a thorn in your step-mother's side."

"A whirlwind, you say? Hans, have we extra horses boarding with us then?"

"We have! Two very fine mares, one groomsman, and a well-endowed lady-in-waiting."

"And have you spoken to this groomsman?"

Sophia tapped her finger on her cheek in contemplation as she watched his changing expression.

"I have," he chuckled, revealing a mouthful of crooked teeth.

"Come on then, what have you learned?"

"Only that this older woman, who doesn't look a day past thirty, is your long lost aunt. I understand that she wishes to speak to you. She won't accept Lady Wendeline's hospitality, which as you can imagine has the baroness quite upset."

"My aunt has arrived?" Sophia bristled, grinning. "Thank you for that piece of news," she said, passing him the reins to her horse. "I knew I could count on you to be my eyes and ears. It would never do to go into the house unprepared. If you'll rub down Maraclese for me, I would appreciate it. I've not seen my aunt in years."

She pivoted to leave. "Hold up there, Lady Sophia. You have some fixing to do before you go to the house."

"What do you mean?" she asked innocently, turning back.

"I'm not of a mind to judge your actions," he remarked, picking grass from her hair. "But if you've been cavorting with some lucky lad—"

Her mouth fell open, her cheeks reddened with shame.

"Come on now, don't get your knickers in a knot. I'm sure you've been lying in the grass studying the clouds. But conclusions can be drawn, and the higher folk would torch a fine filly for lesser cause."

"You'll keep my secret?"

He took his hat off again, smiling. "I don't have the heart to hurt you, Mistress. You've been good to me."

She hugged him gratefully. "I don't know what to say; such loyalty is unheard of," she whispered, straightening her hair. "I'll never forget that you've given me yours."

"You're welcome," he replied, leading Maraclese to her stall. "I've a mind to get back to my chores. But you owe me."

"I suppose you'll want me to put in a good word with Rosa," Sophia hinted, joining in his humor and retreating to the stable doors.

"Ah, my Lady, you are kind."

She stopped at the large double doors, leaned across the frame and peered across the courtyard. Perhaps she was overly anxious and overcome by a suspicious third sense that warned of caution.

Where are you, Alisz?

She gazed upward at the windows. She had little desire to be confronted with an interrogation before she could properly comport herself. Her blouse and gray skirt were fairly straightened, but she wouldn't rest until the heavy layers of her hair were rearranged into a tidy bun.

She walked through the doorway that led to the servants' quarters. Just before the kitchen was a staircase that led to the upper house. Sophia took it and made her way to her room with not so much as a glimpse of her stepsister. She was anxious to see her aunt. Could hardly wait to change into appropriate daywear so she could make her acquaintance.

SOPHIA PASSED through the doorway into her bedchamber, and then shut the door softly behind her. She saw that her chambermaid had been waiting.

"Oh, my gracious, my Lady," Adeline said anxiously, rising from the bench. "Finally, you've returned. But just look at you... You're a terrible mess! Well, that won't do, not when you have a visitor who has come from afar to call."

Sophia smiled, not caring about the state of her undress. She knew full well that she could trust her personal maid. "I know. My aunt has arrived. Isn't it wonderful?"

"She's anxious to see you. Instructed me to escort you to her bedchamber as soon as you arrived home. But she cannot see you like this. Good gracious, what have you been up to?"

"Never you mind," Sophia giggled.

Adeline turned scarlet, blushing clear down to her roots. Was the truth of her morning escapade that obvious? Her chambermaid walked purposefully to her, stepped in front of her and began undoing the brass buttons of her vest with quick and nimble fingers.

"If I didn't know you better, my Lady..." Her complexion paled, her voice softened to a whisper. "I would be of a mind to wonder if you'd been frolicking with some lad."

Her steel gaze and pinched mouth pierced through Sophia's thin exterior, guessing the truth. Sophia felt guilty under her accusatory glare.

"So it is true. How could you have been so careless? Should anyone learn the truth, you would be ruined. As if this family doesn't have enough to hurt you with already."

Sophia assumed an air of indifference, of strength and courage. "I bit of kissing, Adeline. Nothing to be ashamed of, but the family will never find out. I'll never confide the truth to anyone. Furthermore, I feel no guilt for being in the company of the man I love."

Adeline whipped the bodice from her back, leaving her bare except for her chemise. Already her fingers were tugging at her skirt, loosening the fabric until it fell in a barren heap at her feet. She was angry. Sophia had never seen her so agitated.

"They will find out. Your stepsister will use this information to ruin you. I cannot bear to see that happen. If I have anything to say about the matter, it won't."

"Thank you," Sophia replied, hoping to lighten the mood. "I knew I could trust you."

"No time for trust or thanks. We have to get a man's scent washed off your flesh. I will see that a tub is brought up straightaway. We'll say you took a spill from Maraclese and need some time to properly present yourself."

"That excuse will never work, everyone knows of my prowess as a horsewoman."

"Bah," Adeline disagreed. "Everyone takes a spill from time to time, even the best of the best. Today was your day for such an accident."

"But I'll have no bruises to show for the story."

Whack! Adeline struck her on the thigh with her brush. "There you be."

"That hurt!"

"The truth will hurt more if you're found out. Now, I'll see to your bath."

Adeline left Sophia standing before her armoire in nothing more than her chemise and pantalets, wondering which frock should be chosen for her reunion with her aunt.

The door opened and slammed against the wall with such force, she flinched in panic. China knick-knacks rattled as Alisz made her entrance. The rage was startling, frightening even, seeing her sister's face mottled with a murderous rage.

"What have you done?" She screamed, hands on her hips. "Why is that woman here in this house?"

"I don't know what you mean. Do we have a guest? Who has graced us with a visit?"

She raised her hand, her fingers squeezing into a fist. "Don't lie to me," Alisz shrieked, her voice shrill. "You know the subject of which we speak."

"I assure you," Sophia sneered in contempt, her voice even, "I do not! I have only arrived home from a morning ride in which I took a terrible tumble. Adeline is seeing to a bath to soothe my aches and pains."

Perhaps it was a mistake to alert Alisz to her personal state. Her sister eyed her up and down, sniffing the air in disgust. Then stalked closer, sneering, forcing Sophia to step nearer to the wall.

"I don't see any cuts or bruises. Surprising, for an excellent horsewoman who professes to have had a fall."

Sophia lowered her gaze, pretending to study her manicured fingernails. "I don't bruise easily. Fortunate, don't you think?"

"You lying, cavorting trollop. You cannot hide the scent of a man," Alisz said, ranting. "Your skin reeks of him, leaving no question as to your act of playing the hoyden. Did you lie with your priest, or Franz?"

"What if it was Franz; he was mine first! What I do is none of your business. Mind to your own affairs, you have more to lose."

"I'll kill you if it's true."

Alisz's face turned a murderous red, Sophia became fearful for her safety. "Why do you hate me?" Sophia grumbled, speaking sternly. "Why have you forced me into a position where winning the next punch is all that matters? We could have been friends, should have been sisters."

"I cannot tell you how much I hate you, loathe and despise you. You've always been handed anything that your heart desired, material, maternal, and otherwise. My life has existed in the shadows. A dark silhouette forced to walk in the wake of your brightness. You will never be my sister."

Reaching slowly, extending her arm, Sophia attempted to take her hand in her grip. Alisz pulled violently away, as if the contact of their fingers burned her flesh.

"Why do I bother to try? You don't want my compassion; your heart is frozen to anything but hate. Tiresome enemies, is that all we'll ever be to each other?"

"Yes," she sniveled, her face bright red. "And it's your fault."

"You know, sister dear, I don't in any way discount your feelings, but this sense of foul play to my person is unjust. I have done nothing to provoke these outrageous claims."

"Don't patronize me. You were the benefactor of everything I've always wanted, but was denied, and I beg to disagree."

Sophia had had enough of her disrespect. How dare she act the suffering victim? Because of misdeeds and greed, Alisz was primarily at fault for her current woes.

"Stop it, just stop it," she railed. "You're a spoiled brat! From the time you were born, nothing has been equal to your desires. You always wanted better than could be given. It didn't matter what material bobbles Father gifted in order to please you. He always failed in your estimation, because you were never satisfied. You wanted something that he could not give."

She turned her head slightly away, shaking, balling her hands into fists. When Sophia gazed into Alisz's ice-blue eyes again, tears flowed across the contours of her flesh. She was stunned. Never before had she witnessed her stepsister crying, perhaps this release of emotion was good.

"I wanted something all right." She stepped ominously closer, banging into her. Sophia attempted to step away, but Alisz grasped her chemise, holding her close. "I wanted what all daughters yearn for, their father's love, but failing that, a sister to love me."

Alisz emitted a horrifying scream, the sound residing from somewhere deep within her soul. Her eyes fissured with tears and her mouth shaped into a miniature portrait of abject misery.

When at last she released her grasp, Sophia thought herself safe, but then her fists swung cruelly, pounding on her chest.

"Stop it," Sophia cried out, raising her hands in defense and attempting to block the thrusts. "You're hurting me."

But Alisz was out of control and too angry to halt the onslaught. Two fists connected with the soft tissues of Sophia's arms, and drove into her abdomen with startling quickness, continually slapping at her face.

She had not heard Adeline enter the room. Suddenly she was just there.

"Have you gone mad?" the chambermaid yelled, grabbing Alisz's arm. "How dare you attack your sister! She's done you no wrong."

Adeline grasped Alisz's arm and ushered her to the door.

Sophia attempted to breathe while rubbing the life back into her arms. Bruises would mar her skin, deep purple ugly bruises. She watched Alisz carefully, prepared should she strike again. However, it seemed as if the confrontation was over.

"Sweet Jesu, I hate you, both of you, all of you... But I give you a gift, Sophia. Now no one will question that you fell from your horse."

"She's left me in state of exhaustion," Sophia complained after Alisz left. She walked to the settee and collapsed on its tapestry, scrutinizing her arms and legs, meeting Adeline's worried expression.

"Seems I returned in time. How bad has she hurt you?"

"I'll survive. I will be believed now, apparently thanks to my own hateful sister."

"Half-sister," Adeline stammered coming close, reaching out to inspect the damaged skin.

"I was missing the bruises. One never falls from a horse without carrying a few marks."

"You poor dear," Adeline said with a grimace, "to be fated with a sister who would turn on you like that. I'm glad I came when I did. Your injuries could have been worse."

"Indeed," Sophia sighed as her tub arrived, soon filled to the brim with steaming hot water. "She could have killed me. I know she wanted to."

They waited until the servant placed the porcelain tub in the center of the room. Only then did Sophia rise from the settee. Slowly, she moved toward the tub, feeling like an invalid with each painful step. When there, her fingers inched along the ivory edge. She needed this bath.

"Do you need my help to enter, my Lady?"

"No. I'll be fine."

"I'll take my leave then, returning once your bath is over to help you dress. No one will know what happened here."

"That's all right, Adeline," Sophia replied, removing her chemise and losing her pantalets to the floor. Then painfully slowly, she stepped into the tub and eased her aching limbs beneath the water.

"I really don't care who knows, the truth will only hurt Alisz."

"Yes, well, if you are sure you don't need me, I will leave you to your bath."

"Adeline," she called, "one more thing."

"What is it?"

"Please lock the door behind you."

CHAPTER 19

G owned in a dress of emerald satin, Sophia scrutinized her reflection in the mirror, fingering her hurt cheek. Adeline had done her best to hide the bruising by applying different applications of cold compresses, but herbs and powders had made little difference to the discoloring. After her efforts, a faded purplish-blue mark still underscored her right eye.

"Oh dear," Sophia sighed, stepping away from the mirror. The slight mark was not that difficult to look at, and maybe her aunt wouldn't notice.

Walking across the bedchamber to the door, she smiled in anticipation of her visit. Her luck was improving with her aunt's arrival. Perhaps in a few more minutes, the questions of her heritage could finally be answered.

Grasping the doorknob, she opened the door and stepped into the corridor, searching the dimly lit space for any sign of her sister. She'd had enough skirmishes for one day and wasn't anxious for repeat performances. Seeing that the hallway was clear, she walked to the guest quarters. Once there, she rapped gently on the door.

"Come in, please," a feminine voice responded.

Sophia patted her hair one final time, rearranged her skirts, then with her head held at a proud angle, she swung the door open and stepped into the quaint white-washed room. Her aunt was resting on the settee. A hardier portrait then her once petite mother, she lounged comfortably, sipping wine.

She was fitted in a gown of bluish-gray silk; wide folds of fabric hugged an ample bosom, then tapered to accentuate a full waist. Silver hair swept upward into a tidy bun, softened by liquid blue eyes that shimmered with the onset of tears. Though age had lightened her hair and softened her facial features, Sophia remembered the aunt she had once adored.

"Sophia," she called out, placing her goblet on the side table. "Oh, my dear, is that you?"

Sophia nodded as their eyes met, dismissing her ladylike principles and running to her aunt's side as she once had as a child, lowering herself to her knees at her feet, hugging her close. Breathing in the scent of jasmine, she nestled close to her aunt's neck, closing her eyes and recalling the familiar scent. She could have cried, holding someone that loved and cared for her unconditionally, this affection second only to her own mother's love. She pushed away to look into her eyes to ensure this meeting was real and not a dream. Her aunt's expression softened into a smile, her wrinkled fingers rested on her head.

"Of course it is you," she whispered softly. "I can see your mother's face, my dearly departed sister's image in your emerald eyes. Such a beautiful color for a mother to pass on to her child."

"Yes," Sophia agreed, rising from her knees to join her aunt on the settee. She clasped her aunt's hands within her own. "My mother's legacy has passed on far more than I ever could have expected," Sophia said with a grimace, lowering her head. Though she wanted to believe in her mother's virtue, probable lies plagued her thoughts. What if her aunt only confirmed that her illegitimacy was true? She was almost afraid to ask.

As if in answer to her worry, her aunt pulled a packet from her pocket. "My letter," Sophia exclaimed, "you received it?"

Her aunt tapped the packet on her leg, her expression stern. "It was fortunate indeed. I was preparing to depart when it arrived. I had every intention of coming to see you, regardless of the letter."

"You have read it of course."

"Yes," she ground out, her teeth almost grating. "Several times."

"Then you know what question I need answered. Do you know the name of my true father?"

"My dear," her aunt breathed, sparks igniting her eyes. "I should be ashamed of you for asking such a question. After living in a house turned wicked with lies, and memories of your parents distorted, I suppose I shouldn't be surprised. I should have come to you long before now."

She paused in her speech, her bosom heaving, Sophia waited for her to continue. "Who do you think your father is?"

Sophia lowered her head, clenching her hands, feeling the weight of shame on her back. The effect was noticeable and brought tears to her aunt's eyes.

"I want to believe that Father is my father. But the executor, and Lady Wendeline and Alisz, have been firm in their conviction, insisting he is not."

Aunt Lovisa pulled her hand from her grasp, gently gripping Sophia's chin and propelling it upward in a display of proud determination. "Lady Wendeline and Alisz will be damned to Hell for the lies they have made you believe. Lies that would have destroyed your life had I not come to your assistance."

She grasped her aunt's hands tightly, witnessing a shimmer of hope. "Then Father is my father, and my mother was not an adulterous woman?"

"Sweetheart," Aunt Lovisa cooed softly, as if talking to a child. "Your mother and father were inseparable. They were so deeply in love that they couldn't keep their hands away from each other. That is why their first child, *a love child*, arrived seven months after they were wed. There would have been many more children had your mother not perished during her second childbirth."

Tears filled Sophia's eyes at the startling news. "Then I'm not," she sniffed, "a bastard child?"

"You most certainly are not. I will put this situation to rights with Sterling, your father's legal attorney. But before the day is finished your stepfamily will pay for blackening your name. I promise you that. There is only one bastard child living in this house and it is not you."

Sophia gaped at the statement. "Whatever could you mean by that?"

Aunt Lovisa covered her mouth quickly, as if she had never meant to divulge the information. "I'm sorry," she mouthed, shaking her head. "I promised your father long ago that his secret would be safe and two sisters would never learn the truth. He wanted Alisz and yourself to be true sisters, since you would never have other siblings."

"You are saying that Alisz is not the daughter of my father, but how can that be? Why, I thought he married Lady Wendeline to give his child a proper name?"

"Your father married the money-grubber because she tricked him into believing that the child she carried was his own. An honorable man, he attempted to do right by the woman," Aunt Lovisa ruminated, the recollection obviously evoking some distress. "But when Alisz was born, two months too soon, he realized he couldn't have fathered the child. He could have left the schemer, and he certainly had grounds for an annulment. But he wished to protect the innocent child, so he stayed with the mother, eventually accepting the baby as his own."

"The saints preserve us," Sophia sighed, running her fingers over her hair. "This explains details that I never understood before. Alisz and I have never been close. She's always hated me, resenting my position. Aunt Lovisa, does she know?"

"I cannot say. It was your father's wish that his secret be kept, as much for her sake as for his own. I assume Lady Wendeline wouldn't confide the information in order to protect her daughter. Only the three of us knew the truth, how would she find out?"

"But she must know," Sophia exclaimed. "It can be the only explanation for the crimes she's committed."

Aunt Lovisa's expression became thoughtful. She touched her face, stroking the bluish bruise. "Has she hurt you? Struck you, leaving this mark in her need for revenge?"

"Yes," Sophia exclaimed, glancing away. "After your arrival, Alisz fell into a terrible rage. She expressed her unhappiness."

"I imagine she feels like an animal caught in a trap, with her secrets about to be exposed."

"When the time comes, it will not be pretty. I'm worried about the outcome."

"Sophia," her aunt urged, gripping her hand. "The truth must be told. Regardless of the sparks that fly, I will see your name vindicated. I'm not afraid of your stepsister. Before I realized the details of this sordid affair, I was prepared to travel to see a niece properly wed. I'll not rest until I've achieved that end. I wish to keep your father's confidence, but if Alisz's paternity must enter into the equation to rectify a wrong, then so be it."

"I can't believe I would even say this, considering the harm Alisz has done to me, but if it can be helped, I don't want my sister's name sullied."

"Why do you care after such an awful plot?"

"Because I know what it feels like to lose favor with society."

"But the truth must be told, so the situation can be reversed. I will see you properly wed."

Sophia rose from the settee and backed away from her aunt, putting her hand to her mouth. She wanted the truth of her paternity to be revealed, but she had never considered the negative implications should the truth be discovered. Would her aunt seek to have her wed to Franz?

"Sophia?" she asked, standing as well. "Is something wrong? Have I said something to cause discomfort?"

Sophia sighed, running both hands through her hair, allowing some of the curly strands to escape the bun, the hair falling, twining into ringlets about her neck. Though she could not confide the true reason for not wanting to marry Franz, there was a truth of sorts to be considered.

"Yes and no," she ventured. "Aunt Lovisa, you must understand that marrying Franz was once a realization of a dream come true. But when he chose another, regardless of the circumstances, he hurt me terribly. I'm not sure I want to marry him anymore."

Her aunt approached her where she stood. "Give the man his due. This sordid mess cannot have been easy on him either. Franz Altbusser was pledged to marry you. Committed in every way that mattered. Imagine how he must have felt when his plans were thrown in the air."

Sophia faced her aunt, biting her lip. She could not deny that the circumstances must have proven difficult for Franz, but he could have supported her and offered his protection when no one else would. Only Mathias, the man she loved, had protected her, saved her, stood by her regardless of her position, regardless of her name.

"Do not feel pity for Franz Altbusser. He's not worthy of your concern."

"That may be, but the fact remains that the marriage would be a good pairing. If your father were alive, he would agree that I must pursue this union. At any rate, once the truth is out, the Altbussers' will understand that you didn't break the betrothal contract, and that you're an innocent and pure bride. The agreement will stand like before and you will marry the man."

Sophia laughed mindlessly. Yes, she had been innocent and pure, but she had given a gift of purity to the man she loved. She wouldn't be forced to go through with a farce of a marriage. The thought of walking down the aisle to anyone but Mathias made her angry.

"Aunt Lovisa, you are not listening. After everything that has happened, I have no intention of marrying Franz."

Her aunt grasped her hands, gripping them firmly. "In time you'll understand that this is best for your future. Not all marriages begin as love matches, quite the opposite in fact. In time, you'll realize the fondness you once felt for Franz. I'll not let you forgo the opportunity of marrying this young man. You will be at the height of society as his wife."

Sophia walked to the door and grasped the doorknob, ready to throw the door open and run. Her aunt seemed confused and shocked by her actions, but she couldn't know that another man was at stake. Or that Franz had nearly raped her.

"I care little for society. Please don't force me to do this. For reasons that I cannot reveal, I won't marry Franz. Not now, or ever."

Her aunt marched to the doorway, preventing her from leaving, gripping her shoulder with the palm of her hand. "I'm sorry that we've come to this crossroad. I was hoping that our reunion wouldn't be marred by further unhappiness. You must understand that your father bade me to ensure your future welfare. Therefore, I must direct the path of your life with your best interests in mind. Someday, you will thank me for the steps I take."

Sophia ground her right fist into the door, not caring if her hand filled with splinters and mindless of the skin that suddenly pained. How could her aunt deceive her this way? It seemed her life was entering a black hole.

"Please," she cried out, "show me your mercy. Don't make me go through with this."

"It's too late. The plan is already in motion."

She ripped her fingers from her shoulder, turning to face her aunt. "Whatever do you mean? What have you done?"

For the first time it was her aunt who lowered her gaze as the first hint of uncertainty crossed her features. But her doubt passed quickly. Sighing, she rose to meet her expression once more, holding a determined stance.

"A messenger was dispatched to the Altbussers' estate on my arrival, seeking their attendance at dinner. I mentioned that it was urgent that they grant the request, as information had come to light that affected the futures of our children. I'm certain they will respond."

"How could you?" Sophia advanced, shaking her head. "The sister of my mother, the aunt once loved with heartfelt devotion; is the relative to put a nail in my coffin. I will never forgive you for this interference."

"Don't be dramatic," her aunt warned, sniffing with disdain. "I won't abide with disobedience when I attempt to better your future. Perhaps it's best to refrain from further conversation. Take yourself to your room and prepare for tonight's meal."

"Huh," Sophia huffed with anger, sulking, displaying one final act of defiance. "I will not promise to attend a meal where my fate, doomed by the actions you seek, will be decreed."

"You will be present," Aunt Lovisa responded in kind, showing no mercy, portraying a voice edged with annoyance. "Do not thwart me on this issue, Sophia."

She couldn't remember a moment when her aunt had treated her so cruelly. The cutting words provoked her to tears. Sophia nodded meekly, assenting that she would do as bidden. Then walked from the room with tears cascading down her cheeks, not responding verbally to her aunt's conviction. When she arrived at her room, she closed the door, locking it, then walked to the sanctuary of her bed to lie down, placing her head on her pillow.

The tears fell, leaking to the cotton coverlets. In her despair, she tried to understand why her aunt felt so strongly about this union. If only she could confide the truth, but that was impossible. The relationship with Mathias must be kept a secret.

But there must be a way out of this farce of a marriage that was about to be foisted on her. Surely a plausible solution would come to mind. For appearances only, she would play along with the notion of matrimony. But regardless of her aunt's best intentions, she would never meet Franz at the altar.

Mathias needed to make a decision, and soon.

CHAPTER 20

*U*nobserved, Sophia stood outside of the dining room, contemplating the seated guests. The dinner table had been set with fine china, matching silverware and crystal goblets, and all pieces had been meticulously arranged on a white embroidered tablecloth. Sophia acknowledged that her aunt put on a pretty show. Hosting a gathering with such care hadn't happened in a long time, and she imagined that the food would be served with a similar panache. So sad, that her father couldn't experience it.

Pondering the assembled guests, Sophia stretched further into the room, wearing the emerald gown she'd chosen earlier. It wasn't appropriate for the dinner hour, but after her aunt's declaration, she didn't much care. With her future about to change, *again*, wrinkled silk and a messy bun wasn't a priority, but comportment mattered to Verena Altbusser and she wouldn't like her appearance.

Engaged in amiable conversation, the duchess sat to the right of Aunt Lovisa. Her husband, Duke Albrecht, sitting across from his wife, might regard her with a similar distaste, wondering why a young woman who had been taught feminine decorum from birth had denounced ladylike principles of grace. She had to admit that she didn't much care what anyone thought, least of all, these people.

Franz, sitting beside his father, was too deep in his cups to mind her appearance. Clearly angry, Alisz joined him in his revelry for the drink. Occasionally, they spoke a few words to each other.

Lady Wendeline sat at the end of the table clutching a crystal goblet, tapping it with her finger, and appearing out of place and equally upset. Sophia snickered, enjoying her awkwardness, realizing that Aunt Lovisa had obviously usurped her control.

She placed her hand over her mouth, realizing the foolishness of her laughter too late. The tittering must have carried to the guests, as conversation quieted and each person's movements ceased, directing their attention her way.

"Good evening," she said with a grimace, striding to them. She stood before her chair with both hands clutching the backrest. "Aunt Lovisa, Duke and Duchess Altbusser. Franz, Alisz."

Standing beside her aunt, she directed her gaze firmly at her stepmother, knowing that by addressing her last, she slighted her. "Lady Wendeline."

Oblivious to the telltale sniff of disgust from her stepmother, Sophia pulled out her chair and sat down, sliding it closer to the table. She placed her napkin on her lap, and then reached for her goblet, taking a sip of fruity wine and then extending the crystal into the air.

"Cheers everyone," she greeted gaily, looking to her slimly amused aunt. "Cheers."

"Ahem." Aunt Lovisa cleared her throat, directing everyone's attention. "Thank you for joining us, Sophia dear. Our guests have been kept waiting too long. Our dinner has been on hold for a considerable length of time."

Sophia looked at her aunt and then glared at Lady Wendeline, taking another sip of wine. "Please," she beseeched extending her hand. "Permit me to apologize for my tardiness, I must have fallen asleep. But now that I'm here, let the festivities begin."

Her aunt shook her head, and then waved to the footmen standing by the door. "Gentlemen, dinner may now be served."

The doors opened and a procession of servants walked into the dining room, each carrying an extravagant dish. Stuffed game hen was placed on each of their plates, followed by rutabagas and grated cooked cabbage. Sophia was reaching for a bun when Duchess Verena Altbusser cleared her voice, intent on speaking.

"Lady Lovisa, now that everyone is seated, please share why this meeting of the minds is so urgent?" The duchess sat as regally as an opinionated queen, wearing a gown of red silk damask with glistening rubies draped around her neck. Her fork yet to be lifted.

Sophia sliced an ample portion of game hen, and then placed it in her mouth, enjoying the flavor. She was anxious for her aunt's reply, yet could not help intruding on the question.

"Delicious," she replied, staring at the duchess, taking another sip of wine. "And you have yet to reach for your silverware."

"Young woman," the duchess scolded, "have you no manners?"

Sophia laughed awkwardly, noticing how Alisz's eyebrows drew upward with interest. Her aunt on the other hand, used her napkin to dab at her strained face. "I'm merely dabbling in dinner conversation. No slight was intended, Verena. Oh my," she corrected. "Duchess."

Duke Albrecht threw his napkin to the table and rose angrily, red in the face. "Young woman, you will apologize to my wife immediately, or we are leaving."

"You will do as you're told," Aunt Lovisa insisted, also rising. "This attempt at abominable behavior will not alter my course."

Not wishing to reveal any outward signs of intimidation, Sophia cut another slice of game hen and quickly put it in her mouth. Closing her eyes, she savored the taste of the meat, as if nothing could come between her and the flavor. The dining room grew quiet, the guests waited for her response.

She opened her eyes, delighted to see Alisz deftly stabbing the table with her fork. "Very well," she said to no one in particular. "I hardly care if you stay or leave, but I do confess, I am dreadfully sorry if my tardiness or my comments have offended. Now, Aunt Lovisa, please inform the Altbussers' the reason for this assemblage."

Sophia had their attention, but Duke Albrecht had yet to return to his seat. Aunt Lovisa sat down, sighing deeply. She didn't reply until she had taken an ample swig of her wine.

Alisz jumped up, her fork clattered noisily to the floor. "I will not be entertained with lies."

Franz stared pointedly at her from across the table. Swirling his wine, he licked his lips. The scandalous guise made Sophia uncomfortable and suggested in a blatant manner what the churlish man desired. She trembled under his scrutiny.

"Sit down, Lady Alisz, you too, Father," Franz managed. "It's not unusual for Sophia to model childish behavior, but surely there's a reason for her display. Come on, Sophia, enough teasing, out with it."

"Very well," she countered, holding her head proudly and never taking her eyes from Franz. She rose from her spot, dropped her napkin on the chair and went to stand beside her aunt, placing her palm on her shoulder. "It seems that we have been made to suffer a slight due to the unkind hands and questionable nature of Lady Wendeline and Alisz. They have incorrectly portrayed that my birthing was illegitimate, that my father was not my father, and my mother a trollop. I don't know how they managed the scandal, but it's a lie!"

"The nature of your bastard heritage is true!" Alisz condemned. Lady Wendeline fanned herself, nodding in agreement with her daughter.

"This has gone far enough," Aunt Lovisa quipped. "I apologize, Duchess, Duke Albrecht, but your family has been led on a merry chase. My niece's heritage is certain. She is the offspring of Dedrick and Lurleen Baldemar. I swear this on my life."

She took a tentative sip of wine before continuing. "A betrothal contract was struck between the Altbusser and Baldemar family years ago for the hand of Sophia. As she is not illegitimate, and has not broken the contract in any manner, I insist that the agreement for Sophia's hand in marriage be honored."

The duke and duchess seemed to give Aunt Lovisa's words serious consideration. Franz smiled like a cat that had its victim in reach and tipped his cup at Sophia as if he was about to taste her. She shuddered as her stepmother howled.

"How dare you utter such preposterous lies! The girl is a trollop. Anyone can see that by her outrageous display. But if your claim is true, where's the proof? Surely you have something more substantial than a few choice words."

"My sister was a chaste virgin when she greeted Dedrick Baldemar in his bed," Aunt Lovisa replied angrily. "I assure you, she never engaged another lover during their course of marriage. I know this, for during their first year of wedded bliss, I resided in their house, privy to every loving word my sister shared with her husband. She was faithful to the man and do not attempt to tell me otherwise."

Duke Albrecht cleared his voice, finally eating his game hen, as if this distraction would relieve him from the current crisis. "If what you say is true, there is much to consider."

Sophia shook her head at the portly man. "All that needs to be said," Sophia stated unequivocally, "is that I'm not a bastard. Alisz is free to marry your son, as is her wish. I no longer want a man, or a family, that will not stand beside their future daughter-in-law when lies are communicated. I'm not interested in marrying your son."

Troubled, Duchess Verena twisted her jewels about her neck. Sophia imagined it must be difficult for a societal snob to be brought down a peg. She could tell that the only consideration occurring to this woman regarding this nasty business was how her family would fare once the news reached her society peers.

"Albrecht," she pleaded. "Whatever are we going to do about this mess? We'll look like laughing stocks if we honor the contract."

Now that the truth was out, the duke looked more concerned with the fare that tempted his pallet. "Dedrick Baldemar was a good man, a friend of mine." He chewed deliberately, thinking. "It seems we have no choice but to honor a contract that was made in good faith between two families."

"But you heard what the girl said, she'd be satisfied with her sister marrying our son. Think of the scandal, Albrecht. Could we leave the situation as it is?"

He seemed to consider this carefully. "Perhaps," he responded.

"Absolutely not!" Aunt Lovisa declared. "I will not entertain this slight on my niece's reputation. Whether she agrees to this union is immaterial. I will see the betrothal contract honored, Sophia will marry your son."

"This cannot be happening," Alisz cried out suddenly. "I have been wronged."

"Hardly," Sophia insisted. "But don't worry, sister, I won't go through with it."

"I will fight this union." Lady Wendeline protested. "I won't permit my daughter to be cast aside."

Franz waved his hands, pleading for calm. "Has the groom no say in the choosing of his own bride?"

"Speak up," his father urged, swallowing his food with a mouthful of wine. "Perhaps my son is the best person to solve the dilemma. Were it your decision, my son, which bride would you escort to the altar?"

Sophia glared at him, hoping to state with her expression that his choice was not to be her. But the man was daring indeed. He rose from his chair smiling, his intentions clear. Approaching her where she sat, he bowed in a grand flourish with his hand extended outward.

"My Lady Sophia," he beckoned, reaching for her hand, gripping it tightly. "It is my desire to escort you, the bride that resides within my heart, to the altar. Once we are in the sight of God, I will pledge my troth and become your husband. If it takes the rest of my life, I will re-earn your trust for the grief I have caused."

"No!" Sophia and Alisz said at the same time.

"Sorry, Alisz," Franz responded, glancing at her. "There's only one woman for me and it can't be you."

"How dare you turn on me," Alisz glowered, unshed tears marring her expression. "We slept with each other, you took me to your bed."

"And you were astounding, my dear, but a man must negotiate far more than pleasure when choosing a wife."

"It really is sad you cannot have both of these vixens," Duke Albrecht stated, sipping his wine. "Perhaps one of the sisters would consider a position as your mistress?"

"Really Albrecht? Did we require more inappropriate conversation?" the duchess screeched.

Alisz jumped up from the table and stormed to Franz. "Look out," Sophia attempted to warn him, but she was too late. Franz turned his head in time to greet Alisz's fist, smacking him right below his left eye. Then she ran from the room with her mother in hot pursuit. She never muttered another word. Sophia snickered into her hand, her sister having finally done something to please.

"Serves you right," Sophia emphasized, while the duchess saw to her son's eye. "I could have warned you to stay out of Alisz's bed. My little sister packs a strong punch."

Angry, Franz brushed off his mother's hands, and then came to stand at her feet, sneering. "Sophia, we will next meet at the altar. Henceforth, you will be the woman adorning my bed. Let me tell you something, sweetheart, I can hardly wait to have you there."

"I will never share your bed, Franz Altbusser."

He grasped the bottle of wine and refilled his goblet, then downed the red liquid in three swigs. He refilled the glass and proceeded to the entranceway of the dining room, taking the glass with him.

"Don't worry," Aunt Lovisa exclaimed, running from the table, angrily glancing back. "Sophia will be made to see reason. She'll be your bride if I have to steer her to the altar myself."

"I never doubted that for a minute," he countered, and then left the room.

Sophia stood, leaving the table to see to her aunt, her hands knotted at her sides. "You are selling me to the devil. You have no idea what situation you're placing me in. If you had a care for my welfare, you wouldn't pursue this match."

"I'm doing what I think is best."

"I wish you had never come. You have taken my life from a terrible mess and made it so much worse."

Aunt Lovisa appeared stricken, angry or hurt, Sophia couldn't quite tell. Her expression turned ugly. Pinched. She suddenly struck Sophia across the check. Her skin burned with shame and humiliation, having been punished in front of the Altbussers. Liquid pooled in her eyes, but didn't release. This wasn't the help she'd hoped for.

"Why are you doing this to me?" she asked, trying to leave the dining room. Once in the hallway, she grasped the banister, ready to flee up the stairs.

"I'm doing what I think is best, what I believe your mother and father would request of me."

"You cannot make me," Sophia cried, climbing the stairs with tears streaming down her face. "You simply can't..."

She trembled, escaping her aunt, attempting to decide an appropriate solution to the new dilemma. Pulling the hairpins from her hair in an act of defiance, she allowed the thick auburn layers to fall about her shoulders. Hurrying to her bedchamber, she massaged her head where the heavy mass had been coiled in a tidy bun.

What was she to do now?

One person might have a solution. Though she had promised Mathias his privacy, gaining him the time to consider their future together, or apart, he was the only answer to her current dilemma. She had to see him.

Sophia retrieved her cloak and then left her bedchamber, exiting the manor house by way of the back stairs. Hurrying to the stables, she soon mounted Maraclese. Leaving the mare unsaddled, she took flight into the night, rushing to the man who might yet be her salvation.

CHAPTER 21

Sophia had hoped to find Mathias at his house, but the interior had been dark, quiet and empty. Panicked, she fled to the church, hoping she'd locate him inside. Lingering at the threshold of the sanctuary, she sighed in relief when she glimpsed candlelight flickering on the altar.

"Mathias?" she called out, walking tentatively along the aisle-way, grasping each pew, and edging closer to the altar.

"Sophia?" he replied, his voice a whisper in the darkness. "Is that you?"

"Yes," she said with some relief, standing before him. "I know I promised to give you space, but I desperately needed to see you."

"I've not stopped thinking about our last encounter. Truth be told, I'm not upset that you're here. Quite the opposite in fact."

Sophia edged her way between the pews and sat beside Mathias, leaving a respectable space between them.

"I'm glad, for I'm in need of your counsel," she breathed, nibbling at her lip. "Much has happened since I left you," she sighed, her voice shuddering. "And though I respect your need for privacy as you consider our future, together or apart, I knew no other place to seek advice, or any other person to turn to with what has happened."

He slid closer to her, filling the space she had purposefully left empty. Taking her hand, he held it tenderly before bringing her fingers to his mouth for a kiss. Her heart skipped a beat, her face surely reddened as he trapped her hand against his whiskered cheek.

"What's happened?" he asked, kissing her fingers a second time. "Trust in me, I won't fail you."

Sighing, she relaxed against his shoulder. "I hardly know where to start."

"The beginning is usually best," he said, still clasping her hand, but bending nearer still, he was soon threading his fingers through her hair.

"Well—"

She closed her eyes, concentrating, aware of his touch. "My aunt has arrived."

"Your aunt? Did you know she was coming?"

"Yes and no. A fortnight or so ago, I received a letter from my Aunt Lovisa regarding the upcoming wedding with Franz. She stated her desire to assist me with the preparations, only she didn't know that the circumstances had changed, and that Alisz was the bride, not me."

He continued fingering her hair. Now and again, he touched the side of her cheek, eliciting tiny shivers that spiraled down her back.

"Did you respond to her letter, alerting her to the truth?"

"I did. But in the telling of my story, as I saw it anyway, I posed a few questions—regarding my heritage. I had come to believe that Alisz might be lying about my past. I was determined to learn the truth. It occurred to me that my aunt might be able to answer my questions."

"Is that why you're not yourself? Was the truth difficult to bear?"

He released her hand and laid his arm across the back of her shoulders, hugging her close. "They lied to me," Sophia said, huffing. "I don't know how they managed it, but I'm not illegitimate. I am the daughter of Lord Dedrick Baldemar."

"Wonderful news," he affirmed, "but why the long face then, when the truth has been revealed?"

Sophia lowered her head, wanting to remain strong, but the water pooled in her eyes.

"Come now," he appealed, urging the rise of her chin. "Can it be that bad?"

"Yes, it can," she stated unequivocally, meeting his warm expression again. "My aunt has not only confirmed the truth, but also seeks to do justice. This evening, she surprised me by inviting the Altbussers' to dinner. Mathias, she will see me wed to Franz regardless of my feelings on the subject, and she's taken steps to ensure her wishes are carried out."

MATHIAS CONTEMPLATED SOPHIA'S NEWS. It was horrible, yes. But people could be disconcerting when they were afraid of losing something valuable.

"Mathias? Do you understand? My aunt has dissolved the betrothal agreement between my stepsister and Franz. I'm being forced to marry a man that I detest, despite my feelings to the contrary. Albrecht and Verena Altbusser have given their blessing to the marriage. Franz has accepted his responsibility, too."

Mathias decided that the change of affairs was shocking. He didn't like it. The thought of the woman he loved, joining herself in matrimony to anyone but him was upsetting. But what did this alteration really mean?

"Not so long ago," he mulled over the past, "we met inside this very chapel. You were grief stricken. You claimed to love the man."

"What of it?"

"Have you buried the feelings that upset your tender heart and brought you to tears? Is there a part of yourself wanting to take back what is rightfully yours?"

She stared at him, openmouthed, obviously shocked by his question. "How can you ask such a thing after what we've shared? Besides that, the bastard attempted to rape me!"

"I'm sorry that I must press for answers," Mathias remarked. "But because we've shared an intimacy, I require the truth of your commitment. Our future depends on the answer."

"Very well, I'll attempt to satisfy," Sophia sighed, swallowing. "I thought I loved Franz. I confess that I've kissed his lips, too, but the emotions were nothing more than a passing fancy. Love is based on far more than a handsome face and tender kisses, you taught me that."

"What have I taught you about love?" Mathias muttered, resting his forehead against her soft skin. He sucked in a breath when she kissed him sweetly, a quick peck on the lips.

"Well, you know, a foundation of faith, kindness, understanding, and hope, hope from your gentle touch."

"Human contact," he groaned, aware of the ache that longed to be sated. Their lips were much too close, but he desired it so. He wanted her to kiss him again. "Love is based on more than the weakness of the flesh, but if I were free to love you, our life wouldn't be one of wealth. Lord Franz Altbusser could offer so much more. Perhaps, the path your aunt seeks is a better choice."

"No, Mathias," she appealed, kissing him again, her fingers caressing his cheek.

"You need to think about it, being with the other man that is, regardless that the thought upsets you."

"No. I don't. There's only one true path for me, if you'll have me. *I love you!* You're the only man I want to share my life with."

"Sophia, I don't have much. A house, a church and a congregation of like-minded people, that's been my life. To be with you, I'd have to seek a dispensation to leave it all. What financial security could I offer my wife, my children? I know aught else but my vocation."

"Baldemar Manor and its surrounding lands will be enough of a dowry for us to live happily. But any home will do, no matter how big or how small, as long as we share it together. There's a way to remedy this situation, a way out of this mess."

He kissed her on the mouth, relishing her young figure and quicker mind. If only his decision could be made without consideration for his actions. He would follow the urges, acquiring a partner and a wife in the bargain. Accepting her love, saying: *yes, I will marry you without regret.* Yes! We will raise a family and grow old together. *Could he do it?*

But regardless of the sweet emotions he had come to know with Sophia, the vows spoken to God must not be taken lightly. He was a priest, first and foremost, a fact that worried him repeatedly these days.

"I need to make sense of the vocation I've chosen, and come up with answers to secure my future. There's rumblings in the religious community that might offer a solution to our dilemma."

"I'm aware of the controversy, if you're talking about Father Luther."

Father Martin Luther, a more radical priest, was seeking a reformation of sorts in the church. His campaign had begun nearly two years ago, when the Father had posted 95 theses on a church door, thereby encouraging the debate over the legitimacy of the sale of indulgences.

"Indulgences," Mathias said with a frown. "I know which side of the issue I'm on."

"As far as I'm concerned," Sophia sighed, "indulgences are no more than a means to create more wealth for the church. Funds cannot possibly forgive an individual's sins and offer them a seat in heaven."

"They won't aid the passage either, but the Roman church, hoping to gain funds to renovate St. Peter's Basilica has responded predictably, branding Father Luther's teachings heretical," Mathias said with a grimace, shaking his head, "but his writings are impressive, and his teachings seem to have roused a group of Saxon priests to his views. I'm especially excited that he's translating the Bible into the Germanic language. Just imagine, the people reading the Word for themselves."

"Yes," Sophia exclaimed, excited by the prospects. "It makes sense to have closer contact with the scriptures, to say Mass in German, *not Latin*, so the people can understand God's message."

"It's an exciting change, but I think the Pope is threatened by the idea. My point is—if I join the reformation movement, perhaps I could align with other priests seeking to reform the Roman Catholic Church."

"It's a risk, Mathias. You could be branded a heretic. I wouldn't want to see you hurt, not even to be with me."

He released her somewhat, and then slid his fingers around the neckline of her bodice. "Everything's a risk," he said as her breathing quickened. "But I'd sacrifice all—everything—for your love."

A heated longing came painfully to life beneath his robe. God forgive him. He wanted to submit to her temptation. The future had arrived and he was grateful. Father Luther assumed a bold stance, an honest path, but Mathias admired the priestly commitment toward change. A break with the past couldn't happen without courage.

"Not at the risk of your life, Mathias. I couldn't bear it."

"I don't want you to marry that man," Mathias said, playing with her neckline. He closed his eyes as her fingers tousled the hair at the back of his neck.

"I don't want him. It's not my wish to marry a scoundrel whom I do not love."

"The way you claim to love me?"

"Yes," she stated emphatically. "Precisely."

He slipped his fingers inside the cleavage of her emerald dress and massaged the rounded breasts rising and falling with each inhalation. In that moment, the empowering need of her passion likened him to a predator stalking its prey. He wanted to bind her to his heart, leaving no doubt as to which man should reside beneath her blankets. "What are we to do?"

"I want to be with you," Sophia said, gazing thoughtfully at him. "Can I please stay, if only for a little while?"

He cupped her cheek. "I want you to stay with me for the rest of your life. I should say no to your request, you realize, but your womanly curves are far too tempting."

"You'll permit me to stay?"

"The hour grows late, too late for a woman to travel alone. You cannot leave. I must have you, again."

"I feel it, too," she said, pressing closer to his chest. "A need to be close to you, to hold you."

"Come with me," he said, beckoning, rising from the pew and grasping her hand. "I need to leave the church, embrace our future."

He escorted her to the aisle-way. Together, they walked the path between the pews, hand in hand, leaving the sanctuary for another refuge.

"Where are you taking me?"

"I'll show you, soon," he hinted, squeezing her fingers.

Mathias could not answer her question outright. His emotions were in turmoil. Each step led them toward his priest's house, his bedchamber, and he knew what act beckoned should they arrive in that quarter.

He supposed he struggled with a male dominance issue. Though his mind battled over the rightness of the path now traveled, his heart had come to a decision. He should be honest with Sophia and reveal his intent, but she would know soon enough.

They left the church, crossed the courtyard, and soon entered his house. He led her to his private bedchamber. "I'd like to take you inside," Mathias said, apprehensive in this choice, standing at the doorway of sin, "will you go with me?"

"I will," she said, nodding. "If you let me stay the night, and promise that there will be others, too."

He led her inside his bedchamber, seeking change, closing the door on the past. "I promise, I will never forsake you." Releasing her hand, he lit a candle, allowing soft cadences of light to flutter on the walls and the ceiling like butterflies dancing.

Turning to her, he cupped her face in his hands. "I shouldn't be asking this, but I want to touch you."

Shyly, she glanced away, but then sought his attention again, licking her lips. With a nervous giggle, she reached to him. "Yes, please..."

He was overjoyed with her response. So happy, he didn't contemplate the consequences of his actions, only the sweet need that spurred him to touch. With nary a breath, he undressed her before the candlelight, permitting her emerald dress to slip from her shoulders and fall to the floor in a pool of satin. She stood before him wearing a fine lawn chemise and cotton pantalets. Gauging her approval, he gently, slowly, removed these items too, amazed at the modesty of the woman who unabashedly came into his arms.

He led her to his bed and laid her down against the coverlets, savoring her beauty and nakedness.

How could God deny a man such purity? Even if that man happened to be a priest.

"Is it wrong?" she asked him.

"I won't think of the right or wrong. I need your love; I need to make you mine."

Sophia watched him as he stripped off his robe. Mathias wasn't uncomfortable bearing her scrutiny, or her heady stare. Forgotten, priestly garments lay on the floor, and he the man stood proudly before her in appeal, naked and ready.

"You're beautiful," Sophia breathed, waiting for him, her eyes alight with passion. He came to her and she pulled him close, cradling his head in the crook of her arm as he lay beside her on the bed.

Stroking her hair, he studied her facial expressions, her eyes more beautiful then emerald gems, high cheekbones, sweet rosebud lips. "I love you," he gushed, sliding closer. "Regardless of what happens after this night, I will always be your shoulder. You can rely on me."

She kissed his lips. "I know, my darling, and I thank you for sharing your thoughts. That you could promise such a treaty gives me comfort."

He returned her kisses. "I'm committing more than my strength. Tonight, I mean to give you my heart."

"Oh, Mathias," she cried, calling out his name as his lips descended on her mouth, preventing further conversation. He pulled back, cradled her head with his hand, touching her earlobe, taking pleasure from the soft tissues of her mouth that responded to each kiss, matching each caress.

He slid closer, nudging his leg provocatively atop hers, groaning with the excitement of his manhood rising against her thigh. She must have become conscious of the contact, for she reached, sliding her hand along the length of his pelvis to grasp his shaft.

"Oh," he moaned, as she stroked him. Squeezing gently, her fingers tickling the nest of pubic hair, then massaging to the base of his shaft to the lick of his scrotum. He could not help the gentle thrusts, pressing his penis into her massaging fingers.

She took his hand and placed it at the side of her breast and he responded to the invitation, stroking the silken mounds. As she kneaded his masculinity, he found her nipple. He circled the rosy areola with his tongue, teasing the bud to further height. Taking the nipple into his mouth, he tasted the sweet perfume of her flesh, pulling, licking, gently nibbling at times, suckling as a babe might, he supposed.

His left hand shook, kneading, attempting to give the matching breast equal measure. He twisted on the bed, rising above her, pressing both mounds to his face…

"Oh, my sweet goodness," Sophia declared.

"So soft," he replied, trailing downward, across the softness of her belly and lower still to the downy hair of her mainstay.

"'Tis wicked where you're going."

He laid his hand on her sweet petal folds, fingering her moist skin. She shuddered against the contact, arching against his hand.

"Mathias—" she moaned in ecstasy. "How I want you..."

He closed his eyes, rising upward, returning his lips to her mouth, kissing her anew, but his hand stayed put, parting folds slick with dew. She groaned as he slipped two fingers inside, sheathing them, stroking her intimately in a canal of moist heat.

"I will make you mine in every way that matters," he responded in kind, breathing heavily. "I too, long for the joining of our bodies."

Thinking only of another part of his anatomy that longed to replace his fingers, he slid them in and out of her slick sheath. Kissing her lips, fondling her breast and pressing his shaft against her leg.

She grasped his back then, urging him to come astride. He answered her need, spreading her legs with his hands, making a place between her thighs. She appealed for him to take her then, but he was not ready. Instead, he came between her knees, growing hungrier still while gazing at her perfect body.

An overpowering desire came over him to taste the liquid honey of her sweetness. The idea received from the testimony of sinners, from men in the confessional booth. He lowered his head to where his fingers thrust, her entrance wet with honey. Greedy, he replaced the appendages with his swathing tongue. Very suddenly, her knees went rigid and her hands clasped his head.

"Mathias?" she breathed heavily. "What are you about?"

"Sweetheart," he cooed, licking the honeyed nectar, thrusting his tongue deep inside her core, further heating with each swathing. "You taste, exotic. But if you're uncomfortable, I will stop."

But already her knees were relaxing, spreading wider, her hands urging him to continue.

"No," she purred, running her hands through his hair, relaxing. "This is surely a sin. It feels—wicked. But, you may… continue."

"Are you sure?" he appealed, kissing her nub.

"I trust you," she cried out. "Oh. My. God…"

"Don't use the Lord's name in vain," he mumbled, licking, snickering.

But soon she demanded more. His excitement boiled into a fevered pitch. Agitated, he came fully atop of her claiming her breasts with his mouth, kissing her lips, his shaft more than ready.

But before he could enter, Sophia reached between their bodies and grasped his shaft. "I want to kiss you, too," she appealed. "Like you kissed me. May I, Mathias?"

The vision of her soft lips making contact to his tip, even once, was enough to make him burst. But he didn't want to disappoint, and so he complied, sliding backward onto his knees to sit on his buttocks. "I cannot say no to you, but no one has ever grasped me so, I cannot know how I'll respond."

"Neither have I so been kissed," she giggled, coming forward on her knees, her eyes studying her immediate desire. "I shall be careful," she responded breathing hard. She grasped his waist with both hands, and then she kissed the tip of his penis.

"Oh, sweet love," he groaned, closing his eyes.

He was so excited from the contact that he thought he might find his release, but he surprised himself with some restraint.

She kissed him again. "You're wet, Mathias."

"Well, thanks for that good news," he laughed, hoping that he wouldn't burst, while leaning backward. She wasn't satisfied with just a kiss for soon her tongue was stroking. He gripped the sheets, knotting them between his fingers while she lathed him, circling his tip, her lips grasping, caressing. "Christ's nails," he cried out. She sucked at him, too.

"My sweet Lord," he gasped as she took her fill, taking his shaft deep inside her throat. Soon, she had swallowed him whole.

"Darling, exquisite torture. I can take no more of it. Please…" He withdrew from her lips, and urged Sophia onto her back.

"I have to have you—now!"

"I know," she replied. "I feel the wanting, too."

Sophia reclined to her back, spreading her legs wide. In one quick stride, he was inside. He groaned, resting his hands on the bed, her hands holding tight to his upper chest. In and out, burying deeper with each thrust. It didn't take long before her screams broke through the silence, indicating she had found her release.

The sound was joyous. Soon after, he found his own release, spilling his seed into her womb. He removed himself shortly thereafter, his shaft so sensitive he couldn't bear to nudge her skin. Lying on his back, he nestled beside her, pulling her to him, hugging her.

She sighed in contentment, gazing at him, overwhelmed by the joyous rapture, and the wonder of the orgasm they had shared. "I love you," she purred, gently rubbing his cheek.

He rose from the bed beseeching her to do the same. Opening the sheets, he urged her inside the layers, then joined her on the bed and hugged her close to his chest. He kissed her on the forehead. Closing his eyes, satisfied, ready for sleep.

"My darling, I'll never let you go. You're mine now. I love you, too!"

"Does that mean what I think it does?" She yawned sleepily.

"I've no regrets. I won't turn my back on what we've found."

"I'm glad to hear it as you've completely and efficiently defiled me."

"I have, haven't I," he said with a grin, his fingers stroking her belly. "And soon, we might receive the greatest gift our love could behold."

"What is that, Mathias?"

"A child. A daughter or a son, a baby born of our love that will carry my name."

"Only if we marry, so we can be together, officially."

"Yes," he replied, hoping his Heavenly Father would understand. "We'll find a way to become man and wife. You'll not marry Lord Franz Altbusser. No matter that your aunt thinks it best."

She relaxed against him. "I knew I could trust you."

"No more worries, my darling," he soothed, brushing curly strands away from her eyes.

She smiled, comforted by his words, he supposed. He held her close, listening to her breathing as she slipped into sleep. Precious, she was a wonder to behold. He watched her sleeping peacefully, listening to her breathing for some time, refusing to release his hold, but then he couldn't escape his rest any longer. Yawning, he joined her in slumber, counting the hours until morning.

CHAPTER 22

*S*ophia awoke to sunlight streaming inside the bedchamber through a small window. She was almost surprised, finding Mathias nestling close to her side, quite nude and snoring loudly. A gentle nudge in the ribs and the nasal tone subsided.

She stared at him in wonder, having never before slept with a man. Mathias, his solid form, keeping her warm all through the night had brought her a sense of security. A blanket of protection shielded her, cradling her from harm's way. A life without such tenderness would be a lonely existence.

As his breathing quieted, she stroked the morning growth of bristles on his cheek, running her fingers along his jawbone and the cleft in his chin. His sandy hair was a matted mess, and she attempted to straighten it with her fingers.

"So handsome," she whispered, yawning. "Even with the first light of dawn and a mess of disheveled hair."

She shouldn't take advantage of his present state, but she

couldn't help the sexual yearning that coaxed her to explore. She massaged the muscled sinew of his arms, sliding her fingers across his elbow and lower to the indentation at his waist.

He chuckled in his sleep and at first Sophia thought she had awakened him, but his eyes remained at ease, closed. His lips seemed to move into a pleasant, if not roguish smile.

Pressing closer, she studied the wry face that seemed to materialize. Suspicious, she carefully slid her hand over his buttocks, squeezing the flesh. Perhaps, he was awake. She watched for any change in expression, but he only nuzzled closer.

She drew her fingers along the contours of his pelvis. He groaned when she grasped him; surprisingly, he was fully erect.

"If you touch me there, we're bound for a repeat performance of last night."

Not deterred, she continued stroking, her fingers smoothing a tour from the base of his genitals to the tip of his swollen manhood. Grasping him tightly, she embraced his shaft, shuddering as his manhood pulsated in her hand.

"Every great performance should occur more than once," she giggled as his fingers came alive, touching her belly.

She released Mathias when he moved to settle between her legs. He grasped her hand, pressing it into the sheets, his knee urging her legs wider. She scrutinized his amber eyes, inches away from her face, even as the tip of his penis prodded at her entrance, probing to come inside.

He knelt closer, his shaft entering her slightly, his lips descending on her mouth to kiss. "And do you desire such a performance?"

She grasped his buttocks, squeezing, pulling him to her, her hips rising in invitation. "I do."

"I'll fulfill your desires," he insisted, entering her fully, thrusting deeply, reaching a nub of passion that throbbed and pulsated against his contact. The pleasure received as each thrust sought a sacred juncture spurred her to further heights of passion. Her hips rose a little higher meeting each thrust; her fingers grasped his buttocks, pulling him urgently forward, helping him to a higher pinnacle.

And he complied. Each thrust was measured at first. Gentle as he entered and withdrew, taking his time to provide her with enjoyment. But soon, he lost control and could no longer direct the movement. He became frenzied in the act of their love play, thrusting in and out with a force that should have caused pain.

Yet surprisingly, the action had achieved the opposite effect —pleasure.

"Oh my, darling," she cried out, her heart racing, her breathing loud, riding a sensation of passion. She was brought to a bold height before gently floating back to the ground.

"Ah," she sighed, kissing his forehead in gratitude, while her lover reached his own zenith.

Holding firm, he stopped thrusting, buried deep. "Sophia," he said with a groan, plunging two or three more times before falling atop her, cradled within her warmth. She held him, squeezing, holding him close.

"Darling," he beseeched, withdrawing, chuckling. "I know not how you manage that cincture, but I would enjoy it more were I not so sensitive."

"We could attempt contact later when your sensitivities are returned to normal."

He laughed jovially, in good humor. "I wish we could, my love. But as you can see, the day has begun and we must move with it."

She playfully punched him in the chest. "I suppose that means you want to get dressed."

"I would stay like this, deep inside your love without a care in the world. But unfortunately, the world would intrude. I have to prepare to say Mass and it wouldn't do well to have the few parishioners that come weekday mornings to find their priest in bed with a woman."

"You are right on that account."

He bent forward and kissed her. "And my dear, you must return home. Hopefully, no one will be the wiser to your night away."

"I could never be that fortunate. If Alisz has her way everyone already knows that I didn't sleep in my bed last night."

He threaded his fingers through her hair, contemplating the situation. "What has happened to your sister to make her hate the world? Is there any room for goodness in her heart?"

"I've only just learned the reason for her hatred. Mathias, she's not my sister by blood. We're only related through marriage. My aunt claims that Alisz is neither my sister, nor my father's daughter. She revealed quite by accident that my stepmother seduced my father into believing that the child she carried was his."

"And your father, he kept this secret to the end of his life?"

"Yes. My aunt claims he knew that he'd never father another child, and he wanted me to have a sister, a companion. He accepted Alisz as his own, but we were never as close as he had hoped."

He reached for her hand and kissed it, enfolding her fingers within his palm. "After your father's sacrifices to give the girl his name, why do you think she holds such bitterness?"

"She must have learned the truth of her heritage somewhere along the way," Sophia sighed. "I think she became jealous of the relationship between my father and me. It's the only plausible reason. In her need to become a true heir of the Baldemar fortunes, she had to discredit my position and good name. Once her stratagem was achieved, she would have the family name she had always wished was hers."

"Can you forgive her sins?"

Sophia thought about that question for a moment, but the answer was not long in coming. "Maybe," she stated. "I might be able to forgive Alisz, because in a roundabout way, she has saved me. Had she not attempted her cruel games, I would be marrying Franz. Mathias, we would never have fallen in love."

"Who would have thought," he said, shaking his head, smiling slimly, "that because of the schemes of a woman, our destinies would alter course. We should thank her, I suppose."

"Well," she attempted. "I don't know about such expressions of gratitude, but I did have in mind a form of penance. That is if Alisz can be persuaded to a scheme that could not only benefit each of us, but also secure our mutual futures."

He rose on his elbows, studying her expression. "Sophia," he urged. "What is your quick mind contemplating?"

"Plenty, I assure you. I will apprise you of the details as soon as I know them myself. If everything goes as I believe it will, you won't want to miss the drama."

He prodded her chin upward, gazing at her with a serious expression. "Promise me, you'll be careful."

"Of course," she smiled, kissing him, "I promise."

"Father," Edda interrupted, knocking on the door. "Your breakfast is ready. Do we have a guest with us this morning?"

His face went white, all sense of humor extinguished from his expression. But then he surprised her by smiling, tickling her chin and kissing her lips. "It seems we've been caught, my love."

"So it seems," she agreed, "but Edda will understand."

"Yes, there is no servant more faithful than my housekeeper."

It became apparent that the servant they spoke about was growing impatient to be answered. They could hear her foot tapping on the wooden slats outside the door. She knocked again, harder this time. "Will the two of you be rising anytime soon, then?"

"Yes," Mathias replied. "We will break our fast shortly."

"I have a fresh gown for Lady Sophia. I will leave it outside the door." She paused shortly. "Her sister Alisz brought a change of clothing this morning. Apparently, she's joining you for breakfast."

Sophia shot upward on the bed. "It cannot be," she cried out. "How can Alisz be here?"

Mathias said not a word in response. He climbed from the bed and walked to his wardrobe, quickly dressing in a fresh robe.

"A better question might be, why is she here and what does she want?"

Sophia slid to the edge of the bed and dangled her feet over the side, soon touching the floor with her toes. "I hope she doesn't do something outrageous." Her voice rose in distress. "She could really hurt our relationship, finding us together, Mathias," she said, biting her lip. "Is it obvious what we've shared?"

"Your lips are swollen from my kisses."

"They are?" she asked, touching them.

His smile slipped away, replaced by a serious expression. "We can't hide from this. We must face the truth."

He sat beside her on the bed, patted her hand, and then pulled black kid leather shoes onto his feet. Then he turned to her and enclosed her hands in his, squeezing, trying to offer reassurance.

"When I invited you into my bed, I acknowledged the consequences. I had hoped to postpone revealing our relationship to the parishioners, but if the truth comes out, so be it."

"The truth could hurt us."

"I love you; and you love me, that's all that matters. The worst that could happen is that I'm forced to leave the priesthood, but that's going to happen anyway. Don't worry, Sophia, we will see this through, come what may."

He released her hand and rose from the bed, opening the door and taking up the gown that rested on the floor in the hallway. He closed the door again, then handed her the frock and matching slippers.

"You mean everything you say, don't you?" she whispered, standing, reaching to him.

"Every word."

She took the silk damask gown from his hands, and then stepped into the yellow saffron garment, her eyes clinging to his earnest expression. When she was only halfway into the gown, he reached to her, taking her in his arms. Kissing her heatedly, passionately, seeking her lips as if he wanted to possess her again.

"I take my promises seriously," he said, speaking forcefully. "I'll find a way to share the good news, but regardless of the trouble that arrives at our door, or meets us at our breakfast table, or who learns of what we've shared; I will not turn tail and hide from the truth." He grasped her shoulders and held them firmly. "Do you understand? I love you, Sophia. I won't be ashamed; I don't care what people think."

He turned her away from him and began the task of lacing her ties. After his proclamation and declaration of love, she didn't know what to say.

"I hope I never do anything to disservice your affection," she mumbled, while he placed kid leather slippers on her feet. "I'm fortunate to have your care."

He reached for the brass handle, taking her hand, holding it tightly. "Are you ready to make your first appearance at my side?"

"I think so," she confirmed. "I've been waiting for this moment my entire life."

"Then let us go to breakfast, together."

IT WAS difficult to maintain a brave front. Why would Alisz confront them like this? Why had she come and what was her purpose; she always had a purpose? Her visit would certainly reveal a devilish scheme.

But what really made Sophia worry about the arrival of her stepsister was the damage that Alisz could cause. If she revealed their relationship to the community at large, the gossip would destroy them. Would she be that evil? It seemed they would find out soon for as they approached the kitchen, Sophia got her first glimpse of her sister, and the expression on her face made her feel like a mouse that was about to be pounced upon. Edda, who stood in the background, would be no match for this viper.

"Good morning, Sophia, Father Mathias," she snickered. "I had thought to take in Mass this morning, but it seems I have come across a lesson of another sort. Did you sleep well, or were you too busy fondling each other to find your rest?"

"Look," Sophia said, lurching forward angrily. "I'll wipe that petty smile from your face."

"There will be no fighting in this house," Mathias said grimly, holding her back.

"She's spoiling for a fight. Look at her."

"You started this," Alisz quipped, raging. "But I will finish it."

"Whatever has occurred between Mathias and me is none of your affair."

"As one who resides within his community of faith, I'm making it my affair. You couldn't leave well enough alone. Because of you, my plans are ruined. You'll pay a heavy price for your interference. When society learns of how you sullied a priest—"

Mathias released Sophia, walked to the sideboard and poured himself a cup of ale. He faced both sisters, leaning against the counter, his head raised in a confident stance. "Your scheming was bound to be revealed, but you're not coming into my house and threatening my vocation, or the woman I love. Our relationship will be revealed to the parish sooner or later. If you choose to share our romance on this day, so be it."

"Aye, well put, Father," Edda praised, removing her apron. "It seems you have things fair of hand. I will be taking my leave then, if you don't need anything more."

"Thank you, Edda, that will be all."

After the housekeeper left, Alisz continued her charade, but Sophia could tell that much of the heat had left her battle. Her sister assumed a look of desperation. "You don't mean what you say, Father. You know how people will respond when they learn that their pastor is cavorting with a known trollop. Your life will be destroyed."

"I beg to differ. My congregation will understand. The church is reforming, perhaps there will be a day when even the worshippers will accept such a love."

"Hah," she ground out cruelly, "wishful thinking. It will never come to pass."

"Alisz, if you so much as…"

"Sophia," Mathias interrupted, gesturing with an open palm. "Leave this to me."

"You're fooling yourself. The Pope will never rescind the celibate rule."

"Perhaps not in my lifetime," he agreed, sliding his fingers through his hair. "But the day may come when a religious man not only marries, but also serves his God. Perhaps the title of priest will alter its name to suit a new and better way. So you see, trying to take our truth and use it as a weapon, will not hurt us."

Alisz lowered her head into her hands and at first Sophia thought she would cry. But she should have known better, for Alisz rose up again, looking directly into her eyes. "I suppose I'll have to take my chances, for I won't allow my half-sister to marry Franz. He is mine. If I must be forced to desperate measures to win him back, I will take my chances."

Sophia fetched a cup of ale and went to sit at the table, sliding a chair next to her stepsister. She took a sip before speaking. "No desperate measures required," Sophia implored, smiling. "You are welcome to the man for I will not marry him."

Holding the cup of brew in both hands, Sophia knew that her statement surprised her sister. Alisz's eyebrows arched dubiously upward, obviously questioning her motives. Could they overcome the past to bring peace into both of their futures?

"Come now, Alisz, surely you're not surprised. I'm in love with Mathias. He's the man I want to spend the rest of my life with. Can we not for once put our differences aside and work together to seek a promising solution for both situations?"

Now Alisz was interested; she sipped her brew before replying. She sighed, struggling over a hidden dilemma. "Why would you help me after all I've done to you? After the trick I've played."

Sophia shifted on her seat. "I don't know how you achieved it, but changing Father's Will to suit your own purposes was mean-spirited and cruel. However, our father never wanted this hurt between us. He wanted us to be whole, not half. It would demolish him to learn the lengths you have gone to destroy me."

"He was not my father. He never cared about me. He never loved me. His name need not come into the picture now."

"So, you know."

"Yes, I know," Alisz said, rising from the table, her voice becoming shrill as the pain of yesteryear revisited her face. "I have known I was not his daughter since I was a young child. I overheard a heated conversation between Father and Mother. You have no idea how his words of truth hurt me."

"I'm sorry," Sophia murmured, shaking her head. "Sorry that you were hurt."

"This is good to get these feelings out," Mathias implored. "You must continue."

It was time that wounds were healed. For the sake of her father, she had to attempt it. "Alisz, you have to know that Father loved you and accepted you as his daughter. It was his fondest wish that we would be close, as two sisters should be. It would kill him to know the pain that exists between us."

Sophia hesitantly reached to Alisz. "That is why he never told me or anyone else the truth. I learned of your heritage only recently from my aunt. You have my word that I will never reveal it."

"Why should I trust you to remain silent about my illegitimacy, you have much to gain by acknowledging the past. If I were you, I would use the information to seek revenge."

"I would never do that. Have you not heard a word I've been trying to say? Our father gave you his name when he made you his daughter. He accepted you! Not your mother because of her trickery. That would explain the heated conversation you overheard. It was Father's decision to make. I will not dishonor his choice."

Suddenly, Alisz looked like a little girl again. Forlornly, she bowed her head, wringing her hands in her lap, shielding invisible tears. A child longing to be saved, did she have the strength within herself to attempt it?

"Why, Sophia? Why do you attempt these niceties? I've been so cruel."

"Because together, we can solve these problems. You should have come to me long before now. I have a plan that could positively affect our futures. Will you at least hear me out?"

Alisz shrugged her shoulders, but it seemed she was finally ready to listen. "I suppose I have nothing to lose by listening. What is your plan, Sophia?"

Sophia took her stepsister's hands into her own and for the first time in her life Alisz didn't pull away. It was a start. "A scheme that will knock society on its knees. But it can only succeed if we work together. And if everything goes as planned, each of us will receive everything that we want. Are you ready to play my game?"

"I don't suppose I have any other choice. You've got my attention. Yes, I'm ready."

Sophia chuckled softly as she relayed her plans. The information seemed to rush out of her in a torrent of ideas. Alisz didn't interrupt her until she had finished.

She released the grip they shared, smiling. The look of amusement portrayed on her face was promising. "You mean this? It's not some sort of final game you play to get even?"

"This is real, I assure you."

"Well then." Alisz chuckled, smiling slimly. "Your scheme could actually work. But it's going to upset a lot of people at the moment of discovery."

"But that's the beauty of it. It will be too late to undo the pledge by then and you'll have a chance for happiness. So will I."

"I'm not sure I can be a party to this scheme," Mathias complained, taking a chair at the table. "We're attempting to bind a man to a situation that he does not want. Surely this is a sin."

"Huh," Alisz responded. "I wouldn't feel too sorry for the young buck, Father. He was promised to both of us and he will reap the rewards of the rightful one. Pardon the expression, Sophia, I meant no slight."

"No slight taken. As long as the right sister makes her way down the aisle to the groom. Mathias, you won't do anything to prevent this wedding, will you?"

"Who am I to stop what God has brought together," he sighed, shaking his head. "Two sisters. But, it will be difficult to stand at the altar and proclaim them man and wife. Alisz, is this your wish to marry this man? Are you sure you want to go through with this charade?"

"Yes," she confirmed. "This is what I want, and I want you to understand why. When I marry Franz and take his last name, I will finally hold my heritage. I can build a solid future, providing my children with a name that will stand up in the community. A name they can be proud of."

"You should have told me your feelings sooner," Sophia whispered, downing the last of her ale. "We could have come to an understanding before my aunt arrived, preventing this debacle."

"In my mind, I couldn't trust anyone, least of all you."

"Do we remain enemies after the battle is done, or do we call a truce?"

"I think too much time has passed for us to be friends, but I'm tired of hating you and fatigued from our continual fighting. For once in my life, I long for peace."

Mathias came to the table and sat down between them. Sophia didn't think too much of it when he grasped both of their hands. "I didn't think it possible, but I can see promise from this conversation. Alisz, your life has careened out of control long enough. It's time for you to make amends for your sins, so you can lead a normal life. You have sinned against your sister. Will you chart a new course by repenting and beginning anew? Will you ask Sophia for forgiveness?"

Alisz released his hand, her face constricting in pain. She wouldn't look Sophia's way. "I don't think I can."

"It's all right, Alisz. You need not apologize," Sophia murmured, though she wished she would do just that.

Father Mathias took on a serious tone, facing her. "Your plots have been cruel, though in many ways, your actions have secured two futures. If you want me to proceed with this charade the two of you have planned, I must insist you repent your sins."

Sophia held her breath, waiting.

"I'm sorry," Alisz managed to say.

The statement surprised Sophia. Words she'd thought to never hear.

"I'm sorry, too." Sophia wiped a tear from her eye, not believing that this was happening to them. But she was grateful. They were starting anew and she wouldn't harm their progress, progress could easily fall away like a wall of sticks.

"Welcome home," praised Mathias. "From this day forward you begin anew. May God go with you."

He stood then, reaching for the jug on the sideboard. He filled three goblets then replaced the jug to its proper place. Sitting between them once again, he raised his goblet to them.

"To your futures, ladies; may God bless your strategy and forgive me for my part in it."

"Cheers," Sophia saluted, swinging her mug.

"The future," Alisz repeated in kind, toasting. "And to the day when I capture the man who will secure my goals."

"And by this act of marriage, my goals as well," Sophia foretold. "But there is much to be done before we can toast to our success. Each step leading up to the wedding must be guided and planned with caution. We cannot appear as if we're working together. That would evoke unwanted suspicion. If my aunt ever got wind of our plans..."

"Not a problem, sister dearest," Alisz said, rising from the table, taking a final sip of her drink, then placing the empty goblet on the table. "I'll never have difficulty maintaining a nasty demeanor. Now if you asked me to be nice, that would be quite impossible."

"I would be shocked if you were anything but headstrong."

"Let us make one element of this affair clear, here and now," Alisz retorted. "I go along with this scheme because it accomplishes my goals. Do not get the notion that after the repast is complete, that we will be bosom sisters. Regardless that our dead father might have wished it so."

Sophia raised her hand not wanting their conversation to divert into a direction she could not control. Their discussion had gone well and she didn't want their progress set back.

"Rest assured, you will receive no fight on that account. After all that has passed between us in recent months, I find it difficult to believe that we could ever be close. However, a truce preventing further warring in our lives, seems a fair enough prize."

"Then we are agreed on that subject at least. I shall be on my way home then; will you join me on the ride, Sophia?"

"No, Alisz, traveling with you would be unseemly. I will depart soon after you leave."

"Will neither of you be staying for Mass then?" Mathias questioned.

"Not me, Father." Alisz laughed, shaking her head. She walked to the door, imparting one final statement before leaving. "Sunday is the only day I will suffer the scriptures within the presence of the chapel. I will see you then, for the sake of appearances and social graces only."

Sophia chuckled, placing her goblet on the table surface as well. She turned to Mathias, seeing those quizzical lines beginning to develop along the planes of his forehead. "You'll never save the likes of my stepsister, Mathias. Why even try?"

"Perhaps not today," he agreed. "But there is hope for redemption on another day. As a shepherd of God, it is my destiny to search for a means to the dilemma."

She turned into his chest, wrapping her arms around his neck. "A noble quality, Mathias, and one that I admire about you. But Alisz is content in her sin. Let her sink or swim in her corruption for now. There are more wondrous circumstances for us to consider."

"Hmm," he whispered, intently studying her eyes while cupping her face within his hands. "And what circumstances would we be bearing in mind?"

"Our future, of course. After I've satisfied my stepsister, and a problematic Franz tossed into the bargain, we can start our life together."

While eyeing a serious countenance, he lowered his lips to her mouth, kissing her subtly. "Our path will be difficult, Sophia. I can only promise that we will share our life together, always."

She kissed him fully on the mouth, enjoying the sensation of his arms circling her waist, pulling her closer. "Your love and companionship is all I need and all I'll ever ask for."

"After hearing your vocal support, I hate to request that you leave; but I must prepare for Mass."

"Of course," she replied, pulling away from his arms, sad that she must leave and hating the moment they separated. "I understand. I should be leaving anyway. There's much to accomplish in a short period of time."

"Before you leave, Sophia, there's something else you should know."

"You look so serious, Mathias. What is it?"

"This Sunday, I will share with the congregation that I have broken my celibate vow. I will reveal my intention to leave the Church."

"You will? Are you sure? Are you ready for this?"

"I have to be."

Sophia grasped his arm. "I don't know what to say."

"Say you'll be my wife."

"Oh, Mathias, are you asking me to marry you?"

"I am. What do you say to that?"

"Yes," Sophia said, hugging him close. "I will be your wife."

CHAPTER 23

The horse-drawn carriage arrived at the manor house as the sun peeked through a gray sky. Alerted by the clip-clop sound of hooves striking against the cobblestones, Sophia walked to the window still dressed in a wrap of gossamer white. Her stepsister stood calmly by her side.

"My, my," Alisz remarked. "Our groom appears in a hurry to have his bride relocated to his residence."

Sophia glanced at her sister, expressing her curiosity, and then took in the courtyard where the carriage had come to a full stop. The footman approached the door and lowered the minor staircase. As if on cue, the door swung open and Franz stepped to the ground.

He chanced to look upward while walking to the main entrance and caught her scrutinizing expression. Sophia stepped to the side of the window, noting the provocative intent he directed her way.

"Yes," she agreed, twittering with laughter. "It seems the groom has direct intentions. From your experience, do you think he would attempt liberties prior to the ceremony?"

Alisz paused in thought, a remembrance crossing her face. "Knowing the nature of this man as I do, he might attempt an intimate overture before the nuptials. You must be firm when in his presence. And for heaven's sake," she scolded, as if speaking to a child, "do not find yourself alone with him."

"Not on your life," Sophia responded. "Franz Altbusser will have little opportunity to consummate a union before a right and proper wedding can take place. And since I'll not be his bride, I wish you luck on that score."

Alisz chewed her fingernails nervously, walking to the door. "He is apt to be angry when the bride is revealed, but he will recover soon enough. And even if he doesn't approve and seeks to have our marriage annulled, I have gained an advantage."

Sophia pushed away from the wall and walked to her sister, her expression raised in question. "What advantage? What dirty little deed will render Franz helpless against your advance and likely trussed up like so much wild fowl? Curiously, I wish to dwell on your stratagem."

Alisz sniggered, shaking with laughter, holding her belly with her hands. "Revealing the details to you would only jinx my plans. But don't despair over the possibilities, all will be revealed in time." Alisz approached the doorway, ready to take her leave.

"Not even a clue?"

Alisz clicked her tongue disapprovingly, shaking her head. Finally she pointed a suspect finger in Sophia's direction. "It's my last hurrah. Not even you will deprive me of the reward."

With her final words, she fled the room, leaving Sophia astonished but not surprised. They were working together to achieve a mutual end, but they had yards to go before they might realize trust.

It was not much longer before an anxious Adeline came rushing into the room. "Your groom has arrived, Mistress, and he's in a terrible hurry to fetch his bride. We must dress you quickly."

Sophia walked to the settee and sat down. Adeline reached for a gown that had been chosen with particular care. The rest of her belongings had been temporarily moved to another room while Alisz's menagerie of goods had been packed in trunks, ready for departure. They were probably being loaded onto the wagons already.

"Adeline, I won't rush on his account. He will have to wait. Perhaps we could ring for tea to be brought up."

Adeline turned to face her, holding the intended dress of ivory satin, her face a gentle crimson. "Oh no, that would be inappropriate. A bridal feast has been prepared and is waiting for you. Your aunt will not let the groom take you away until the delicacies have been tasted. But I swear, that man looks as if he has other edibles on his mind."

Sophia stood and Adeline began to remove her sleepwear. "Yes, well, I hope he will not be too disappointed if the flavor is not to his liking."

She stepped into the dress, turning her back to Adeline, who made quick work of the fancy laces while rambling on. "'Tis obvious that food has escaped his hunger for a woman's stronger appeal. He's a lucky brute. I hate to see you leave, not because I'll be losing my position. Well, only because I don't believe he deserves a woman of fine moral character."

Sophia turned and faced her maid. She couldn't reveal the truth of the situation, but she wouldn't have Adeline believe that her position was in jeopardy. "Forget about Franz. What is this about losing your job? Surely you realize that regardless of what becomes of me, your position here is assured."

"Well, I appreciate the thought. But with Lady Alisz controlling the running of the manor, I'm sure she'll be asking me to leave."

Sophia grasped her hand and held it firmly. "That will never happen, let me assure you. Promise me you will not resign your post."

"How can I make such a promise?"

"Adeline, I will not be stepping foot into the master's carriage until you make your promise."

Adeline released her hand, raising her own in amazement. "Very well then, my lady. I promise."

"Good," Sophia smiled, satisfied. "Then shall we make our way down to my wedding breakfast?"

"But my Lady, I have not tended to your hair."

Sophia only laughed, realizing that Adeline could not possibly understand that the state of her hair hardly mattered. But she supposed she should at least attempt to look excited about the coming match. "Well then, brush it out and secure it into a tidy knot. That will have to do until later."

Adeline smiled, claimed an ivory comb then went about the labor of freeing chocolate tresses of incessant tangles. "You never cease to amaze me, my Lady."

"I never cease to amaze myself," she chuckled in response, scanning every inch of her bun for loose tendrils of hair. She yearned to have this situation at an end. It was time to have this nasty business underway.

"There," Adeline commented, stepping away. "It's done. I swear; I've never seen you look more radiant."

"Thank you, Adeline."

Finally she was ready to make her entrance. Leaving the protective surroundings of her bedchamber, she walked to the main staircase. She was surprised to find every household staff member awaiting her presence. They lined each side of the staircase, forming a tunnel that she must pass through. Slowly, she began her descent, taking caution with each step.

Parlor maids holding dust mops dabbed at fresh tears. The cooking staff, plump from their culinary expertise, rubbed at teary eyes. Chambermaids and the like portrayed similar portraits of grief. Young Rosa broke down at her approach.

"Come now," she voiced, gripping Rosa's hand. Her words were as much for her as for everyone else. "No one has perished; we only prepare for a wedding."

"Oh, but, my Lady," Rosa cried, tears streaming from her eyes. "We will miss you."

The emotion caught her unaware. "Perhaps you won't miss me half as much as you think."

She released Rosa's hand and proceeded to the bottom of the staircase, nodding approval at various servants as she passed them by. And if she had been surprised to see the household staff assembled, she smiled in amused delight to see the upper crust awaiting her presence at the door as if Lady Wendeline and Alisz could hardly wait to see her depart with the anxious-looking groom. Only Aunt Lovisa looked unquestioningly happy.

She stepped toward the entourage. A dashing Franz, impeccably groomed, bowed in her direction, placing a wet kiss on her hand. She attempted to maintain a pretty smile. Though he was a handsome man, she could barely keep herself from pulling backward or wiping his kiss on her skirt.

"Good morning, my fated bride. If you are ready, we shall depart for my residence."

Sophia chuckled, clearly amused, raising her hand to tickle the undergrowth of his chin. "Are we in a hurry to see the deed achieved?" she voiced so everyone could hear. "I'm anxious myself, but my staff have prepared a wedding feast and we shall sample the flavors before we take our leave."

He frowned, came beside her and placed his palm on the small of her back, edging her toward the open door. "Sophia, I'm eager to leave. Make your apologies and let us be on our way."

But she would have none of it; she backed away from him not allowing his grip to linger on her back. "But they have worked hard to prepare this meal," she appealed, turning to the staff. "Would you slight them by rushing your bride away?"

Every person directed an ugly eye at the groom, raining his or her thoughts down on him. She knew he had little choice but to yield. "Very well," he conceded. "If the bride desires a wedding breakfast, then the bride shall have her wish."

"Did you hear that?" Sophia called out to everyone. "We are to hold a wedding feast and I wish my servants to be in attendance to share in the meal. Let us make this a day of new beginnings and celebration."

A whoop of joy spontaneously erupted from the throng. They began their descent down the staircase, making their way to her. Ready to escort the supposed bride and a dashing groom to the dining room table. Sophia reached for Alisz's hand, winking at her, oblivious to the stunned stare she received from Franz.

"And in honor of the coming nuptials," Alisz announced. "I give every staff member the day off with pay."

Another cheer rose from the crowd. The merriment continued until everyone was settled in the dining room. They stood either around the table or casually sitting on the sofa or armchairs. Sophia took a seat at the head of the table while Franz continued to stand. He poured a generous amount of wine into two goblets and presented one to the bride.

Conversation ceased when he raised his glass. "To my future wife," he said with some seriousness. "May we be blessed with happiness."

"And to the man I wish to call husband," Sophia proclaimed, toasting Franz, Alisz, and then the other celebrants. "May God bless a chance at this happiness."

A footman placed a plate before them then, filled with the delicacies of freshly baked pigeon pie, sausage, bread and cheese, and savory snacks. Franz chose a miniature pigeon pie from the assortment and brought it to Sophia's lips, giving her no other option but to bite. She was equally tempted to nip at his fingers, but thought it wise to refrain from this hurtful action.

Instead, she chewed the tender cuts of meat, watching his changing expression. Rather than offering the remaining portion of pie, he placed it in his mouth and chewed, his focus on her.

"A bit of sauce stains your lip," he whispered.

She attempted to wipe the liquid away with the back of her hand, but he clasped her fingers in a firm grip. A terrible shiver weaved its way up her spine when he lowered his lips to the crease of her mouth before she could voice a complaint. She placed her hands on his chest as he descended, feeling the contact of his mouth pressing against her own, first kissing, and then sliding his tongue around the contours of her lip.

"Oh my," she gasped, remembering the last time he had gripped her this way. She forced herself not to recoil. Franz must have sensed her disquiet, for he seemed stricken. He broke their contact, leaving her fingers suspended in the air.

"My regards to the chef," he regaled, "the pigeon pie is excellent. A better flavor I have yet to taste."

"Yes," Sophia agreed, her voice stilted, lowered. "Nicely done."

The chefs murmured their thanks then Franz had the floor again. "I thank everyone once again for their efforts in this feast, but the time has come to escort my bride to my residence. After we have departed, please share in this meal as you have shared in Sophia's life."

"Yes," Sophia agreed, "It's time to leave."

She rose from her chair and allowed Franz to escort her to the door. Though she would be returning to this home before the sun set on the horizon, she hated to leave these people like this. She hoped they wouldn't be disappointed when she arrived home later—with Mathias.

Her aunt waited at the door, her arms extended, tears glistening in her eyes. "My beautiful niece, you are bound for an exceptional future."

"If you say so," Sophia replied, stepping near her aunt. "You think you have acted in my best interests," she whispered, "but only I can account for my future. I enter into a new relationship today. I hope you'll support me."

Franz grasped her elbow.

"Of course," Aunt Lovisa acknowledged as she was led through the door and outside to the waiting carriage. Everyone exited the household and stood in a line in front of the manor house. Franz opened the carriage door and assisted her inside. He joined her shortly thereafter, and then the carriage moved away.

She waved frantically to the household staff and they responded, waving back. Some ran behind the departing carriage until they could no longer keep up with the quickened pace of the horses. Sophia sat back, resting her head on the wall tapestries, permitting Franz to hold her hand. She closed her eyes attempting to find rest.

The wheels moving awkwardly beneath the frame of the carriage carried her toward salvation and a new beginning, but the altar couldn't come soon enough.

CHAPTER 24

F ast asleep, Sophia awakened after the carriage jostled over a rut, suddenly aware that her head rested on Franz's shoulder. He played with the tendrils of her hair, winding the strands around his finger. Angered at his audacity, she pushed his fingers away and slid to the further wall of the carriage.

"I'm sorry, Franz," she began, attempting to regain her composure. "I must have fallen asleep."

"Not as sorry as I," he drawled. "It took an interminable amount of time to see you safely situated within my carriage. I had hoped for a favorable interlude once we were alone, but you became quiet. Is there something you wish to tell me?"

She refused to meet his eyes, and stared blankly beyond the carriage windows at the passing prairie. "I was tired. Excitement, I suppose; I barely slept last night."

His fingers sought her face, turning her portrait to him. Desire was stirring, shading his hazel eyes with smoky hues, concerning her. "Perhaps there shall be little slumber this evening as well. I aim to take you on a journey of sensual enlightenment, one that you may never wish to awaken from."

She peeled his fingers away. "Franz, until I stand at the altar of commitment, I refuse to think about such intimate business."

His eyebrows drew dubiously upward. "The way you speak, in the second sense, I might be forced to question whether your pledge of loyalty was for another gentleman. Do you play a game with me, Sophia? Are you scheming against me?"

She huffed, not caring what he thought. This would be the last time she came this close to Franz Altbusser. "I enter into this union reluctantly. And if an opportunity presented itself to rend myself free, I would..."

"Ah," she cried as he grasped her clothing, pulling her close, bruising her against his chest.

"You'll do nothing of the sort. Don't think to cross me, as you'll pay dearly if I'm denied."

"You cannot force me against my will. Let me go, you great brute."

He yielded then, but the anger creasing his features into a disturbing façade frightened her.

"Very well," he grated, releasing her. "But be warned. Let nothing disturb what is finally within my reach, our marriage."

"You're unpredictable. Your actions frighten me."

She wondered how he might respond to the coming nuptials. What might happen when he lifted a heavily shrouded veil, ready to kiss his desired bride, finding instead…

"Give me what I request, and all will be well."

She swallowed, choosing not to reply, pitying Alisz. But what if her sister backed out of this farce of a marriage, what then? She urged herself to remain calm as the carriage stopped before the Altbusser residence.

A broad castle-like dwelling, it towered upward in straight linear lines with few windows for light. It was almost as if the designers of the structure had constructed the rather plain-looking piece of architecture with invaders in mind. She equated the layers of stone to be more in keeping with a stately mausoleum and was glad she wouldn't be calling this place home.

The footman opened the door. Franz took her hand and led her outside, assisting her to dismount from the carriage steps to the graveled ground. Taking a deep breath, she gazed at the household staff, who had assembled in a straight line in front of the castle. She reflected on their inescapable portraits of seriousness; not one person smiled.

And so she smiled, attempting to break through their gloom, while Franz led her to them, but dashing her hopes, each person remained sullen, their expressions frozen.

"Your attention," Franz bellowed, affecting the younger women to skip to alertness. "Please acknowledge, Lady Sophia of Baldemar Manor, my soon-to-be wife."

Sophia lowered her scrutiny, maintaining a stoic expression, curtseying deeply. Then rising again, she searched their expressions for some sort of favor. Many nodded, but one man in particular; who she assumed held a position of some importance, stepped forward.

"We welcome you to the residence, my Lady. It's our fondest wish that you'll find happiness within these walls."

He stepped back into the line, his straight expression never changing. "Thank you for your kind words," she responded, gesturing to every person assembled. "I'm sure, I'll be pleasantly happy."

"You may go about your duties," Franz ordered, and then turned to face her.

"And you, my sweet, may get ready for our wedding. It shall occur within the hour."

"But Franz, there is much to be done in preparation. I cannot possibly be ready in such a short period."

"I hardly care if you come to me bejeweled or plain, or even with your dress crumpled." He pulled her against his chest. "We will be wed at the groom's convenience, not the bride's."

"Franz?" she asked, her heart beating too fast. "When did you become such a lecher?"

Cold eyes bereft of spirit bored into her soul. Then he lowered his lips for an excruciating kiss, leaving her mouth bruised and her mind confused. "I'm the man I've always been. Term me with disrespect if you must, but later, you shall be singing my praises, love."

"We shall see," she chided loudly.

"I could beat you into obedience, but what good would that effect. There are other ways for a man to achieve his ends. Come now, I shall see you safely escorted to your bridal suite in preparation for our wedding."

He grabbed her arm and led her up the steep steps of the castle none too gently. Though she attempted to walk willingly beside him, she lapsed slightly behind, falling into silence. In a way, she thanked him for speeding up the wedding. She was tiring of this charade and longed for the game to be over.

Once they entered the large foyer, marbled in white, Franz presented her to the manservant who had spoken a welcome previously. "Escort Lady Sophia to her bridal chamber forthwith."

"As you wish, my Lord," he spoke flatly.

Without looking at her, the servant approached the white-railed staircase that rose upward from the middle of the room. Wide stairs loomed before her at the bottom that gradually tapered, narrowing at the top. Sophia hurried to follow his quick easy strides, finding it difficult to keep up with his longer legs. Franz called to her when she had nearly reached the top.

"I expect you to be at your most beautiful, Sophia. Do you think you can manage it?"

She laughed, unable to conceal her mirth. Placing a gloved hand to her mouth, she turned on her heel to face him. "Beauty is in the eyes of the beholder, Franz. Prepare to behold the likes of which you have never seen before. Or perhaps you have witnessed a disguised beauty but just didn't appreciate it overly."

"You speak in riddles, woman."

"Goodbye, Franz, until we meet again."

"Aye, my love," he called to her.

The manservant led her along a considerable length of hallway, and then inside a large bedchamber. She laughed in astonishment, mostly for effect at seeing the beauty a groom had inspired. Floral arrangements occupied every countered space of the room, filling the air with the aromatic smell of lush perfume.

Rose buds littered the floor and were scattered over every square space of the poster bed, comforted in frosted white. Flounced lace veiled the bed in a canopy of sheer snow, tied in huge white bows that swayed downwards from the corner posts of the bed.

"It's simply beautiful," Sophia gasped, feeling a momentary guilt.

"And quite overdone. A waste of foliage that would be better placed in the garden," the manservant replied, sniffing the intoxicating air with contempt. "I shall leave you to your own devices. If you require anything, just ring the bell cord. That is," he smirked, "if you can find it among this rubble."

"Thank you for your assistance." Sophia laughed out loud. "You may take your leave."

"As you wish, my Lady."

After he left, Sophia turned to the bed, once more amazed at the great scene that bloomed before her. It really was too much and a great waste of cut flowers. Oh, but she could not deny that it was beautiful.

A noise startled her, shifting her gaze to a large wardrobe. With little announcement, the doors sprang open and Alisz nearly collapsed on the floor.

"Thank God that waspish man left. I didn't know what would kill me first. The mustiness of the confined space, or these damnable flowers."

"You're safely arrived," Sophia said with delight. "How did you manage it so quickly?"

Alisz stood, shaking out her heavy skirts, stepping to her. "'Twas easy," she gasped, pinching her nose to dislodge the scent. "I traversed across the land as fast as Midnight could run. I arrived quite a piece before the two of you."

"And you're changed already, dressed in the most beautiful bridal gown I've ever seen. Alisz, you have never looked so, so beautiful."

"Let us hope the groom thinks so too," she groaned, frowning, releasing her nose.

Alisz's statement brought back a memory. "That reminds me," Sophia began. "I'm worried about Franz, and the manner in which he might react when he learns he's been duped. He has a temper; he might harm you."

Alisz approached her awkwardly, the heavy lace of her train dragging behind the gown. "Do I detect a note of kindness and consideration for me?"

"It's not a time to question my motives. Honestly, he can be a brute of a man. You don't have to go through with this charade. That's all I'm trying to say."

Alisz scratched her head in contemplation. "Do you want him for yourself then, is that it? Has this display of frippery won his appeal of your hand?"

"No, not at all," Sophia said. "No offense, but I wouldn't marry Franz if he were handed to me on a silver platter. I only wish to warn you of his hurtful nature, should you face his wrath at the altar. I won't have you suffering because of me."

"I accept your explanation, but don't worry terribly. I will face the repercussions. I'm more than an equal match for the likes of that boy. He won't best me."

"If that's your decision, then we must hurry and prepare you as time is short. Alisz, you will be the wife of Franz Altbusser, and within the hour."

"If you do little else for me sister, please pray. I fear I may require the strength of a higher authority before the day is done."

As THE BRIDE didn't have a father to escort her down the aisle, Duke Altbusser came for Alisz at the top of the hour. Sophia hid in the wardrobe, as Alisz had done before her, waiting for the couple to depart.

She was shrouded in white and no one would recognize the pretty face hidden beneath the veil. It was a wonder that Alisz could see the world she passed by with the lacy layers of netting so thick. Sophia hoped her sister wouldn't trip, or hurt herself as she left for the small church that was situated on the property.

Sophia waited to exit the wardrobe until she believed it safe, and then gently eased the large wooden door open, stepping out. Draping herself in a cloak of midnight blue and a matching veil that hid her image, she moved to the door, ducking outside quickly to ensure that no one wandered the hallway before she departed.

Noting that the path was clear, she entered the corridor. Finding the servant's stairs, she descended, stepping softly until reaching the bottom. Peering around a corner wall, she watched women busily preparing what must be the wedding feast in the kitchen.

As luck would have it, a servant girl dropped delicate pastries on the floor. In the commotion of her scolding, Sophia hurried across the hallway to the outer door. Gratefully, she passed by the staff unnoticed.

Now, she opened the barrier door and breathed in the fresh air of the outside. Holding herself with a stern demeanor, she proceeded to the chapel, wanting to see the outcome of the ceremony. Arriving at the door, she was soon greeted by none other than Verena Altbusser.

"Welcome to the marriage of my son." The duchess smiled, offering her hand.

Smiling beneath a veil, Sophia simply nodded in silence, grasping her hand. Then she moved past the duchess and found a seat next to the aisle at the back of the church.

"Who is that woman?" she heard the duchess request of another guest. But perhaps the question went unanswered for no one approached her. She settled down to wait, nervously clasping her hands in her lap.

It didn't take long for the service to begin. A woman at the front of the chapel plucked the strings of a harp, accompanied by the twang of a lute.

She turned her head to watch the procession of people who made their way down the aisle. Father Mathias came first, followed by the Duke and Duchess Altbusser, and then finally, Aunt Lovisa.

After the respective guardians seated themselves on the front pews, the groom made his way down the aisle with the bride, *Alisz*, on his arm. Sophia crossed herself as they passed, watching them proceed to the altar. When the music ceased, Mathias opened his Bible wide and began the service.

"We've gathered here today," he said with a grimace, "to unite this man and this woman in holy matrimony. If any have just cause as to why they should not be wed, speak now, or forever hold their peace."

Seconds passed, but the guests remained quiet. Sophia could think of a number of reasons to speak up, but she chose to remain silent. Instead, she feasted her eyes on the man she loved, waiting for him to continue.

Mathias reached for the couple's hands, indicating that they should rest their palms on the Bible. Sophia held her breath, praying that Franz wouldn't notice the difference. "As God is your witness, is it your intent to marry before these witnesses?"

"It is," they both responded.

"Then will you please turn and face each other."

Sophia couldn't help the anxiety that caused her heart to beat faster. When Mathias requested that they face each other, she not only sucked in a breath, but also dug her fingernails into her palms. She examined Franz's expression for any sign of recognition. Surprisingly, though a quizzical frown crossed his features, he otherwise remained quiet.

Mathias placed his hand over top of the bride and groom's hands. "My Lord, as you stand before the altar of Christ, in sight of these witnesses and before God, do you take this woman to be your wedded wife?"

"I do," Franz replied, stating his intent loudly. "I take this woman to be my beloved wedded wife."

"And you, my Lady, standing before the altar of Christ, in sight of these witnesses and before God, do you take this man to be your husband?"

"I do," Alisz replied softly, almost inaudibly, clearing her voice. "I take this man to be my husband."

Mathias removed his hand, withdrawing the Bible as well and leaving their hands clasped in midair. Sophia took a deep breath. This was the moment of truth.

As if even Mathias knew what was coming, he took a step backward. "What God has joined together, let no man put asunder. With this in mind, I pronounce you man and wife. You may now kiss the bride."

Franz tenderly reached for the veil, his fingers shaking as he lifted each layer of netting. Frowning, he lifted the last layer, holding it high above her sister's head. A sheepish Alisz was revealed.

"What manner of dastardly business is this?" Franz yelled, addressing no one in particular.

While he waited for a reply, occupants of the small church craned their necks to favor a better view of the unexpected bride. Wondering, as she did also, what might happen next?

Duchess Verena frantically waved her handkerchief in front of her face. "Albrecht," she called out to her husband. "I think I might be ill. I feel, fain…"

Aunt Lovisa, perhaps made of firmer character, rose from her seat and turned, directing her vision to Sophia, while Franz bent to attend to his mother.

"Sophia," she breathed fire. "What have you and this villainous woman done? I know a scheme when I see one."

Sophia was not deterred by her aunt's anger. Rising from her seat, she removed her veil, permitting the fabric to float to the floor. "That would seem obvious. I had no desire to marry this man, and yet I didn't want him disappointed at the altar." She smiled sublimely, stepping away from the pew and into the center aisle. "Alisz kindly agreed to take my place."

Franz left his mother in the care of his father, and then turned to face her. "How dare you do this to me. I could…"

"Do what?" Sophia yelled, unafraid, stepping closer. "Do something to hurt me? You have already hurt me, and in ways I'm sure, you would rather not have revealed. And anyway," she continued. "Why should it anger you overly that Alisz should meet you at the altar. She's beautiful, too… And it seems like mere days have passed since you, once my beloved, shunned me for my sister. Now I shun you for the same woman. A fine tit for tat."

Franz turned away from her, facing Mathias and Alisz whose expressions shone with curiosity. His mother was coming to. "I want this farce of a marriage annulled, immediately."

"That will take time," Mathias replied, rubbing his head, mastering a bewildered expression.

Alisz maintained a prim posture. She lifted her head to her husband, displaying a winsome smile. "That would be quite impossible, mine husband."

He raised his hand high as if he might strike. Alisz shrunk away, her expression turning to one of alarm. If Sophia didn't know her stepsister better, she might have been inclined to believe the fear was real.

"No, Franz, you must not. Our baby, mine husband, you could hurt the baby..."

"Huh," Sophia retorted, wondering if Franz was fully snared. So this was the tidbit of information that her stepsister had chosen not to reveal, at least until now. Duchess Verena took to the vapors once more.

"What lies do you tell? Father Mathias, I insist that this farce of a marriage be annulled immediately."

"But Franz," Alisz pleaded. "Would you deny your child the benefit of your name? Or would you leave him or her to certain ridicule, to be entitled a bastard."

Mathias interrupted now. "Franz, do you deny that you have lain with this woman?"

He shifted his feet from side to side, refusing to look at Mathias. "No, Father," he admitted. "I cannot deny that I have taken this woman to my bed."

"And did you discuss the possibility of children and her good name before you lay with her?"

"At the time, Father, I believed our union safe. I thought she was going to be my wife, but then everything changed."

Mathias raised his hands to the assembled people. "As the groom has freely admitted, he has violated this woman before their wedding day and begot her with child. I can only determine that this marriage has been consummated. Therefore, no annulment can be granted."

"Ladies and Gentlemen," Mathias announced the stricken couple: "I present to you, the bride, the groom, and a future heir to the estate. Franz and Alisz Altbusser. Though you have already pleased the bride," Mathias whispered to Franz, "you may kiss her now if you're of a mind to do so."

"Come on, Franz," Sophia pleaded, overhearing. "Give your wife her reward and kiss the bride."

"Yes!" Someone from the congregation shouted. They had come to see a wedding and were not about to be disappointed. Soon the guests began to chant. "Kiss the bride, kiss the bride..."

Franz looked like a helpless boy. A sullen expression stained his cheeks where he stood with his bride before the altar. Alisz leaned closer to him with appeal in her eyes. Finally when the taunts grew loud, he surrendered, pecking her on the mouth.

Though slight, it seemed to satisfy him, for Alisz's expression lit into a beautiful smile. A roar of applause sounded from the celebrants. Sophia merely giggled and then stepped forward.

"Let me be the first to congratulate you," she beamed, shaking Franz's hand. He growled in response, taking his hand back and turning from her in disgust.

"Congratulations as well, mine sister," she breathed, embracing Alisz. "I wish you luck in the months ahead. Perhaps you might even grant me a visit once your child arrives. I'd dearly love to become a proper aunt."

"Perhaps," she said, withdrawing. "I might require a friendship of sorts."

Sophia approached Mathias, soon standing beside him, watching the couple intently. By the bemused look on Franz's face, she decided that difficult times were ahead. That became apparent when the groom abruptly left his wife's side and walked to the exit, leaving Alisz to attempt to catch him. In the bat of an eye, they were both gone.

Soon after, everyone who had witnessed the wedding fiasco filed out. Duke Altbusser clutched his wife tenderly, leading her shaken form down the aisle. The look on his face breached no argument. "Young lady, shame on you."

Sophia didn't feel inclined to respond. It was rude, but she turned her back on the man. Aunt Lovisa approached her next, shaking her head. "Why, Sophia? Why would you master such a plot when you could have had it all? Why did you allow such a scheme to lose a fortune that was rightly yours to receive?"

Mathias answered for her. "The answer is simple, my Lady. Your niece is in love and it's time you knew of her intended."

"In love? What hogwash is this? Sophia, is this true?"

She smiled, looking to Mathias for support. "Yes, 'tis true."

"Who?"

Mathias pulled her into his arms, tucking her head beneath his chin. She willingly lounged there, wrapping her arms around his gowned waist. Suddenly, their affair was no longer a secret as intuit and shock registered fully on her aunt's face.

"I think I need to sit down," she said with a sigh, sitting on the nearest pew, attempting to gain a semblance of composure.

"God might damn the two of you for this unnatural love. Do you know what you're about?"

Mathias released Sophia and sat beside her aunt on the pew. "I currently travel uncharted territory, Mistress. I scarcely know what I'm about, or the steps to take to leave the church, but what I'm certain of is the love I feel for your niece. I hope that my God will understand."

"God understand?" she replied. "I barely understand."

"All we ask for," Sophia began, kneeling at her aunt's feet, "is your blessing."

"I suppose there's little choice but to support you. Therefore, I give you my blessing, however grudgingly."

"There's one more matter we wish you to be a part of. Will you be present when I take Sophia as my bride, when I vow to be her husband?"

A tear fell from her eye as enlightenment dawned in Sophia's eyes. She grasped his hands, holding everything she desired. "Are you asking me to accompany you to the altar, Mathias? Do I dare to believe that you are risking everything, possibly your very soul, to make a commitment? To be my husband?"

"Yes," he declared, emotion breaking in his voice. "There are three assurances that are important. Faith, hope, love abide, these three; but the greatest of these is love. I can see this conviction clearly when I look into your eyes. I'm powerless to escape it, neither would I want to. Will you risk it all, my darling? Marry me, right now?"

"But how could that happen. There's no one to officiate and you're still a priest."

"I'll officiate. We'll be married in the eyes of God. Everyone else, I suppose, will think we're living in sin."

"But Mathias, is there any other way?"

"A dispensation from the church won't come quickly enough, and it could be denied altogether. I won't wait for sad news. I want to marry you now. Will you, agree?"

"Yes, oh yes, my love," Sophia replied, with tears of self-renewal raining down her face, blessed by their love.

"Will you be our witness?" Mathias requested of her aunt. "The chapel is ready, the wedding feast awaits at Baldemar Manor, and I'm set on marrying."

Aunt Lovisa rose from her spot on the pew, wiping a tear from her eye. "Is this what you want, Sophia?"

"It is."

"Then, how could I say no after hearing such an impassioned speech. My niece's happiness is most important."

"My parents have come from afar," Mathias said with grin, escorting her toward a humble looking couple. "Sophia, permit me to introduce to you, Lars and Ilsa Rohland."

A silver-haired mother smiled earnestly, a proud and strong father reached forward and grasped her hand tightly. "Delighted to meet you," he said, his voice breaking. "I never thought I'd witness this day."

Smiling, Mathias led them back to the altar. "My father never wanted me to be a priest and there's a story to share with how my vocation came about."

"You'll tell me how it came to pass, won't you, Mathias?"

"We have a lifetime to share our stories, for now, let our ceremony begin. Are you ready?"

Sophia simply nodded her head as the group returned to the altar. She nearly broke into tears when Mathias took her hand into his grip, searching her expression and squeezing her fingers with such gentleness and compassion. The steps he was taking to realize their love amazed her. A Sacrifice for Love, it could be nothing else.

"I stand before you, our family, and before God, asking you, will you be my wife?"

"I will," Sophia responded, staring into his sunshine visage.

"And you," Sophia said simply. "Will you make one last sacrifice, and be my husband?"

"I will," Mathias responded.

"I pray that our Heavenly Father blesses our union, and equally blesses any children conceived of our love. Sophia," he whispered softly, stroking her face. "I proclaim you my wife."

She tilted her head to him as his lips came down on her own, kissing her. He would have continued if her aunt had not cleared her voice, and his father had not whooped with glee, indicating that they should stop. Though she wished to continue, too, Sophia suspended the kiss, and then turned to face her aunt.

"I suppose you'll want some sort of celebration?" Aunt Lovisa declared.

Sophia didn't reply. She merely looked into Mathias's eyes expectantly.

"Make a joyful noise unto the Lord," Mathias sang out. "Yes, dear aunt, it's time for the world, or at least the staff of Baldemar Manor, to know that a new master will be residing beneath their roof tonight. I believe a celebration is in order."

"What about the parish church?" Sophia asked. "How will it fare without you?"

"The new Bishop has appointed a new priest. The Father has already begun the chore of moving his belongings into my former house."

"So fast?"

"Well, I gave the clergyman little choice in the matter. The parish must still be served."

"It seems so sudden. You amaze me, Mathias."

"Don't prop up his head too much." Aunt Lovisa shook her head, readying to leave. "We'll see how your husband fares in time. But we don't want to overstay our welcome on the Altbusser estate. Perhaps we should be leaving?"

"Let's be on our way," Mathias said, agreeing.

"I will take care of everything," Aunt Lovisa continued. "Before the bride and groom arrive, the staff shall be apprised of this new development. I have never witnessed so many tears in my life. I expect they will be glad to welcome their Lord and Lady into their household."

"Thank you," Sophia said with a winsome smile. "Your support means everything to me."

After her aunt left, followed closely by her new husband's family, Mathias took her by the hand and led her down the aisle, leading her outside of the church to where a horse and buggy waited. He assisted her to climb to the driver's box, and then took his spot beside her, holding the reins loosely in his hands.

"I meant what I said inside the church, mine wife. Our love is my primary consideration, for love is most important. But God has played a vital role in my life. I must find a way to serve."

She rested her head on his shoulder, closing her eyes, gladdened by his warmth. "Faith will find its way."

He kissed her forehead. Shifting closer, she lifted her chin to have his lips alter course and seek out her own. "I love you."

She held tight as he stared into her eyes, a tear shining in his depths. He said little then, just flicked the reins and encouraged the two mares into a tidy trot. Ahead of them lay the path to home. They took it together.

Suddenly, the chirruping of a bird caused Sophia to shift toward the sound. She soon sighted the feathered friend flying through a bright blue and sun-drenched sky. Excitedly, she pointed at the bird but Mathias saw it too.

A snow-white dove flew peacefully, aimlessly above them in the billowing breeze. "Perhaps it's a sign that God is not overly angry, and that our love is not forbidden?"

"Perhaps." Mathias smiled, embracing the symbol of the dove as a peaceful sign of hope to that end. "Perhaps indeed, my work is not yet done."

CHAPTER 25

*L*ittle Marcos Rohland was born in the early morning hours on the first day of spring. Sophia had labored long, with Mathias refusing to leave her side, finally giving birth to their son. Even before the midwife had cut the cord or bathed the child, he'd taken the crying boy into his arms.

He'd insisted on blessing his son with a name straightaway, naming the baby after his brother. The thought that she could give him this gift, and this new life, filled Sophia with joy, regardless of her fatigue.

His parents waited in the Chintz Chamber, having moved to the Baldemar estate to be close to their family. Sophia welcomed the maternal support, as she still missed her own father.

She knew now that Lars Rohland had long wanted a grandchild, and his wife, Ilsa, seemed excited about the prospect of being a grandmother, too.

Alisz had birthed a tiny sprite of a girl the month before, but Sophia had been too ill to visit her sister. In fact, she hadn't seen her sister since the wedding day charade and didn't know if a future with her sibling was possible. Whether it was because of their difficult past, *or Franz*, she didn't know.

The cries of a new babe filled the bedchamber with the responsibilities of the future, filling their hearts with wonder and joy. Their life seemed complete now, but Sophia whispered a prayer of gratitude, all the same, thanking whomever was responsible for this blessing.

Bless you, and thank you, *Amen*.

Thank you for reading *A Sacrifice for Love*. If you enjoyed Mathias and Sophia's love story, your honest opinion of their romance will support the author's writing career. Please rate or review this book on your favorite book site, review site, blog, or your own social media properties, and share your opinion with other readers. Thank you!

CONTACT SHELLEY KASSIAN

If you would like to learn more about Shelley or her novels, visit her website at shelleykassian.com. Here you can read excerpts from her books, linked reviews, blog posts, as well as discovering her professional affiliations and accreditation.

Shelley enjoys hearing from her readers. If you'd like to contact the author, send her a message at: shelleykassian@gmail.com.

FOLLOW SHELLEY ON SOCIAL MEDIA

facebook.com/ShelleyKassianAuthor

twitter.com/@shelleykassian

instagram.com/shelleykassian

amazon.com/author/shelleykassian

goodreads.com/shelley_kassian

bookbub.com/authors/shelley-kassian

pinterest.com/shelleykassian

NOTES

CHAPTER 7

1. Martin Luther, *Our Father, Thou in Heaven Above, 1483–1546*
2. Martin Luther, *Our Father, Thou in Heaven Above, 1483–1546*

ABOUT THE AUTHOR

SHELLEY KASSIAN has been writing timeless love stories filled with romance or dark fantasy (romantasy) for more than twenty years, novels that include her recent beach read, *A Sea for Summer*. A history enthusiast, she's traveled far and wide to explore secret gardens and medieval castles, having an avid interest in the Tudor period. Her prose has been described as "near rhapsodic," "pitch perfect," and "stylishly straightforward, rarely relying on complex turns of phrase." Reviewers have said her narrative conveys "imaginative fantasy," "fascinating characters," and "refreshing romance."

Shelley's taken creative writing courses, holds board positions within professional associations, and retains a Professional Editing Certificate. Drawing on her expertise, she has mentored novice writers, but her passion comes alive while scribing her stories into novel-length fiction. Shelley shares her life with her husband, adores her adult children and three grand pups, and when not relaxing at her seaside cottage, lives in Calgary, Alberta, Canada.